## "Is something wrong?" Deacon asked.

The night was dark, the moon late to rise. The car's headlights showed the road in front of them, but there were no other vehicles, and where they sat in the Audi was a bubble, one out of time.

"No, nothing wrong. Just... This is like a magical thing. Like it's not really me. A life that isn't mine, but for one night, it is."

He shot a glance at her. "And that made you sigh because...?"

"Because it ends. Which is stupid, because of course it does, but sometimes I wish it didn't."

Deacon nodded. "I wish it didn't as well."

Jess turned to look at him. "You really don't like working for your family, do you?"

"No. I've enjoyed the law I practice here much more. But I also have responsibilities I can't ignore back in the city and in the firm."

If that's where he felt he had to be, she admired him for following through.

"I get it. I'm sure these kids are going to make me want to walk away sometimes. But I won't."

Deacon put his hand on hers. "I know you won't, Jess. You're going to be a good mom. These babies are going to be very lucky."

Dear Reader,

This is the fifth Cupid's Crossing book I've written, which is so exciting! I'm happy to feature some of the characters from previous books enjoying their happy-ever-afters, while two new people find theirs.

Family is a theme in this book. Jess's family disintegrated when she was still a teen, leaving her at a disadvantage, but she's fought her way despite the hardships. Deacon is from a privileged family but is caught up in the expectations his family has placed on him.

When Jess finds herself pregnant, she returns to Cupid's Crossing to make a family of her own. Deacon has been sent to the Crossing as a kind of punishment, and he has to decide how much his family's needs offset his own. Both of them want to be loved and accepted for who they are. Don't we all?

Sometimes you have to make the family you need. Jess and Deacon work on that in this book. I hope you've been able to find or create the family you need as well.

*Kim*

# HEARTWARMING

## *An Unexpected Twins Proposal*

—

*Kim Findlay*

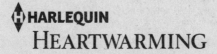

# HARLEQUIN®
## HEARTWARMING™

Recycling programs for this product may not exist in your area.

ISBN-13: 978-1-335-49091-9

An Unexpected Twins Proposal

Copyright © 2023 by Kim Findlay

For questions and comments about the quality of this book, please contact us at CustomerService@Harlequin.com.

Harlequin Enterprises ULC
22 Adelaide St. West, 41st Floor
Toronto, Ontario M5H 4E3, Canada
www.Harlequin.com

Printed in U.S.A.

**Kim Findlay** is a Canadian who fled the cold to live on a sailboat in the Caribbean and write romance novels. She shares the boat with her husband and the world's cutest spaniel. Bucket list accomplished! Her first Harlequin Heartwarming novel, *Crossing the Goal Line*, came about from the Heartwarming Blitz, and she's never looked back. Keep up with Kim, including her sailing adventures, at kimfindlay.ca.

### Books by Kim Findlay

### Harlequin Heartwarming

#### *A Hockey Romance*

*Crossing the Goal Line*
*Her Family's Defender*

#### *Cupid's Crossing*

*A Valentine's Proposal*
*A Fourth of July Proposal*
*A New Year's Eve Proposal*
*A Country Proposal*

Visit the Author Profile page
at Harlequin.com for more titles.

# CHAPTER ONE

IT WAS DEFINITELY FLAT.

Deacon stood at the side of the road and glared at the offending tire again. Passenger side front. He wished desperately that this time it could be fully inflated, but no. It continued to mock him, the rim almost touching the gravel on the side of the road. He'd managed to pull off the road safely, but now he was stuck.

He turned his gaze to his surroundings. They were lovely. Upstate New York, a quiet country road, a mild October day. A chill in the air, enough to hint of winter to come without being uncomfortable now. Leaves were a riot of red and orange and brown, with evergreens contrasting dark patterns among the colors. It was a piece of paradise in the middle of nowhere, which was exactly the problem. Deacon checked his phone for the fifth time and found there was still no signal. No one else driving past. Just Deacon and the car and the flat tire, and he had no idea how to fix it.

This was…mortifying. He'd graduated from Harvard. Not top of his class. Much closer to the bottom, but still, he had the degree. He'd passed the bar here in New York State. He was thirty-four years old, healthy, reasonably intelligent—and he was helpless because his phone couldn't call AAA.

He kicked the offending tire but got nothing but a sore toe and a scuff mark on his leather shoe.

If he could go back in time, he'd add a basic car maintenance lesson to his driving instruction course. It hadn't seemed necessary at the time: he lived in New York City and rarely drove. If he did have problems, there was AAA to provide assistance, or the garage that cared for the family vehicles. There were taxis and buses and Ubers and people, but here, nothing. No one.

He hated this feeling of incompetence. If he could get some cell reception, he'd look up a video on the phone to learn how to do this himself. It couldn't be that difficult. He was a good student. Just a bit of help…

A sixth check of the phone showed no more bars than any previous attempt. Stupid phone and stupid car and…stupid Deacon.

His free hand fisted. He wasn't stupid. He had to stop that voice in his head.

Another glare at the Audi.

"If you needed to draw up your will, I could do that for you. In fact, maybe you should consider that, because I'm going to have to try to change this tire on my own, or drive you like this. It could get ugly."

The car didn't respond. Deacon leaned against it.

"If not a will, how about an employment contract? A loophole in an NDA? I have skills, I swear."

Except none of them was going to get the car back on the road. How badly would he damage his vehicle if he just kept driving on the flat tire? Would it be dangerous on these twisty back roads?

He patted the metal under his hand. "I do have a will, just so you know—"

He broke off when a distant growl made him aware that finally someone else was driving this road, and also that he was talking to his car.

The rumbling of the engine was from the same direction he'd been coming. He had a few moments to consider who else might be traveling on this quiet road, and his brain, inspired by the true crime podcast he'd been listening to, chose to remind him that this might be a serial killer. If so, Deacon's only weapon to hand was the cell phone that still (seventh time) had no signal.

Serial killers could probably change tires. Maybe he could make a deal: don't kill me and I'll help you find a good lawyer when they catch you. *If* they catch you.

The vehicle that appeared was a beat-up van. The kind people camped in. Well, not Deacon's people, but other people. He bet camping people knew how to change tires. This van was old enough that Deacon guessed the driver didn't bother with AAA.

He raised his hand in what he hoped was a friendly, please-help-me way and finally noticed the driver was a woman. Would she stop? She might think *he* was the serial killer, using a flat tire as a ploy to lure his victims. He didn't think there was any way he could indicate to her that he wasn't competent enough to be a serial killer. After all, if he was driving his latest victim to stash somewhere, he'd be in trouble when his car got a flat tire and he was stuck with a dead body in the trunk.

Either the woman could tell he wasn't in the midst of a series of grisly murders or she was naive and helpful. Maybe she had lethal ninja skills so didn't need to be afraid. She pulled her van off to the shoulder of the road ahead of him. The van door opened, and the woman stepped out.

She was of average height, but she was thin. Not the way his mother and cousins were thin. Thin enough that her dress hung loosely, making her torso appear broad and her arms and legs sticklike. She marched toward him with a surprising amount of confidence, considering that he could be a serial killer. As she got closer, he could see the dark hair of her ponytail was lank, the striking gray eyes had dark circles underneath and her skin was pasty.

He thought he could take her, if she was the serial killer, unless she really was a ninja. A tired one. Unfortunately, he wasn't looking for a victim himself, and she didn't seem strong enough to change his tire. But maybe she could call AAA once she got to a place with cell coverage.

He'd ask her for a lift, but he didn't want to abandon his car with so many of his possessions packed inside. And that might be too close to serial killer tactics. He really needed to find another podcast.

She'd reached the front of his car now. "Are you okay? Any trouble?"

He liked her voice. Deeper than he would have expected from her slight frame. Her sleeveless dress bared arms that were surprisingly muscled for being so skinny.

He turned his head to the flat tire, and she stepped to stand beside him.

"Gotcha. No spare?"

His cheeks warmed. "Uh, I think I have one. I just…" Could he really tell her he had no idea how to change a tire? "I don't have any phone service here, so if you could call AAA when you get a signal, that would be very helpful."

The woman stared at the rows of trees climbing the hillsides beside them. "Yeah, not a surprise that this place has no towers. I have no idea when I can call, or how long they'll be, so maybe we should just see if you've got a working spare?"

He liked the sound of *we*, but he didn't like to expose his ignorance. What else was he going to say? The chances that his car didn't have a spare were slim. And if he sent this woman away, when might someone else come along?

He nodded and pulled his fob out of his pocket, tapping it to open the trunk. It was full—suitcases, golf clubs, a bag with shoes. Moving to a new town, even if it was just for a year, meant his car was packed.

He opened his mouth to apologize, explain,

something, but his companion had reached in and tugged at the handle of the top bag.

"Oh, let me—"

The bag was already sitting on the ground, and she was reaching for another. Deacon jolted into action, grabbing his golf clubs, which were ready to fall out. It took only minutes for the trunk to be empty, and the woman was peeling up the carpet, exposing the spare tire.

Deacon heard that voice in his head again, calling him stupid, but he'd known that's where the tire was supposed to be. He also understood there was a jack to lift up the car to enable the flat tire to be removed and the spare put on.

He just didn't know the practical aspects. The stranger reached for the tire, and he lurched forward to grab it first. He might have no idea how to change it, but he could at least take the tire out of the trunk.

He set it on the ground and looked at it. It was smaller than the tires he currently had. At least, to his eyes. "Is it okay?"

"Yeah, it's a doughnut. You'll have to get a proper tire as soon as you can. And drive carefully on these roads."

He nodded. Now that she mentioned it, he'd seen cars driving around with small tires like this. He mentally added getting a proper spare tire to his settling-in list.

She reached in and pulled out some other items buried in with the spare. One thing that must be the jack, and other things that would remove the old tire? Hopefully. And put on the new one. She passed him the jack while she picked up the other tools.

He stood, holding it, desperately trying to figure out how it worked and where on the car he needed to put in. Somewhere near the tire, on the frame, but not where it would impede removing and replacing the tire. What he wouldn't give for a few bars on his phone and a quick video tutorial....

"I've never done this," he admitted and risked looking at her. She didn't look surprised, just jerked her head for him to follow and walked around the side of the car to the flat. She set down the tools and turned to face him.

"So, I can do this for you—I've done it more times than I care to count—or I can show you how to do it, so you're ready if this happens again. Your choice."

She looked thin, and tired, and there was no way he was going to stand here watching while she did all the work.

"Would you tell me how to do it? Please?

I'm happy to do the labor—I just don't know how."

She nodded. "First thing, let's find a rock."

"A rock?"

"We're on a slope, so we need something to block the back tires from rolling if the jack slips."

That sounded smart. He set down the jack and walked into the brush beside the road. He came back with what he thought was a good-size rock, and she nodded. Then she told him how to place it.

That's how they worked. She instructed him in a patient, neutral voice, and he put the jack together. She explained where to put it and why. Once the car was jacked up, she removed the first lug nut, and he did the rest.

Again, he was impressed by the strength in her slim arms. Those lug nuts were screwed on tight, but she handled them.

Flat tire off, spare tire on. After she checked that the nuts were tight again, they lowered the car and put everything away. She offered to handle the flat tire, since it was dirty, but he kind of liked the idea of being a little messed up from doing a job like this. Something outside his normal. Something that made him feel competent in an arena he didn't usually work in.

Once the flat tire was back in the trunk with the tools, and his luggage rearranged on top, he turned to thank her. Again.

"Could I reimburse you for your time? You've been so helpful."

She shook her head. "Nah. Just pay it forward sometime."

She strode back to her van, opened the door and climbed in. With a wave of her hand, she pulled onto the road and was gone.

He hadn't even asked her name.

*THAT WAS STUPID.*

"Pay it forward?" Jess muttered to herself. The guy was driving an Audi. He had money, obviously. His clothes, the golf clubs—everything indicated that he had enough cash that he didn't worry about where his next meal or place to stay was coming from. But instead of saying, *Sure, I'll take a hundred*, she'd wanted to impress him. Show him she wasn't a nobody he could pay off and forget.

Which was ridiculous, because he wasn't going to remember her. They'd never see each other again. And if they ever did, she'd learned her lesson about guys like him. They stuck to their own.

She was on her way to Carter's Crossing. No, now it was Cupid's Crossing, renamed to promote it as a romantic destination. If she didn't find her brother there, she'd keep on going. Her brother was the only reason she had to return to that town. Well, that and the fact that the new romance business they had created to replace the former wood mill meant there would be lots of work for someone like her.

Someone who knew how to wait tables, clean rooms, handle a reception desk: Jess was a master of those kinds of jobs. If her brother was still in town, which an online article had indicated was the case, then it might be worth settling down here for a while. For the first time in years, she was looking to connect with her family. Some of them. Maybe. Depending on what they were like now.

Her hand rested on her abdomen for a moment. She had someone else to look out for now.

She wondered if the rich guy in the Audi would stop to get a new tire in the Crossing. It had been almost fifteen years since she left, so she had no idea what resources the town had now. But even if he did, the local garage was not where she was going.

Actually, she had no idea where she was going. According to the article she'd found, her brother Ryker had married Rachel Lowther in

Cupid's Crossing just before Christmas last year. Jess wasn't sure if the happy couple had stayed in town. She wasn't totally sure how Ryker would react to the news that he was going to become an uncle, either. She hoped he'd be supportive. He'd been that way in the bad old days, growing up. When their dad had been drinking, when seven kids had been jammed in that house after their mother died. Jess had been so young she didn't remember the woman.

They'd all escaped: Ryker to the air force… Jess wasn't sure where the rest were now. In any case, if Ryker freaked or turned out to be a jerk when she saw him face-to-face, she could survive. She'd been surviving on her own for a long time.

She slowed down when she hit the limits of Cupid's Crossing. The sign was new, which made sense, since the name change was recent as well. Jess drove past the mill, noting that it looked drastically different as an event venue. And busy. It was where Rachel and Ryker had gotten married. That might be a place to find a job, if she stayed.

Then another mile or so and she was in the business section of Cupid's Crossing. That also looked different from her memories. A lot had changed, but for the better. A couple of storefronts that had closed now held new businesses. The rest looked like they'd been cleaned and painted and were busy. Jess found a place to park her van on a side street and drew a long breath.

She was impulsive. Always had been. That was why, when she'd suddenly found herself without a husband and with an unexpected pregnancy, she'd done some online searching, found her brother's name and packed up and driven across the country to find him.

If he was still here.

She checked her reflection in the rearview mirror. She looked terrible. Morning sickness, fortunately limited to mornings, had left her thinner than ever. Her hair was lifeless and her skin blotchy. Whoever had talked about a pregnancy glow was a big fat dirty liar.

Would anyone recognize her now?

She'd run away when she was sixteen. Life at home had been horrible. Her dad was a professional and mean drunk. Ryker, when he'd been there, had been a buffer, absorbing their father's anger and fists for his sisters. Ethan and the twins had never bothered.

But Ryker had his own problems, and he'd crashed a stolen car while drinking. He'd been facing a prison term but had been offered an alternative: signing up for the military. He'd joined the air force, and then there'd been no one to act as a buffer with their father.

Jess left.

She was no longer that sixteen-year-old. She'd grown up, but she hadn't changed that much on the outside. She'd never grown taller, and her precarious existence had left her skinny still. She had the same hair and eyes as most of the family, but did people still remember the Slade family? Remember and judge?

Things had changed enough that Ryker had married the pastor's daughter, so that was hopeful. Rachel had been in Jess's class and had been nice to Jess, so Ryker had chosen well. She just didn't know if they were still here, or if any of her siblings were. She hoped the twins, at least, were still gone, since they'd taken after their father. Ryker was the only reason she had to come back. She wanted family around now that she was going to have her own.

She pulled the keys out of the ignition and dropped them in her purse. She undid the seat belt and straightened her spine.

*You may look like crap, but you always find a way to get by. So go ask if Ryker is here, and if someone says something nasty, well, you can handle that.*

Not the greatest pep talk ever, but it got her out of the van. She'd spotted a diner on the main street, the same one she remembered from before. Someone in there would probably be able to tell her about Ryker, and she could get something to eat.

She mentally counted her cash. Something cheap. Soup?

Her stomach grumbled. *Now* it wanted food. When she'd gotten up this morning, she hadn't been able to face eating anything.

She walked to the corner and paused for a moment to get her bearings. To the right was the town park, looking much better than she remembered. She turned left and wondered for a moment if she'd started hallucinating. Was that a pregnancy thing?

"Ryker?" The tall man walking toward her stopped and turned his gaze her way.

"Jess?" Shock was written on his face. Then he crossed the remaining distance and wrapped his arms around her.

Everything she'd been through the past weeks, months or even years suddenly bubbled to the surface, and she started to cry.

Pregnancy hormones were the worst.

# *CHAPTER TWO*

"WHAT ARE YOU doing here, Jess? Not that it isn't great to see you."

Jess scrabbled in her purse for a tissue. She blew her nose and wiped her eyes. "It's a long story. Could we go somewhere?"

Ryker shook his head as if to clear his thoughts. "Right. I was just going to get Rachel from work, so—"

Relief. They were here in town to stay. "Congratulations, by the way."

"You knew?"

"I looked you up a couple of weeks ago. Saw your wedding announcement."

A smile crossed her brother's stern face, one she'd never seen before.

"Yeah. We're married."

"Happily, if that look on your face is something to go by."

His cheeks flushed. This was fun. He must really be into Rachel. Which was great. Just not what she'd expected from Ryker.

"I'm lucky."

Jess bumped her shoulder into his arm. "She is, too."

His smile fell. "A lot happened since I left." Sounded like it wasn't all good.

"I know. Me, too."

"Anyway, I was just going to meet Rachel—why don't you come home for dinner with us? If that's okay. If you want to talk in private, we could do that after we eat."

Her stomach was about to rumble again. "That sounds perfect. And what I have to tell you isn't really a secret." It wouldn't be for long, anyway. She was about two months along. According to her math, she could expect a bouncing baby something at the end of May.

"Where's your stuff?"

"My van is around the corner."

Ryker frowned. "Do you have a place to stay?"

Jess shook her head. That was the advantage of driving the van. She always had a place to sleep. "Not yet."

"You can stay with us." That was a nice offer, and she would take him up on it for tonight as long as it didn't upset Rachel, but that wasn't why she'd come back here. She wanted help, not to mooch.

"I'd appreciate it if I could have your couch

tonight, but I'll find a place, if I'm hanging around."

His step stuttered as those words worked their way in.

"Okay, we'll talk. Rachel works on the next street. She's a paralegal. Used to work for her uncle before he went into rehab and retired from the practice—now she's been holding the fort till we get someone new. He's supposed to be at the office tomorrow. Rachel's in a bit of a state because she broke her wrist last week and is having problems getting things done."

Jess made note of that. She'd worked as a receptionist and general office help during her temp agency period. Maybe she could help Rachel and make a few bucks as well.

Jess was pushy, she knew. She'd had to be. No one was going to open doors for her, so she had to shove through them herself.

RACHEL HADN'T CHANGED MUCH. She was still the nicest person Jess had ever met. She hugged Jess so tightly Jess almost lost her breath.

"I'd always wondered what happened to you after you left, Jess! Is everything okay?"

Jess pulled out of her tight embrace. "It's been almost fifteen years, Rachel. I've learned to take care of myself."

Rachel blinked back tears. "I'm just glad you're safe and you're here. Can you stay with us?"

Jess glanced at Ryker. "I hoped I could use your couch tonight, but if I'm settling down here, I'll find my own place."

Rachel tucked her arm through Jess's. "Of course you're settling here. At least for a while. And you're welcome to stay with us as long as you want."

That was the Rachel Jess remembered. It was incredible that she was still that trusting and helpful. It would be easy to take advantage of her.

Jess's glance swung across to her brother. His expression was warm as he watched his wife. At least now Rachel had someone to protect her from her naïveté. Jess knew from her own experience that Ryker would step forward to keep anyone he cared about safe.

Rachel and Ryker had a small place close to Main Street. It was clean and tidy, things that the Slades' home had never been, and Jess didn't realize how much that comforted her until Rachel told her to sit and she collapsed on the couch. Her bed for tonight. She was ready to sleep now, but she pushed her fatigue aside.

Rachel stood in the kitchen. "I've got

chicken to barbecue and some salad. We've been trying to take advantage of the BBQ before it gets too cold out. Is that okay? We could go out to the diner or—"

"That's awesome, Rachel. I really appreciate it. How can I help?"

Rachel shook her head, because she was still the same girl Jess had known in high school. "No, it's fine. Ryker is doing the grilling, and the salad is already made. If you've been driving for a while, you must be tired."

Tired was an understatement, since growing a baby apparently wiped a person out. Still... "But you have a cast on your wrist."

Rachel frowned at it. "Ryker made the salad this morning to make sure I didn't try. All I have to do is set the table, and please, let me at least do this. It's bad enough at work, where I don't seem to be able to do anything."

Jess forced herself to stand. "You can be useful by telling me where everything is. Come on, I'm sure your wrist will heal faster if you don't overdo it."

Rachel sighed in defeat. "Thanks, Jess. If it wasn't my right hand, I'd probably be good, but..."

OVER DINNER, Rachel and Ryker caught Jess up on their news. Jess's heart hurt when she heard about her brother's divorces and alcoholism. She was also a little surprised. After growing up with their dad and the way he drank, she'd have expected Ryker to be more cautious about drinking.

He was sober now. Rachel apologized for not having any alcohol in the house, but Jess assured her it was fine. She had always been careful with alcohol, and she wouldn't be drinking now, not for a long time.

Ryker told her their father was in a home. Rachel had gone to check on him, but Ryker refused. The man was lost in the world of dementia, and the house had been sold to a developer from New York City who was putting up a hotel on the property. The money was paying for their father's care.

Ryker watched her as he explained about that. Maybe he thought Jess would care. Jess had no intention to revisit the old place. The memories were almost all bad. The only good ones included some of her siblings, mostly Ryker. She didn't need to see the house to remember that. She wasn't looking for money, either. Not from that place.

When they'd finished eating, Jess insisted on cleaning up, and afterward they sat on the back porch with iced tea and waited for the sky to darken. It was finally time for Jess to talk, and she held in a sigh as her body relaxed in a chair.

"After you left, Ryker, things got really bad with Dad and the twins, so I took off."

Ryker's jaw clenched, and he looked away.

"It wasn't your fault. You couldn't take care of us forever. But when you were gone, there was nothing to protect us."

"Where did you go?" Rachel, the peace-keeper, spoke up. She probably guessed how guilty Ryker felt.

"Albany at first. Then Syracuse, and then I headed west. I found work doing whatever I could—"

Jess broke off when Ryker flinched.

"Not that, brother. I cleaned hotel rooms and washed dishes and waited tables. Learned to tend bar. Worked at a temp agency and did office jobs. I kept myself safe and fed, so it was better than home had been."

Rachel looked ready to cry again. Jess continued her story.

"I got my GED, saved my money. I have a camper van, so I always have a place to sleep if I need to. Before now I was out in Washington State, and I liked that. The Pacific was beautiful."

None of the Slade kids had had vacations

growing up. It was the first time Jess had seen an ocean, and she'd loved it.

"Why did you decide to come back?"

That was the big question. She might as well drop the bomb right away.

"I'm pregnant."

There was a shocked silence for a minute. Jess rushed to fill it before the questions started.

"The baby should arrive in May, 'cause I'm about two months along. I just found out a couple of weeks ago. I looked you up, Ryker, saw you were here and married to Rachel, and thought, if I was gonna do this, I'd like to be near my favorite brother."

Rachel and Ryker looked at each other.

"You plan to keep the baby?" Rachel asked in a quiet voice.

Jess nodded. "I wouldn't have done this deliberately—gotten pregnant—but when I found out there was a baby coming, I wanted it."

She didn't know how to describe that feeling to them. After being on her own for so long, to have someone of her own. Someone to love and care for. Someone to be with. Someone hers.

If she was doing this, she was getting help. She'd stood on her own two feet since she left

Carter's Crossing, but for her baby, she'd ask for help and take it. She'd make the best possible life for her child.

That meant Ryker. The boy who'd stepped between her and her sisters and their abusive father. The guy who'd let their father destroy his own homework to protect theirs. And Rachel? Jess couldn't imagine finding another person who'd be a better help for a single mom.

If they didn't mind. If they'd help.

"The father?" Ryker's voice was level, but it wasn't hard to hear the menace behind it.

"He's not involved."

Ryker growled.

Jess put up a hand. "He doesn't know. I found out after he left, and I don't intend to tell him."

Two sets of worried eyes met hers.

"Please, listen. I've thought this through. I could track him down, I know, and then I could ask for money. And I'd get it, because his family is rich."

Ryker was almost bursting with the need to speak, but Jess knew what he was going to say.

"If his family finds out, they'll want the baby. And they have the money and clout to get him or her. I'm a single mom, with barely a high school education, so I know I don't look good on paper.

"But I'm going to love this kid. No nannies and boarding schools and being paraded out in front of people as a prop. My ex was raised that way, and that's why he left his family. He said it was a horrible way to grow up. But they called him back, and he went. So this pregnancy? It's for me. I like the idea of raising my baby here, with an aunt and uncle on tap, but only if you can accept that this is how I'm doing this."

Ryker sliced a hand through his hair.

"It's not going to be easy, you know."

"Yes, Ryker, I know. I've worked as a nanny."

Rachel's eyes were big. "You've had a lot of jobs, haven't you?"

Jess nodded. "That was another part of the reason I came back. I figured I could find something to do here, since the town is busy. It looked like things have gotten better as I drove through. If I can get a job and a place to stay, this could be a great place to raise a kid."

"We'll help you." Ryker's chin was up, so Jess knew he'd do all he could to make her wish come true.

Rachel looked at Ryker. "You know, the new lawyer is supposed to be in the office tomorrow. And I can't do much with——" She held up her right wrist in its cast. "Jess, you've done office work, right? You can file and answer phones, set up appointments, things like that."

"Absolutely." In between morning upchucking bouts, but she wouldn't mention that. Morning sickness had hit her hard. But it ended, didn't it? Maybe soon?

Rachel was on a roll. "Maybe, at least temporarily, you could help out at the office while you look for something more permanent. Oh, Mariah was looking for help, too, since she's always planning a bunch of things for the town."

Jess's eyes watered. Stupid pregnancy hormones. She was ready to cry at the drop of a hat. But this was so kind of Rachel. She hadn't seen Jess in almost fifteen years, and yet she was prepared to risk her own reputation to get her a job.

Well, Jess wouldn't disappoint.

Ryker squinted at his wife. "Is the place over Benny's empty right now?"

Rachel pouted. "That's too far away. I want Jess close to us."

Jess wasn't sure she was ready for total family closeness when she'd just returned.

She'd had a lot of years with space to set her own rules.

"Do I know any of these people you're talking about?"

"No one has met the lawyer yet, and Mariah is still new. She's in charge of the romance business in Cupid's Crossing and married Nelson Carter. We're friends."

Jess felt her brows rising. Mariah sounded impressive. Would she be someone Jess wanted to work with? If she was a friend of Rachel's, the chances were good. Rachel had been kind to her in high school when kindness had been a scarce commodity for the Slades.

"And Benny was in our year. Benny Gifford?"

Jess thought back. "I remember him. His dad was a teacher, right?"

Ryker nodded. "Mr. G retired, and Benny was in a car accident. He was hurt pretty badly and uses a wheelchair now. He does repairs and rents out the apartment over his shop. I stayed there when I first came back."

"Wow. I assumed most people I knew would have moved on. Sounds like a lot of them stayed."

Rachel shrugged. "I stayed. Benny stayed. Nelson left and came back, like your brother.

I don't know if you'll find many more people we knew in school still around—oh, Dave and Jaycee. And Andie Kozak is here. She's been running the construction company since her dad died not long after you left."

"What about the rest of us?"

Ryker knew she meant their siblings. "The twins are in prison."

Jess grimaced, but she couldn't say she was surprised.

"Ethan went to Europe, but no one's heard from him for a while. Ana went to California, Kat to Australia. Haven't heard from them in a few years now."

"Aren't we just the perfect Hallmark family?" Jess couldn't fault them for leaving—it was what she'd done, after all. To escape her father and the path the rest of her brothers had been heading down.

Ryker put his hand on hers. "We were all dealt a crappy hand. But other people get the same. It was still up to us what we did with it. I'm not proud of everything I've done, but I'm happy to be where I am now."

He smiled at Rachel, and Jess felt a pang of loneliness. It would be nice to have someone like that.

Her hand dropped to her belly. She would have someone. Not a partner, but someone she could love with every bit of her being, and she would. She could do it on her own. She *would* do it.

## CHAPTER THREE

DEACON STRAIGHTENED HIS tie with nervous fingers. The door to Lowther Legal Services was in front of him. First day.

He had no reason to be nervous. He wasn't interviewing for a job—it was his. This was a small-town legal office, not the cutthroat one he'd been working in for the last few years. He wouldn't be responsible for the complex corporate acquisitions and mergers that he'd been dealing with since he joined the family firm. This would be more like the pro bono work he had done for New York Legal Services. The stuff he was good at—simple, straightforward and personal.

But he'd also be dealing with this on his own. No highly trained pool of paralegals and support staff. Just him and one paralegal. Rachel Slade. She'd worked here for years. Hopefully she was fully conversant with all the files he'd need to deal with, and not someone incompetent who'd been kept on by the previous lawyer for reasons of loyalty or—

Enough stalling. Time to begin. He was Deacon Standish—he'd graduated from Harvard and worked in New York City. His father would walk in here and have everyone cowed in moments. It was time for Deacon to channel some of that confidence.

He gave a firm push to the door, and it didn't budge. Two more shoves, and he realized he'd need to unlock it. He opened his briefcase to find the keys that had been couriered to him before he left.

He'd never been the first one to the office before, back in the city. Rachel wasn't in yet, so there'd be no coffee waiting. No one would have a list of the day's appointments and meetings waiting for him. If his father had sent him here to make sure he knew what he was missing back at the family firm, he heard the message loud and clear.

He opened the door and peered around curiously.

His tension vanished. No one was here with coffee, but there were also no expectations. No one giving him that slightly disappointed look. It was…relaxing. He took a closer look at the place where he'd be working for the next six months or year.

It was an old building. That was obvious from outside, but inside he could see it hadn't been updated into a bland, corporate space. There was a large office in the back with an oak door, and a window into the main room, through which he could see a massive wooden desk, a pair of chairs facing it. There was a raised blind, which presumably could be lowered for privacy.

Old-school. It was the kind of desk that would weigh a ton and have brass locks on some of the drawers. It should have an old-fashioned blotter in the middle, instead of the blank surface he saw now. It was the kind of desk a lawyer would have in an old black-and-white movie.

That would be his desk.

Tucked beside his new office was a closed door that could lead to a file room or a break room. Another door bore a sign that said Washroom. In the corner was a table with a coffee maker, a microwave and, underneath, a bar fridge. So probably no break room.

Also in the outer office was a tall shelf with office supplies, a couple of desks, one covered with files and boxes, one with a laptop and printer. A couch was near the door, by him, and a couple of chairs in front of the working desk to his right.

His clients here wouldn't be large corporations. They'd be people who'd come and sit in those chairs in front of his desk, and he'd talk to them. He could take the time to discuss their problems, their families... No one would be looking over his shoulder, urging him to rush through, get more done, bill more hours, get bigger and richer clients.

This was supposed to be a punishment for him. He'd been shunted out of the city until the "big mistake" blew over and he could return to the firm he would head one day. Hopefully a day far, far in the future, since Deacon wished his father a long and healthy life. His father enjoyed what he did and thrived on the stress and competition.

Deacon didn't. That was another reason to wish his father's tenure continued. But there were things that needed to change at the firm, and he was the only one who could both see the need for it and would someday be in a position to make those changes.

He sighed. It was a responsibility he wished wasn't his.

In any case, that wasn't going to be a problem until he'd done his penance here in Cupid's Crossing and was back in Manhattan with a chance to speak up. Stepping up and making his voice heard was not something he relished, so he didn't mind this temporary banishment. He'd have a chance to practice the law he enjoyed—personal, small and, to him, meaningful. Then he would return to fulfill his destiny and set right some wrongs. He could push that future away for a while.

He turned when he heard a noise behind him. A woman stepped in through the door. She was about his age, with brown hair and eyes. Quietly pretty, with a welcoming smile on her face.

"Mr. Standish! I'm Rachel Slade. I meant to be here first to welcome you."

Her smile warmed him.

"Call me Deacon, please. I'm looking forward to working with you."

Rachel walked past him to drop her purse and bag on what was obviously her desk.

"I'm so glad you're here. I've been doing my best to find lawyers from nearby firms for clients as they come in but having someone with your credentials here in town is really going to help. Let me get the coffee going and I'll get you up to speed."

"Thank you."

She took the coffeepot into the washroom to fill it. Deacon tried to picture that happening at the family firm in New York and couldn't even imagine the expression on his father's face. A glance at the table reassured him that there wasn't any instant coffee or artificial powdered creamer. He didn't think he was a snob, but he'd rather drink water than that stuff.

Rachel returned from the washroom, the carafe of water held awkwardly against her as she closed the door. That's when Deacon noticed the cast, mostly hidden by the sleeve of her cardigan.

"Let me help." He let his briefcase drop to the floor and rushed over to grab the pot.

"Thank you." She managed to put coffee and a filter in the machine (quite clean, he was relieved to see) and indicated he should pour the water into the reservoir in back. She snapped the lid closed and took the pot from him to slide into the machine.

"There's milk in the fridge and sugar in the cupboard."

Deacon leaned over to open the door of the fridge and grabbed the container of milk. "I don't use sugar."

"I can get creamer, if you prefer. Do you like the flavored ones?"

Deacon held up a hand. "Milk is fine. It's what I normally have." Well, often milk that had been warmed and frothed by a barista, but he didn't use creamer.

Rachel opened the cupboard and pulled out a mug, setting it down before getting another.

"I'm slow, because, of course, if I break a wrist it has to be the right one."

Deacon watched her wave the hand with the cast in front of her.

"You're right-handed?" he guessed.

She nodded.

"Should you be working? Don't you need to rest your hand?"

Rachel smiled again. "No, I don't need to stay at home. You're going to want me here at the office to get you started, and I'd be bored at home unable to do most things. Here at least I'm of some use."

The coffee finished burbling. Deacon reached for the pot, unwilling to have Rachel try to pour with her weaker hand.

"Thank you." She said as he slid the filled cup over to where she was standing. He filled his cup, adding in milk after Rachel had, stirring it with one of the sticks provided.

"Can I carry that for you?"

She frowned at the cup for a moment, then nodded. "Why don't we go into your office, in case someone walks in? We can close the door so no one will hear us talking."

Deacon grabbed a cup in each hand and followed Rachel to the office. He was relieved to hear she valued confidentiality. He set her cup on the visitor side of the desk and his in front of the large leather office chair on the other side. Rachel went back out to grab her bag while he settled in the well-used chair.

Once they were seated, each with a notepad in front of them, Rachel took a sip of coffee and a deep breath. Deacon picked up his pen, ready to take notes.

"I didn't book anyone to come in today, so you'd have a chance to look through the files and get an idea of what's going on here. That doesn't mean someone won't come in, but we can hope."

Deacon smiled at her. She was very kind. He hoped she was also very competent.

"That sounds good. I appreciate that. So, what do we have to deal with?"

Rachel was more than competent. She'd spent most of a year juggling files, finding lawyers from nearby towns to outsource and handle the details while she did the face-to-face meetings and made sure the invoices and payments were handled and the filing kept up. It was a lot of extra work when everything was funneling through different law offices. He understood why she was so grateful he was here.

Cupid's Crossing was looking for a permanent lawyer. Abigail Carter, matriarch of the Carter family who had founded the town, had brought in new business as she made Carter's Crossing into the new Cupid's Crossing, a place for people to come for romantic occasions. As a result, there was a definite need for someone in place to handle the legal affairs that arose.

He wasn't sure why they'd had a problem finding anyone so far. But that wasn't his concern. He was here because Abigail Carter was involved with Gerald Van Dalton, and Gerald Van Dalton did business with Standish Legal, PLLC. When it seemed advisable for Deacon to lie low, this opportunity to help Gerald was serendipitous.

Deacon spent a couple of hours making notes and listening to what Rachel had to tell him about files that were currently in the office and needed to be dealt with. Some mortgages and deed transfers. A couple of wills to be changed, a couple more to prepare. Contracts for a new hotel being built, involving the architect, and the construction firm as well as a dispute between two neighbors.

"Wouldn't that be handled in small claims court?" he asked Rachel.

She held back a grin. "My uncle was kind of an ad hoc judge for problems like this. The older residents here in town knew him and believed what he told them about the law. It saved going into Oak Hill. I think people will still expect you to make those kinds of calls for them."

Deacon wrote down *mediator* on his list. That was a new one. But it could be interesting.

"Can you bring me the files for the people with appointments tomorrow? I'd like to review them before they come in. And anything you have on the new hotel."

Rachel stood and then paused.

"I'm having some difficulties with tasks like that." She held up her right arm, showing him the cast again.

"If you need to take time off—" He repeated the offer, and she raised a hand to stop him. He hoped she wasn't going to agree this time. He absolutely needed her help to get through this first week. She knew all these people, and her assistance would be invaluable.

"I wondered if you'd approve hiring on a temporary office assistant. Someone who could make coffee and copies and file things that are difficult for me. We'd get more done, and that should cover most of the extra cost. I could still advise you as well as supervise that person, and I think it would help make the transition smoother."

His respect for Rachel grew. "That sounds like an excellent idea. Is it possible to get someone like that to start soon?" If the town hadn't been able to lure in a lawyer, would they have office temps on tap?

Rachel's cheeks turned pink. "I, um, I may have someone. If you're okay with it."

He didn't understand why she was hesitating. They obviously needed the help, and if there was someone available...

"Is this person competent, trustworthy and available? Would they be willing to work for a reasonable rate?"

Deacon hadn't dealt with payroll before, so he didn't know what that reasonable rate would be. Did he need to take a look at the firm's financials before he committed to something? He was supposed to be a gun for hire, but maybe he should check on those things. Or was that overstepping?

"It's, um, my sister-in-law. She's done some office temp work, and she's just arrived in town, so I think she'd be willing to help out while she sorts out something more permanent. And my husband and I would like to do what we can to convince her to stay."

Deacon hesitated. This sounded...messy. Involving families. But, in a town this size, were there many people with sufficient skills ready to work?

"Why don't you ask her to come in, and we can discuss it with her?"

References and employment history—that should cover most of what they needed to know, right? He could write up an employment contract easily enough, but he had never hired anyone. Or fired them. Human resources had always dealt with that.

Rachel was now chewing on her lip. "Would you, maybe, like to join us at the diner for lunch? I was going to meet Ryker, my husband. It would give you a chance to see a bit of the town, and if Jess joined us, then you could get a feel for if you want to interview her."

Right. Lunch. He'd planned to find someplace to get takeout but didn't know what the town had to offer. He should stock up his rental with some groceries but hadn't yet done so. He needed to arrange for a new tire as well.

Should he go out to lunch with his paralegal? Would that cross a boundary? He wouldn't do this back in the city. It wouldn't be deemed appropriate. But he was in a two-person office, maybe soon to be a temporarily three-person office. He didn't like the segregation in his family firm, the unwritten boys' club rules that were stifling to the people who worked there and weren't old boys.

People like Meredith. And he was supposed to be changing that.

He told Rachel he'd be happy to join her. Then wondered if he was making another mistake.

JESS GRINNED ACROSS the diner table at her brother.

"I cannot believe it! This place looks exactly the same!"

Ryker gave her his rare smile. "It was strange for me, too, the first time I was in here after I came back. They've obviously updated the place but managed to keep it looking the same."

Jess checked the menu. "Not the prices."

"I'm sure the operating costs aren't the same, either."

Jess set down the menu on the table and looked around the diner. It was clean and busy. She wasn't sure she recognized anyone working, but it had been a long time. She hadn't been able to afford meals out before she ran away from Carter's Crossing.

"Maybe I could get a job here, if this thing with Rachel's lawyer doesn't work out."

Ryker's lips thinned. "Not sure. Do you remember Jean, the woman at the counter over there?"

Jess looked at the middle-aged woman making a pot of coffee. She shook her head. "No, should I?"

"She wasn't very happy when I came back."

Jess sighed. "Something you did, or we did, or Dad did?"

Ryker nodded. "I don't know exactly, but it was something. She's come around. I'm not afraid she's gonna spit in my coffee anymore, but I don't know if she'd want a Slade working here."

Jess bit at her thumbnail. "Was it a mistake for me to come back? Are we going to be Slades here forever?"

Ryker reached for her hand and wrapped his larger fist around it.

"People had more reason to be suspicious of me than you, and I've found a place here. It should work, but I wanted you to be aware some people still remember. I hope you stay."

"But you had Rachel in your corner, helping you."

Ryker's whole face softened, lips turning up in another smile. "Yeah, I did. But you do, too."

Jess suspected Rachel was a real force

around town, though she'd never push any-one. "She is *so* nice."

Ryker held up a finger. "Don't let her hear you say that. She got tired of being nice."

"Why? It's, like, the best thing you could say about someone."

"She was trapped by that reputation. It wasn't all…nice for her. But, here she is now, and I think that's the new lawyer with her."

Jess looked toward the door. Her new sis-ter-in-law was coming in, followed by a man in an expensive suit. Something Jess could recognize from working at hotels and fancy restaurants where those kinds of suits were found. Or sometimes on the side of the road when that guy couldn't change his tire. As her eyes ran upward, she recognized the man wearing the suit.

It was the Audi man.

# CHAPTER FOUR

JESS WAS WATCHING as Rachel pointed to the table where she and Ryker were sitting, so she saw the man's reaction when he recognized her. His jaw dropped, then a smile began and, as he made the connections his brow creased slightly before his face became a polite mask. Rachel was at the table by then, the lawyer behind her, and she made the introductions.

"Deacon, this is my husband, Ryker Slade, and my sister-in-law Jess Slade. This is Deacon Standish, our interim lawyer."

Huh. Deacon Standish. It was one of those rich, preppy names, which wasn't a surprise. He looked like a Deacon Standish. Tall, medium build, with brown hair and soft blue eyes. Well-groomed, well-dressed and well cared for. Rachel slid into the seat beside Ryker, leaving Mr. Deacon Standish to sit beside Jess. He did it carefully and, she thought, reluctantly. Not that there was anything she could criticize. He had beautiful manners.

He hadn't had a chance to mention recognizing her. She'd bet her van that he did, but she wasn't going to wait for him to decide how to play this, if he wanted to let on they knew each other.

"Did you get your tire taken care of?"

He turned to look at her directly, and from the corner of her eye, Jess saw Ryker and Rachel's startled expressions.

Deacon's ears turned pink. "Ah, no. I haven't had a chance to yet."

Right. It had been less than twenty-four hours. Jess felt her cheeks warm. "Well, don't forget. It's not safe to be driving around on a doughnut."

Rachel asked. "Have you two met before?"

Jess hadn't bothered to tell anyone about the tire encounter—who would have guessed she'd ever see the guy again?

"Ms. Slade helped me change my tire. It was on a stretch of road with no cell service, and I'd never had to change a tire before. I was at a bit of a loss. She was most helpful."

"You did most of the work." Jess had been tired and almost kept driving when she'd seen the man and car at the side of the road. She'd been more than happy to provide instruction and let him do the labor.

"I may have used some muscles, but I'd

still be on the side of the road if you hadn't stopped and helped."

That was patently untrue. The stretch of road was quiet but not totally deserted. "Glad I was there at the right time."

Rachel had a big smile on her face. "That's great, that you've met. I already told Deacon about you, since we need help at the office."

Jess held on to her smile, but she tried to message Rachel with her eyes not to push the guy. It had been one thing, to consider working in a legal office when she'd thought it would be a normal guy. Well, whatever normal was for lawyers. But this guy? With his expensive suits and preppy name, he was in a whole other league, and it was one Jess preferred to avoid.

"Why don't we order?" Jess tried to divert the conversation, hoping to avoid the working question until it was time to leave. She'd find another job.

Deacon opened his menu with alacrity. "What would you recommend?"

Jess kept her mouth firmly shut. She was new in town as well, but this was a diner. Avoid the fancy stuff and order what diners were known for. She had already decided on a bowl of the daily soup. She hadn't been able to keep anything down this morning, thanks to the peanut, and she hoped she could sneak soup into her body before it rebelled.

Deacon was inspecting the menu. "They have organic vegetables for the special—do they use organic ingredients for everything?" He was reading the description carefully.

"Nope," Jess said.

Deacon lifted his head. Rachel shook hers. "I don't think so. The diner just started dealing with Everton Farms—it's one of the new contracts—but I think they're mostly finished for the season."

He nodded. Jess told herself that just because her ex had also expected fancy food like that didn't mean he and Deacon were the same kind of people, but she was wary.

"What about the bread—would it be baked in house?" Deacon's foot was jiggling beside her, another indication that he wasn't comfortable.

Rachel looked anxious. "I doubt it?"

Rachel was clueing in to the fact that Deacon came from a radically different background.

"I'm sorry." Jess was surprised to hear Deacon apologize. "I must sound very fussy. I'm sure everything will be good."

It was a nice thing to say, but Jess could still feel his leg moving beside her.

A part of her wanted to offer assistance, help him learn to navigate the limits of a small town. To fit in and feel comfortable, which he appeared to want to do. But she didn't need to do that. Deacon obviously had money—he was a lawyer, which meant he was smart, and he was a grown, white, privileged male. The last time she'd felt sorry for someone like him, out of his element, she'd ended up with a not-quite-legal husband who'd abandoned her when his family called and an unexpected pregnancy.

So she bit her lip, let him order a grilled cheese sandwich and hoped the soup would stay down.

THEY TALKED ABOUT neutral subjects while they ate. Travel. City life. Jess had been to a couple of larger cities but tended to prefer smaller places. Deacon came from money— the places he'd been and the way he'd experienced them were different from Jess's hand-to-mouth travels and Ryker's tours in the air force. Rachel had never traveled far, but Ryker promised her they would.

Jess would never have admitted wanting to travel to any of her bosses, since there was a good chance she'd have been let go. But Rachel was essential to the law office right now, and Jess knew she'd be good at what she did. After all, they'd been classmates back in high school.

Rachel was the one who brought up Jess as a prospective temporary employee again.

"Jess, I told Deacon that you might be able to help us out in the office while I've got my hand in a cast."

Jess could feel Deacon's foot start moving again. He didn't want her working for him, so she'd make it easy for him to say no.

"I don't have a lot of office experience."

Rachel gave her a puzzled look. "You said you'd worked as a temp."

"Yeah, but I've got more experience waitressing. Or cleaning." Blue-collar jobs that this man would expect someone like her to have done.

"How long did you work as a temp, Ms. Slade?"

Jess paused and finally admitted, "Two years." Closer to three, but she wasn't inflating her experience and skills only to be caught out later.

"And what did you do, and what kind of offices were they? Any lawyers?"

Jess shook her head. "No, nothing with legal work. I was a receptionist at an insurance agency and did some filing and data entry for an accounting firm. Couple of veterinarians and a dentist."

Deacon studied her for a moment. "That sounds like you have experience in an office setting. Do you enjoy that kind of work?"

Why was this man asking questions like he wanted her to work for him? She'd felt him tense when Rachel brought the idea up. It wasn't her job to figure him out, though, so she went with honesty. "I enjoy work that gives me the money I need to live."

A muscle ticked in his jaw. She wasn't sure what part of that had gotten to him. Was he more accustomed to prospective employees sucking up to him to get a job? Obviously, that would have been the smarter move. She had to stop sabotaging herself because he reminded her of her past mistakes.

"I just mean, I'll do any kind of work that's honest and pays."

His jaw ticked again, but she'd tried to be nice. She should pay more attention to Rachel to learn how to do that better.

He swallowed. "Why don't you arrange a time with Rachel to come in and see how it works out? You'll mostly be working with her, so if she's happy, we'll be fine."

He was going to give her a trial? That was good. Absolutely.

Rachel and Deacon went back to the law office after Deacon won the battle over who would pay. Jess followed Ryker out to his truck. He had offered to take her over to see what Benny's rental was like, so she could work out a place to live. She didn't want to take advantage of their offer to stay with them.

Once they were in the truck, Ryker started the engine but asked her a question before pulling out.

"Is there anything you want to tell me about that lawyer?"

"No, why?"

Ryker turned to her. "You were a little on edge with him. Did he do something when you were helping with his flat tire? Do I need to worry about Rachel with him?"

Jess shook her head vigorously. "No, no, nothing like that. I don't have anything against him—really, I don't. He's just… Well, he's rich, and he reminds me of some rich guys I've known. And a little of my ex, the baby daddy. And right now my hormones are messed up, so…just ignore me. He's been nice enough to offer me a chance at a job, so I need to put all that behind me."

Ryker continued to watch her and then

grunted and backed the truck out of the parking stall. "Okay, but if he does anything…"

"Thanks, Ry, but I'm sure it's going to be fine."

WHEN JESS STEPPED into Benny's repair shop, her gaze immediately went too high, then dropped to see Benny in his chair.

"Jess!" Benny said, with every indication of pleasure in seeing her.

"Benny! Wow. Things have changed."

Benny patted the arm of his wheelchair. "Yeah, they have."

"Not just that—you got older! I mean, it's good to see you. Sorry. I never got the tact gene."

"I remember, Jess. You, of course, look just the same." There was a grin peeping at the corner of Benny's mouth.

Jess rolled her eyes. "Nice try, Ben. I've seen myself in the mirror. But things will get better—did Ryker tell you I'm knocked up? Once I'm past this morning sickness, I hope to get that pregnancy glow."

Benny blinked, eyes dropping to her waist then back up. "No, Ryker didn't say anything. Are you okay? Do I ask about the father or not?"

"He's not in the picture, so no."

"And you're good with this?"

Jess nodded. "Surprised the heck out of me, too, but yeah, I want the kid. You don't mind if I stay and there's a kid on the premises?"

Benny grinned. "Not only do I not mind, I'll even babysit."

"I'll hold you to that."

Ryker broke in. "Maybe you want to see the place before you commit to it?"

Benny laughed. "Yeah, that's probably a good idea. Key's in the drawer there—help yourself."

"Thanks, Ben." Ryker nodded at the man, then grabbed the key and led Jess up the stairs.

Jess had no complaints to make about the apartment. She'd stayed in much worse. She and Benny argued over the rate and security deposit, since Jess was sure he was giving her a sympathy deal, but finally they came to an agreement. Jess promised to provide some cleaning services to make up for the break in the rent. Ryker said he'd help her move her stuff in on the weekend and find her some furniture. There were a few pieces already in the apartment, but he wanted her to have her own bed.

Considering how exhausted she felt, Jess was happy to agree.

DEACON FOUND HIMSELF on the doorstep of his office on his second day, hesitating again.

He smoothed down his tie and reminded himself he was a good lawyer. He could handle this, his first meetings with clients. He had Rachel to help him, and she'd been tremendously competent, even with a cast on her dominant hand. Today Jess would be there to assist her, so things should go even better.

He clenched his tie at the thought and had to deliberately relax his hand and smooth the fabric.

There was no reason Jess should make him nervous. But when he thought of those light gray eyes and remembered how incompetent he'd been with the tire, he had to force his hand to the doorknob before he messed up his tie again.

This time the door was open. And he found both Rachel and Jess already in the office.

Rachel met him with her pleasant smile. "Good morning, Deacon. I was just showing Jess some filing to keep her busy so we can finalize the details on the clients coming in this morning."

That was a good decision on Rachel's part. Deacon greeted her and told her that before turning to Jess. Jess took one look at him and then ran to the bathroom. While Deacon stood, at a loss, they heard the sounds of someone retching. Obviously, Jess.

"Is she okay?"

Rachel bit her lip. "She should be."

How could she possibly know that based on the sounds they were hearing?

"Is it the flu?"

He didn't need to get sick his first week. And he didn't need Rachel any more incapacitated than she was. He wasn't the kind of boss to insist his employees come in when they weren't feeling well.

"Noooo." Rachel was still biting her lip.

He lowered his voice. "Is she hungover?" He didn't want to leap to conclusions about Jess, but if she was sick like this every day because she was out partying at night, they were going to have a problem.

"No!" This time there was no hesitation on Rachel's part.

The door to the bathroom opened, and Jess appeared. Now that he had time to study her, he could see that she did not look well. She was pale, still with those circles under her eyes, and surely she was too thin. But she pulled her shoulders back, and her chin up.

"Sorry about that. I'm fine now. I'll get the filing caught up if you two need to talk. I can answer the phone if it rings—Rachel showed me what to do."

Deacon wanted to make her a cup of tea and tell her to sit down till she felt better, but Jess almost dared him to offer any sympathy. He nodded and moved to his office. Rachel followed him in, carrying a tablet. She sat down while he pulled his laptop out of his bag and arranged it on his desk.

Rachel held up the tablet. "I can take some notes on this, but most of what you need to know is in my head."

He smiled at her. "That's fine, Rachel. You, uh, you didn't make coffee, did you?"

Her eyes went wide. "I'm sorry—I was focused on getting Jess going and didn't even think of it! Give me a moment—"

Deacon held up a hand. "Maybe we could ask Jess to do that, since she has two good hands, and we can get started?"

"Right." Rachel shook her head. "I'm not used to having help."

Deacon didn't tell her that he was used to an assistant who had his coffee waiting for him when he arrived. He wasn't in New York now, and he wasn't at the firm. And not having coffee ready was a small price to pay for the chance to be here rather than in the New York office.

Rachel stood and moved to the doorway. "Jess, would you mind making coffee? Do you need any help with the machine?"

Jess's voice came back to them. "I'll make a full pot so there's some for clients, too—not a problem. I've used machines like this one before."

Good. Everything was going to be good.

Rachel started to describe for him the papers that their first appointment of the day was looking for, and the smell of the coffee had just reached the office when footsteps raced to the bathroom and the retching noises began again.

Deacon met Rachel's eyes. Hers looked… guilty.

"Rachel, you need to tell me what's going on with Jess. If she's unwell, she shouldn't be here spreading whatever she has to the rest of us. I'm not saying we can't work something out with her, but I don't think she should be here today."

Rachel chewed on her lip and stood up. She moved to the doorway at the sound of the bathroom door opening.

"Jess, maybe you should come here. Deacon thinks you might be contagious, which is making him worry about you being in the office."

There was a pause, and then he heard Jess's footsteps coming this way. Rachel backed away from the door.

Jess stepped in. She had a cracker in her hand. She crossed her arms, and her chin was up again.

"I'm not contagious, and I'm not sick. Not really. I'm pregnant."

Deacon's mouth dropped open.

"Are you going to fire me now?" She shoved the cracker in her mouth.

Rachel put a protective arm around Jess, and the two women faced him, braced for him to tell Jess she couldn't work here if she was pregnant. The irony struck him. He wouldn't be here if he hadn't helped someone else sue for wrongful dismissal for being pregnant.

They didn't know that, so he needed to reassure Jess and Rachel.

"Come in, sit down and let's talk about this."

Jess shot Rachel a look and then sat down. She swallowed the cracker but still looked pale. Her posture was stiff. She expected him to fire her before she'd even had a chance to prove herself. He wondered what her life had been like to make her expect the worst and contrasted that with her willingness to help him with his flat tire. She'd told him to pay the good deed forward. This was his opportunity. She needed this job, and he could assure her she had it.

"I cannot fire you or refuse to hire you because you're pregnant."

Rachel relaxed, but Jess did not.

"There's some wiggle room if there are fewer than four employees, but I'm not going to even try to use that. I've helped women sue their employers for pregnancy discrimination, so it would be rather hypocritical of me to take the first opportunity to do the same myself."

Jess had her eyes narrowed.

"Also, I'm not that kind of person. You don't have reason to trust me yet, but I try to be a decent human being. Why don't you tell me what you need to make this work?"

"That's great to hear, Deacon," Rachel said.

Jess hadn't relaxed. "Are you doing this because you feel sorry for me?"

Deacon felt sorry that life had thrown her some hard curves, making her suspicious like this, but sorry because she was pregnant? He hadn't thought he should be, but the question made him wonder what the circumstances were behind her pregnancy.

He couldn't ask that.

Instead, he smiled at her. "Someone did a

good deed for me recently and told me to pay it forward. I think this might be my chance to do so."

Rachel looked between the two of them. Jess considered, and then nodded.

"So far, I'm only sick in the mornings. I've got crackers stocked up, and they help. I can stay late to make up anything I miss. It should be over soon anyway."

"Maybe you'd prefer to start a little later and finish later, so that it's easier for you to do your tasks? Can we make that work, Rachel?"

Rachel nodded happily. Jess shrugged and stood up.

"I'll get back to the filing. Can you take care of the coffee, Rachel? The smell of it up close was a problem."

Rachel immediately stood and headed out, Jess behind her.

Deacon wondered what he'd gotten himself into. His paralegal couldn't use her dominant hand, so she was limited in her capability. He had a pregnant employee who was violently ill every few minutes. He might not be able to drink coffee in his own office. He was about to have face-to-face meetings with a variety of people without his efficient assistant from New York to weed through them all.

And he was away from the city and his family and the law firm.

He considered he was coming out ahead.

## CHAPTER FIVE

AT THE END of his first couple of days in the office, Deacon had learned a few things.

Rachel was very good at her job, and with people.

Her uncle, the previous lawyer, had been very bad at his job. Deacon's firm had dealt with higher-profile clients, and there was more care taken with their documents, but Rachel's uncle had let things slide. Looking through the agreements that had been drawn up by his predecessor made him cringe.

This was shoddy work.

His first client had come for a divorce filing. Deacon looked at the previous boilerplate and almost pulled his hair out. It was bad.

He made notes on the situation. Two children, a shared home, spouse cheating. He flagged the file for additional work before the next client was ready, this time for a mortgage.

By noon he could see he was going to be busy for a while. He told Rachel what he'd found and how he wanted to correct the documents. She suggested that after their last client the three of them could discuss how to handle this. Rachel could direct Jess, but Jess would be able to type much faster than Rachel could with one hand.

Jess went to the diner to get them some takeout for lunch. Deacon stood and stretched, stepping out of his personal office to clear his head.

The place looked better. It hadn't been bad before, but the filing had obviously fallen behind. He'd known there would be some catch-up since Rachel had been on her own for a while and then injured, but it was incredible what Jess had done in a couple of hours.

"This place looks—"

"Better, right?" Rachel smiled at him. "I'd let the filing pile up, what with everything else I had to do, and then once I did this—" she indicated her arm "—things were getting worse. Jess worked really hard to make up for being sick."

Deacon didn't want her to overwork herself. The woman was pregnant and much too thin. "I hope she didn't overdo things."

"I don't think so. I'm trying to keep an eye on her. She's Ryker's sister, but they haven't seen each other for years, and he's very protective of her. I think she likes to be busy, and she appreciated that you gave her a chance."

Deacon felt the heat on his cheeks. "It's what any decent person would do."

"I'm not sure she's met a lot of decent people." Rachel looked sad, and Deacon wanted to ask more, but Jess returned with their sandwiches and he remembered he was a professional. He was curious, though. He wanted to know what had made Jess the way she was, and he still wanted her to sit and rest.

However, the next client showed up early. Rachel brought him into his office, and he was pulled into a property dispute. Mr. Rankin was determined to sue his neighbor over the trees that dropped debris onto his driveway.

He wished he could have had Rachel in to take notes, but she couldn't with her hand. He would ask her if he should have Jess come to take notes—was she able to write quickly? She probably wouldn't know shorthand—did anyone use that these days? Did the office have equipment to take dictation? He hadn't seen any signs of the technology being updated, but maybe there was a voice-to-text app they could try so he wouldn't need to rely on his memory or his own atrocious notes later.

Once his client had expressed his anger, disgust and desire to pursue a case that Deacon wasn't sure would end in success, he asked about Jess.

"Is that one of the Slade girls you have out there?"

Deacon wondered if Jess and Ryker's family might have information to help the man's case, if he knew them.

"That's Jess Slade, yes."

Mr. Rankin's lips almost disappeared. "Not sure you should have someone like that working in your office."

Deacon's first reaction was to defend Jess, but he didn't know her. He couldn't assume the best about her, even if Rachel supported her.

"I'm new in town, and I thought Jess had just returned as well. Is there some reason she won't be able to perform her job assisting Rachel?"

The man harrumphed. It wasn't a sound Deacon had heard before.

"The Slades are all bad news. Rachel married Ryker when he came back, but before, when he was a teenager? He had to leave town after stealing a car. The oldest boys are in prison. The whole family is trouble."

"I'm sorry that the family went through

some difficulties, but that doesn't mean that Jess has a criminal record or is likely to be dishonest."

Mr. Rankin stood up. "You're new, so I'm trying to give you a heads-up. The Slades are rotten, and we were well rid of them. Now Ryker is back, and Jess—who knows when the rest of them will turn up? We've just started to bring the town back to life. We don't need anyone like them around here."

Deacon stood as well. "I appreciate your concern, but I'll take responsibility for what happens in this office. In the meantime, I suggest you speak to your neighbor and try to resolve the issue amicably. I don't think you have much chance of success in your suit, and it's best to be on good terms with your neighbors."

"I've known my neighbor for thirty years, so I'm not begging him for anything. But I'll tell you, if you're going to have a Slade working for you, I'll take my business elsewhere. There are two kinds of people, and if you're with the Slades, that tells me a lot about you."

Deacon thought the comment revealed even more about Mr. Rankin, but he held back his temper and showed the man out.

This interval as a small-town lawyer wasn't going to be all sunshine and roses. Maybe

Deacon wouldn't be able to do a good job here. That bothered him more than it should, considering this was a short-term position.

Jess HID IN the file room until Deacon had returned to his office. Then her body sagged.

She was tough. She'd never had an easy time of it, and she'd learned to stop complaining long ago. But right now, whether it was because of the pregnancy or just hitting that final straw, she wondered if she could really make it on her own.

Deacon could let her go now, with perfectly valid reasons not to hire her—she was hurting the business. She'd heard what Rankin had said. Jess would normally be able to find another job, no problem, since she was willing to do almost anything, but with people like Mr. Rankin around, she wouldn't be able to find or keep a job.

Maybe she shouldn't keep this baby. Maybe she should let her ex know. If she couldn't stay here in Cupid's Crossing where she had Ryker and Rachel to help, then maybe she couldn't do this. Call up the ex, let his family take over and…

Rachel's head came around the doorway. "Deacon wants to see us."

Jess swallowed and straightened up. "I'll be right there."

She smoothed her skirt with a shaky hand and wiped the other over her hair. Her ponytail was holding. At least her morning sickness mostly stuck to mornings. She drew in a deep breath and went to face Deacon.

Rachel had provided them all with water. Jess sat down in the chair beside her, across from Deacon, and waited for him to break the news to her. He'd be nice about it, she was sure.

Deacon sighed and adjusted his tie. He was nervous. Probably not used to having to fire someone himself.

"Mr. Rankin was just in here and said some things."

"I heard." She didn't need to hear them repeated.

"I'm new here. I don't know the local politics and gossip. But Jess, you've been gone from town for a long time, correct?"

She nodded, not sure where he was going with this. "About fifteen years."

"I don't believe in judging someone who must have been very young by what her family did. I would like, if you don't mind telling me, to get some idea of why people are upset with your family, just so that I understand what the issues are."

He wanted her to give him the ammunition to fire her?

Rachel spoke. "I can tell you about her brother. When Ryker returned to town over a year ago, he had similar experiences with what you just came across with Mr. Rankin. Ryker, when he was a high school senior, was in an accident with a stolen car he was driving while under the influence."

*Drunk*, Jess clarified in her head.

"He was given a choice of joining the military or facing trial, and so he enlisted in the air force. He served two tours. When he came back last year, people had a difficult time forgetting what he'd done as a teenager and appreciating the service he gave and the changes he'd made to become the person he is now. At this point, most people have accepted him."

Rachel looked at Jess. "I know you wouldn't want to tell what Ryker had done, but he'd be okay with Deacon knowing. And you didn't do anything—it's just what your father and brothers did that people judge you by."

Jess swallowed a lump in her throat. Pregnancy hormones, making her want to cry just because someone was kind.

"May I ask if there's anything else that people might find fault with?"

Jess raised her chin. If Rachel could fight for her, she could fight for herself.

"My father was, or is—I don't know because I haven't seen him since I left—an obnoxious drunk. He stole things and wrecked things. He also hit us sometimes. I haven't seen anyone in the family but Ryker since I was in high school, but he told me the twins are in prison. I'm not surprised. I don't know what the others have been up to."

Rachel spoke again. "Ryker hasn't heard from them, either. I don't think anyone here in Cupid's Crossing knows where they are or what they've done."

Deacon folded his hands together. "None of that sounds like it has any bearing on Jess's work here. Is there anything else I should know?"

Jess met his gaze. He seemed sincere. Like he wasn't going to toss her out even if some of the old town busybodies thought she was a bad choice for him to have working in his office. Maybe he was for real. If so, she'd let him know the last bits that might affect her working here.

"I haven't broken any serious laws."

"Serious laws?"

One shoulder humped up. "I've broken the speed limit and parked in places I shouldn't. Might have used some water and electricity that wasn't meant for public consumption."

"Recently?"

She shook her head. She hadn't been that desperate for a while. "No, that was years ago. When I didn't always have food or a place to sleep."

She was sure this man had never been in a situation like that. The way he was blinking at her backed up her opinion.

"If that's a problem again—"

"We'll take care of it," Rachel said fiercely.

Jess gave her a smile of thanks. "I can take care of myself now. It was just when I first left that things were bad."

She turned back to Deacon.

"And about this baby. I'm not currently married to the father, and I'm not in contact with him anymore. That will upset some people."

Deacon sat up. "There are laws about that. He should at a minimum provide child support. That's something I can do for you."

"No." Jess spoke firmly and loudly. "He doesn't know I'm pregnant, and if he finds out, his family will get involved. They'll want to take the baby from me, and that's not going to happen."

Deacon had a crease between his brows. "But—"

"No," Jess repeated. "If that's a deal breaker, I'll leave, but I'm not budging on this."

Deacon smoothed his tie with one hand. Jess would have bet his leg was moving as well. "I won't try to force you, obviously, but if you change your mind, I'd be happy to help. Now, is that everything we're likely to encounter?"

Jess shrugged. "I don't know what people are going to say, but that's all I know that they might get upset about."

Rachel added, "I think that's all there is. People are judging Jess because of her family."

Deacon smiled at them. "Then let's get back to work. You're feeling okay, Jess?"

Jess nodded. She wasn't going to complain, no matter what. Deacon talked a good game, but so had her ex. She just had to remember not to count on it.

She had a chance to make a home for herself and her baby. She'd give it all she had.

THE NEXT TWO weeks went fairly well.

Fairly.

Rachel was a godsend. Deacon wondered why she'd never considered studying law herself, because her knowledge of the issues covered by the office was impressive, and her people skills were top-notch. There was no way this office would survive without her.

Deacon had to give Jess points for trying. He understood why she was so thin. The number of times she bolted for the bathroom with morning sickness was concerning. And he had given up having coffee at the office, since it never failed to send Jess running for the restroom.

She was smart, as well. When she was told how to do something, she remembered. She was able to type up documents in good time and was excellent at filing. Her reception skills were a little...rough.

He cringed when he overheard her saying, "Yeah, yeah, I got it. I'll give him the message, don't worry." That was nothing like the polished responses he was used to hearing at his family firm.

He did receive some complaints about Jess. Most were from older, conservative clients who were concerned about the Slade family's reputation. He used the same argument as he had with Mr. Rankin (who had not returned to pursue his claim) about Jess not having done anything, but he soon found that referring to her as Rachel's sister-in-law had the best chance of stopping the complainer.

Rachel was beloved in town, and Ryker was the best computer technician available. He'd heard Rachel explaining to people that Ryker worked mostly with software and applications, but there was no one local who was better at the hardware side, either. The world was so dependent on the internet now that no one wanted to be at the bottom of Ryker's list.

At the end of two weeks, Jess no longer had to run for the bathroom. Her skin and hair cleared up, and the shadows were gone from under her eyes. Her clothes were less baggy on her, and she had a tendency to rest her hand on the slight bump forming under her waistline.

Deacon couldn't avoid noticing that Jess was actually very attractive.

Not that he hadn't been around attractive women in his life. He had. Frequently. His mother was a beautiful woman, and so were many of his cousins. He'd gone out with some stunning women himself. He'd been more focused on work than dating, so those occasions were more likely to be some kind of formal, family-related event, and often the women were daughters of clients or other lawyers in the firm. None of those women had ever unsettled him the way one look from Jess's gray eyes did.

Since he was unsettled, he decided his best plan was to keep his distance from her. At least, as much as was feasible in a small office. He needed to be professional. He discussed the work with Rachel, which was sensible, because Rachel knew everything and she was the one who'd be here permanently. If he needed a file, he'd ask Rachel, and she would get it from Jess, instead of him asking Jess directly. Neither woman called him on it, so he hoped they put it down to the process he was accustomed to from working at his firm in the city, rather than anything connected to Jess.

He finished a meeting with his divorce client, having adjusted the paperwork to what he considered to be a satisfactory level of diligence. He'd stood his ground on some issues her soon-to-be ex-husband had tried to bully her over, and she was flatteringly grateful. He stood to open the door for her to exit and, after watching her leave the office, turned to call for Rachel.

Rachel wasn't there.

"Rachel had a dentist appointment." Jess

looked up at him from her laptop. "You're stuck with me for a bit."

Deacon felt his cheeks warm. He swallowed. "That's not a problem. I'd just forgotten she'd be out."

One corner of her mouth quirked, and her eyebrows lifted, but she didn't say anything. It was clear she had noticed how he'd done his best to avoid her, and he hated that she was resigned to it. She expected it.

That wasn't fair, and he needed to do better. Maybe if he just didn't look right at her eyes.

He leaned against Rachel's desk and smoothed his tie.

"Has everything been going well, Jess?"

He tried to watch her mouth rather than her eyes, and he couldn't miss the way her lips pressed together. Was she angry—or laughing at him? Either wasn't good. Wanting to know the answer to that question, he looked directly at her. She was holding back a laugh.

"Everything has been fine. Do you have any concerns you want to talk about?"

Deacon opened his mouth to respond but didn't know what to say. He was saved by the telephone on the desk.

"Lowther Legal Services. How may I help you?"

There was no complaint to be made about

her initial greeting. That wasn't the problem. It was after, when people wanted to book appointments or speak to him. Should he bother trying to correct her on the way he was used to the phones being handled when Rachel would soon take over everything?

"Mr. Vogler, hold on, just hold on. Deacon…er, Mr. Standish is right here. Explain it to him."

Jess passed the receiver to Deacon, and his jaw dropped.

This was not the way things should be handled. Passing the phone to him, not checking the schedule, not following any kind of protocol…he didn't even know who Mr. Vogler was.

Jess shook the receiver in her hand, and with a frown, he took it from her.

"Mr. Vogler?"

For heaven's sake, he'd never met the man. He was sure he'd seen the name somewhere, but…

"I need help! He's trying to cut down my trees!"

Jess might not have followed the usual protocol, but she had said it was Lowther Legal, not the area arborist.

"Please calm down, Mr. Vogel. Who's cutting down your trees, and why did you call a lawyer?"

"It's Rankin. He's got some kind of legal paper and he's got a chain saw and my wife is standing in front of the trees to try to stop him—you have to help me!"

Suddenly Jess was shoving the notes from his meeting with Rankin into his hands.

"One moment—I need to check something." He skimmed the notes. No, nothing that would give Rankin the right to remove his neighbor's trees.

Jess gave him a shove. "I can call the cops, get them to come and deal with Rankin. The man has always been a misery. You go and legalese him till the cops get there."

Legalese him? A man with a chain saw?

Jess grabbed the phone from his hand. "Mr. Vogler, go help your wife. I'm calling the cops, and then we'll be there as soon as we can."

Jess disconnected and called a local number. At least she wasn't calling 911 about trees.

"This is Jess at the lawyer's office. Rankin has a chain saw and is trying to chop down Vogler's trees even though he has no right to. We're heading over, but you probably need to come."

Deacon was still holding his notes, watching Jess with his mouth hanging open. She hung up, then came around the desk.

"What are you doing?"

She threw up her hands. "Mr. Vogler has been growing those cherry trees since before I was born. They're like, descended from his great-grandparents' trees. Rankin hates everything and just wants to get rid of them to make Vogler miserable. You have to stop him."

"But—I'm a lawyer."

Jess glared at him. "I know. But Rankin was here to try to do this legally, right? Now he's probably told lies to another lawyer in Oak Hill and he'll have destroyed the trees before things get sorted. So just go and tell him habeas corpus or carpe diem or something until the cops get there to stop him."

*Carpe diem?*

She grabbed his arm and began to push him out.

"I don't know where—"

"I do. Now come on before Rankin hurts someone."

## CHAPTER SIX

JESS REMEMBERED MR. VOGLER from when she'd been a kid in Carter's Crossing. Back when they were growing up, constantly hungry, she and some of her siblings had raided those cherry trees. He'd found them climbing the lower branches and, instead of calling the cops on them, told them the cherries were sour and likely to make them sick if they ate them raw. Then he'd brought them out a loaf of bread and some jam his wife had made from the cherries, well sugared to make it taste better.

They'd stayed away from the cherry trees after that. Jess was pretty sure Ryker had cracked a branch trying to climb them, so it was likely they'd get hurt if they tried to climb again, and if the fruit wasn't edible unless you cooked it, then there wasn't much point in climbing the trees anyway. But Jess had never forgotten that kindness, and she was determined to do something for Mr. Vogler now.

Jess managed to get Deacon out of the office, but not without a lot of wheedling and pushing. Once outside, Deacon had stopped resisting and let her tow him the two blocks to where the Voglers and the Rankins lived. Once they got close, it wasn't hard to find the location of the dispute, since Mr. Rankin was revving up the chain saw periodically.

Two Victorian houses, well maintained, with Rankin's driveway separating the two. There was a low fence marking what was presumably the property line between them. On Vogler's side, a row of cherry trees was set back a few feet from the fence. The trees were now grown enough that the branches had reached the fence. Rankin stood on his driveway, chain saw in hand, while a red-faced Vogler faced off against him. A gray-haired woman pressed herself against the nearest cherry tree.

When the chain saw wasn't growling, there was a lot of shouting going on between Mr. Vogler and Mr. Rankin. Neighbors had come over, attracted by the loud noise of the dispute, making a crowd of more than a dozen people. Jess noticed that most of them were on Mr. Vogler's side, and several were standing in front of the trees along with Mrs. Vogler.

Deacon came to a stop beside her. The

shouting continued, and Mr. Rankin buzzed the chain saw again. Deacon's eyes were wide-open, and his jaw had dropped. Yeah, this probably wasn't something he was used to in his fancy law firm in the city. But she knew he was smart, and he cared about people, so she just had to get him going. As soon as the chain saw sound died again, Jess seized the moment and put her fingers in her mouth to send a loud whistle through the hubbub.

Everyone stopped and turned to look at the two of them.

"Here's the lawyer. He'll settle this." Jess crossed her arms and glared at Mr. Rankin.

There was a pause while everyone waited for Deacon to speak. When he remained silent, Jess nudged him in the ribs.

Deacon cleared his throat. "What seems to be the problem?"

Jess rolled her eyes, and Rankin and Vogler started shouting again. She brought her fingers back up to her lips and whistled. It worked just as well this time.

"Show Mr. Standish that paper you've got."

Rankin took a step forward.

"And put down the bloody chain saw!"

Rankin glowered but finally took his chain saw back into his garage before returning with the wrinkled document he'd been waving around.

"Here it is." He shoved the paperwork into Deacon's hands. "I've got a right to get rid of the trees messing up my property."

Deacon opened the papers and started reading. Jess looked around and saw that everyone was focused on the lawyer, awaiting his pronouncement as if it was holy scripture. Deacon merely stood there in his expensive suit, reading papers, but everyone waited quietly. She fought back an inappropriate giggle.

She noticed Deacon's hand stroking his tie and recognized that as his tell. He was nervous. Which made sense. He was facing a whole group of strangers, one of whom had been wielding a chain saw. Jess had dragged him into this mess with no preparation.

She could only guess what his law practice had been like back in New York City, but she'd have bet a lot of money that he'd never had to deal with a chain saw before.

She pulled out her phone and sent a quick text to Ryker, asking him to come over. He was big and tough-looking and must have learned some fighting skills while he was enlisted. Not that she really thought these two men would start a physical fight, but she'd gotten Deacon into this mess, so she had to try to help.

Deacon flipped back to the first page and looked up at the crowd watching him. Jess noticed his flushed cheeks and moved closer, ready to offer support.

"To be clear, this is not a legal document. It's merely a printout of the state law referring to tree trimming and property lines."

The crowd turned their heads toward Rankin.

Rankin's chin came up. "I can cut his trees."

Deacon pierced him with a sharp gaze. "No, what you can do is trim branches that hang over your property line."

Everyone's head swiveled to the fence between the two properties. Deacon frowned at it.

"Does that fence follow the property line?"

"Yes." Rankin and Vogler spoke in unison.

Now everyone was looking at the two branches that intruded into Rankin's yard by a couple of feet.

There was a quiet moment.

"I can chop those two branches down!" Rankin sputtered.

Deacon lifted one eyebrow. It was a surprisingly effective move.

"You are entitled to *trim*—" Deacon emphasized the word carefully "—the portions of those branches that have grown past the property line. I don't think the chain saw will be necessary."

A titter went through the crowd, and Rankin's face flushed.

"But if you read the entirety of the law, not just what is on these two sheets, you'll discover that first, you may not trespass on your neighbor's property. That means that you need his permission to access anything on his side of the fence, which he is not required to provide."

"Never!" That was Mrs. Vogler, still in front of one of the offending trees.

There was a murmur from the crowd as they discussed how the branches could be trimmed without entering the Voglers' yard.

"And secondly—" Deacon raised his voice, and all eyes returned to him. "You may not damage or kill the tree. If you do, you have to pay a fine of three times the stumpage fee."

Rankin's glance shifted around.

"I don't know if you're an arborist, with the skills to trim these fruit trees without causing harm, but if not, you might prefer to use a specialist to save yourself the penalty."

More murmuring.

Jess whispered in an aside to Deacon, "What's the stumpage fee?"

"No idea," he whispered back.

Mrs. Vogler dashed toward the offending branch nearest her and, removing pruning shears from her pocket, deftly trimmed the section of the branch intruding onto Rankin's yard and dropped the bit of greenery into her own.

Someone applauded, and she quickly snipped off the second branch.

"That appears to solve your problem, Mr. Rankin." Deacon spoke to the frustrated man glaring at the trees. "Since you didn't trim the branches, or cause them to be trimmed, you're not responsible for their well-being as a result. Your property is now cleared."

"But what about the mess that still lands in my yard?"

Deacon shrugged. "That isn't covered by state law."

Rankin glowered at his neighbors. "I can build the fence bigger."

"There are laws about spite fences, Mr. Rankin, so I suggest you check those out before doing anything. Now, if you don't mind, I have work to do."

Deacon turned and headed back to the law office, Jess following on his heels. She shot off a text to Ryker, telling him he wasn't needed.

She slipped her phone in her pocket and grinned up at Deacon.

"That was seriously impressive. Like, next-level lawyering."

Deacon stopped for a moment and looked down at her. "We'll talk when we get back to the office."

He didn't look like the compliment had warmed him up. In fact, he looked angry. Jess set her jaw. He was going to tell her off for something. Maybe he'd fire her. Well, he could see how well he did without her. And Rachel would be upset.

She didn't understand why he was so wound up. They'd saved Mr. Vogler's trees, done everything legally—was he just mad that he didn't get to invoice anyone? Too bad. If necessary, she would pay the bill herself. How much did a lawyer charge to face off against a chain saw and tell people about tree-trimming laws?

Jess sighed to herself. She couldn't afford a lot of legal bills. She had to save up for medical costs that were coming. She was going for her first doctor's visit soon, at Rachel's insistence. Jess was willing to wait. After all, she was pregnant. Not a doubt in her mind. What was the doctor going to tell her other than that and to eat the right stuff? She wasn't smoking or drinking, and she knew when she'd be due.

They were silent as they returned to the law office.

DEACON COULD NOT believe he'd just been rushed over to settle a property dispute with two homeowners who were not his clients. And been faced with a chain saw and a crowd. It was…well, it was not what he'd trained for. Had he looked ridiculous? He could imagine how his father and the others at the family firm would react to this story.

Somehow Jess had convinced him that racing over in the middle of the day was necessary. And yes, it could have become an ugly situation if Mr. Rankin had attacked those trees with a chain saw. But he was a lawyer, not law enforcement. Even if he'd been the official mediator, it would have been a civilized meeting in his office, not this.

He hadn't cared for being the center of attention, either.

Rachel had returned to the office by the time he strode through the doors.

"Are you okay? Ryker told me you'd asked for help, Jess."

Deacon turned to glare at Jess. She'd called her brother? Part of him wondered why she'd bothered to force him over there if she could have called her big, kind of scary-looking ex-military brother to take care of things. Another part of him was hurt that she hadn't thought he could take care of it. Did no one think he could handle things on his own?

No, he wasn't hurt. He was just...uncomfortable. This wasn't what he'd pictured himself doing.

Jess met his gaze, then quickly turned back to Rachel.

"Deacon took care of it, no problem. But when we got there, Mr. Rankin had a chain saw out, so I wasn't sure what was going to happen."

Rachel's eyes grew large. "He attacked you with a chain saw?"

Deacon interjected before things got out of hand. "No one was attacked by anything. Mr. Rankin had the chain saw out to trim branches from Mr. Vogler's cherry trees."

Deacon might have intimidated the two men with his legalese, but not Jess.

"No, he had the chain saw out to bully the Voglers. No one needs a chain saw to trim off two little branches. He was either bullying them or he was going to try to cut down the whole trees."

Deacon raised a hand.

"In any case, no one was threatened, the branches were trimmed, I reminded Mr. Rankin of the limits to his legal rights and it's over now."

Rachel sighed. "I hope so, but the two of them have been feuding for as long as I can remember. I'm glad the trees were saved, at least. But how did you get involved?"

Deacon pulled in a long breath, ready to explain how Jess had crossed lines to make this happen, but before he could speak, Jess had already broken in.

"Mr. Vogler called here in a panic, so Deacon and I went over to see what we could do."

That was *not* how it had happened. "No!"

Both women looked at him after that outburst.

"Mr. Vogler called, yes, but Jess dragged me over there without considering whether we should even be involved. Lawyers do not run over to settle quarrels between neighbors. We're not an ice cream truck, wandering the streets looking for business."

He was met with silence.

Jess was blinking her eyes. Oh no, had he made her cry?

"I'm sorry if that was the wrong thing to do, but those cherry trees mean a lot to the Voglers, and I just wanted to help them."

"That's a lovely sentiment, but—"

"I'm sorry." That was Rachel. "I know this isn't what you're used to, but it is the kind of thing my uncle would do. People trusted him to know the law, and he often was called in to help when neighbors were fighting before it had to go to the police. That must be why Mr. Vogler called here."

"This is what you meant by mediating? Not a civil talk in my office?"

He stared at the two women, who obviously did understand how inappropriate this was. And not what he was trained to do. What if the men hadn't listened to him? What if a fight had broken out? People could have been hurt.

"I'm sorry," Rachel repeated. "But it sounds like you handled it well, even if it wasn't very civil, or in your office."

That thought paused his anger. Two neighbors had been in a dispute, and he'd been able to stop any threats of violence by explaining the law to them. And the result was that Mr. Rankin had followed the law instead of taking it into his own hands and causing a lot of stress and damage.

He'd done that simply by explaining the law. Wasn't that a good part of what his job was? The pro bono work he'd done—and enjoyed—had been more like this. Mind you, he hadn't gone hightailing it around the city to meet a chain saw, but no one appeared to find this out of the ordinary. He wasn't going to travel around town dispensing free legal advice as a matter of course, but this had been an emergency.

Jess looked at the ground, biting her lip.

"I'm sorry. If you want me to leave, I will." She shrugged. "I did warn you I'd never worked in a law office before."

That took the last of his anger away.

"No, Jess, I'm sorry. I shouldn't have taken umbrage like that. It's not what I'm used to, and I felt rather...foolish. Just running up, as if someone had called me, and taking over. We should have let the police take care of it."

Rachel smiled at him. "I appreciate what you're saying, and no, this can't be the way the office normally works, but Jess said Mr. Vogler called, so you weren't pushing in on your own. He would call my uncle for things like that. And here, it's a small town, and no one but Mr. Rankin will think any the worse of you."

He didn't really care what Mr. Rankin thought. He hadn't liked the man when he'd come to the office, and there was no chance the man would have ever been a client.

He tried a smile directed toward Jess. "I don't want you to leave. But another time, maybe, you can let me know what's going on? It's just lucky I knew something about those tree-trimming laws off the top of my head."

Jess met his gaze. "You know all that kind of thing, right? Since you're a lawyer?"

He shook his head. "Maybe some people have the kind of memory to store every law in their brain, but it's a vast, constantly changing store of information. I've mostly done contract work for the past several years, not property issues."

"But you knew a lot about them, even the part that wasn't on Rankin's paper."

"It so happened that after Mr. Rankin's visit, I looked up the laws in case he did come back. It was just chance that he'd been in and so I knew what was going on."

A smile started to pull at Jess's lips, and he really didn't need to notice them, or the light in her eyes.

"So you were able to stop him today because he'd come and talked to you? He provided you with what you needed to know to stop him?"

Rachel laughed. "That's wonderful."

"Karma." Deacon agreed. Kind of like paying it forward. Rankin's ill wishes had given

Deacon the tools he needed to prevent him from getting his way.

The phone rang, and Jess answered. "Lowther Legal, how may I help you?" in her best receptionist voice. She glanced at Deacon while she listened to the voice on the other end.

"Yes, Mr. Standish was a big part of settling that dispute. Yes, he is very knowledgeable. You'd like an appointment? I'll see when he's free."

She shot a cheeky grin his way, deliberately being the perfect receptionist. He pulled his gaze away and headed to his office.

"Oh yes, he's very busy. I can maybe find you some time next week?"

Deacon pulled his office door behind him. He'd been frustrated by the strict protocols and procedures at his family firm and had wanted to create a more relaxed and flexible atmosphere.

Well, he needed to be careful what he wished for.

# CHAPTER SEVEN

JESS STARED AT the technician, the one holding a slippery wand in her hand as she rubbed it over Jess's belly. The room was filled with a whooshing noise, and weird blobs appeared and disappeared on the screen beside her.

"That's got to be a mistake. Can you do it again?"

The woman shook her head. "I don't need to. Believe me, I've done this often enough. There are two heartbeats, and if you look here—" She pointed at some blobs on the screen that honestly could have been tadpoles for all Jess knew. "There are two fetuses. You're having twins."

"But—"

There had to be some mistake. Jess had accepted being pregnant. She'd come to terms with the idea of being a single mom—to one baby. But two?

Two was a lot. It was more than one. It was going to make things much more complicated. So much more complicated.

The woman removed the wand and grabbed some tissues to wipe off Jess's abdomen.

"Are there twins in your family? It can often run in the maternal line."

Jess grimaced. "My two oldest brothers."

It made a kind of sense, when you thought about her brothers. But someone should have warned her and her sisters about this possibility. Shouldn't they? Though it wasn't like her father would have passed on any useful information, and Jess had never considered having kids, so she'd never looked it up.

The woman tossed the tissues in the garbage and smiled at her. "That doesn't surprise me. Do you want pictures?"

Jess opened her mouth and tried to find words, but she couldn't respond. Couldn't think much beyond twins. Twins. Two babies. *My two babies*, she claimed fiercely. This was a shock, obviously, and it was going to complicate things, but she'd handle it. She always handled things. And this time she had Rachel and Ryker to help her. Oh, they'd probably like to see a picture—at least Rachel would.

"Yes, please. I might need to prove this to some people."

The woman laughed and returned to the machine.

One of those people being herself. Twins. That wasn't something she'd expected.

The technician passed her off to the doctor, who told her a lot of things that she couldn't absorb at the moment. She should have let Rachel come with her, but she didn't want to leave Deacon without any help in the office. Things had got busier since Cherrygate. She was pretty sure Deacon didn't know they were calling it that, but he'd impressed people.

She was finally free to go, clutching some pamphlets and a sample of maternity vitamins. She had an official due date of May seventeenth, but apparently ninety-five percent of babies chose a different day to arrive. So what was the point of a due date?

Twins.

Jess sat in the van for a moment. She'd planned to go back to the office to work for the rest of the day, but Rachel would want to know how the appointment went, and if she told her about twins, she was pretty sure there wouldn't be much more work done.

She sent a text to Rachel, saying she was fine but not coming back to work. Then she asked if Rachel and Ryker would like to come over to her place for dinner. That would give them lots of time and privacy to talk, and something for Jess to keep busy with while she waited for them.

This early in November the weather was cooling off fast, so Jess took a detour by the grocery store to get what she needed to make chili for her dinner guests. It was simple, filling and there was no problem with quantity if she made a huge potful and froze the leftovers. After picking up that stuff, she bit the bullet and stopped by the vitamin aisle to get some prenatal vitamins as well. She checked out the diapers and formula prices and sucked in a breath. She'd better get more work lined up, since Rachel would soon have her cast off. Rachel would need a couple of weeks to get the muscles going again, but Jess couldn't afford time off, not with *two* babies coming.

Twins.

She carried her bags up the stairs to her apartment over Benny's repair shop. Ryker had insisted on providing her with a bed, and she'd spent a couple of Saturdays checking out secondhand shops to get a few more bits of furniture to fill up the place on the cheap.

She hadn't bothered with a TV yet. Benny had Wi-Fi in the place she could use, so she'd set up her laptop if she wanted to watch something. Ryker had worked on it, and it was faster than it used to be.

A table with a couple of chairs. A dresser that she'd sanded down and painted on a Sunday afternoon. She didn't need much.

She set her bags on the counter in the small kitchen and put the perishables in the fridge. She brought out the cutting board to start chopping onions but set down the knife and walked down the hallway.

She opened the door to the empty second bedroom. She'd planned to make this a nursery and had been looking up nurseries online, trying to find cheap ways to make a pretty room for her baby. She'd been thinking about one crib for *one* baby. Could she use just one? Could babies share? She'd only need a single changing table, surely, and one dresser—baby clothes were tiny, weren't they?

They might be tiny, but she'd need twice as many. Two car seats. Two highchairs. Two times all the dollar amounts. Her thoughts started to get panicky, so she slammed the door shut. She'd deal. She would. But right now, she just needed to chill till she figured out the details.

She went back to the kitchen to deal with what was right in front of her. Making chili. She'd worked in a diner for a time and sometimes filled in for the line cook, so she was confident in preparing basic food. And she'd learned to be efficient. The chili was simmering on the stove, and she still had time before she expected Ryker and Rachel. She needed a distraction, so she turned off the burner and went out her door, down the stairs and stepped into Benny's shop.

Benny looked up from the desk where he was working on a small motor. Jess didn't know what it would be used in, but she wasn't planning to ask Benny for work. Instead, she grabbed the broom out of the closet and started to sweep the floor. Benny was always losing bits of what he worked on. Jess made sure to have him check over the pieces she swept up before tossing them.

"Hey, Jess. You don't have to do that."

She pretended to frown at him. "Yes, I do. The floor is a mess. And then you wheel that chair around grinding everything into it."

Benny shrugged. "Nice to see you, too."

Jess paused in her sweeping. "You doing okay?"

"Same as usual. Why are you here at this time of day? Done with the lawyer's office already?"

Jess leaned back against a table, the one where Benny collected computers for Ryker to deal with. Only one there today.

"Had a doctor's appointment. Decided not to go back today."

Benny cocked his head. "Anything wrong at the doctor's office? You look a little... I dunno, stressed?"

Jess snorted. "I'm pregnant, Benny. That's stress right there."

He smiled at her. "I know. You just seemed a little more on edge. If you want to talk, I'm here. If not, let me know if you see a couple of tiny washers in the stuff you sweep up."

Jess looked at the pile of dust and rubbish she'd gathered, and then back at Benny.

"I'm having twins."

Benny's eyes rounded. "Oh. Stress level explained. You okay with that?"

Jess drew in a long breath. "I will be."

"That's— Well, it's a lot to take on. My offer of babysitting still stands."

Jess swallowed a lump in her throat. These pregnancy hormones were killing her, making her want to cry because someone was kind to her.

Jess hadn't had a lot of kindness in her life. She'd had some: Ryker and her sisters when she was growing up, a woman who'd offered her a job and safe place to stay when she ran away, an occasional friend she'd met along the way. But mostly she'd had to rely on herself, and she was still adapting to the kindness she was finding here in Cupid's Crossing, with Ryker and Rachel and Benny—and even Deacon.

"I will take you up on that. I asked Rachel and Ryker to come for dinner so I can tell them. Do you wanna join us?"

Ryker had been in a bad accident when he was living upstairs from Benny, and there'd been a chair lift installed on the outside staircase. Benny could come up if he wanted.

"That's a nice offer, but my dad's expecting me for dinner. You three can have some family time."

Jess stood, picking up the broom again and grabbing a dustpan.

"You know Rachel is going to flip out over this."

Benny grinned as he leaned over his motor again. "Oh, I know. I might hear her over at Dad's place."

Jess shook out the stuff she'd collected in the dustpan. "You probably will. Are these the washers you were looking for?"

"Yes, that's them. Thanks."

Jess finished the floor and grabbed a duster. Two babies were going to be more difficult, but she could handle it, somehow. She'd figure out the rest. She had to. Because even when people offered to help, they didn't always follow through.

DEACON POKED AT his microwaved dinner. It was supposed to be healthy, but what it might add in nutrients it made up for in lack of appeal. He sighed and put a forkful in his mouth anyway.

Some things here in Cupid's Crossing were working out well. He'd arrived in the middle of October, and it was now the middle of November. Despite Cherrygate, or maybe because of it, work had been busy at the law office. Interesting as well. Not every day included running out of the office to talk to a man with a chain saw, but the work was varied and challenging. Deacon enjoyed bringing the legal documents up to date and providing the expertise his clients were looking for.

He'd known he liked the one-on-one work more than corporate work, and here, he was dealing with events in people's lives, not structuring mergers and takeovers. People sat down in the chair across from him and told him their problems, and he did his best to fix them. There was more immediate feedback. And the way they looked at him, like he was smarter than he knew he was? That was nice, too.

He couldn't get too comfortable, though. This was temporary. He needed to do some reading, keep up on the corporate stuff he'd be dealing with when he went back, because he was going to have to seriously prepare himself to head the firm. He couldn't claim he didn't have time for research. Rachel was irreplaceable and someone he'd be happy to have at the firm back home. With Jess to help, the office was working like a well-oiled machine.

The only problem at work was Jess, and it wasn't anything she did. There was just something about her that distracted him. That something included her eyes, and the way they seemed to look right through him. She was refreshingly honest. There was no guessing what she thought.

She was blunt with clients and terrible at hiding her reactions to what happened in the office, but at least she didn't share her opinions while clients were actually there. He could try to tell himself that he listened to her on the phone because he was worried about what she'd say, but he was too honest to do that. He liked her voice, even when she told clients he was indisposed (in the bathroom) or busy with something more important.

Jess wouldn't be there much longer. Rachel would get her cast off soon, and she'd told him the doctor thought it would be another couple of weeks of physical therapy before she regained enough muscle movement to do her usual work. He knew Rachel was conflicted: she wanted to make sure Jess had enough work while not being dishonest with him about her need for Jess's help.

Deacon worried about Jess as well, though he had no business doing so. He was willing to have her working at the office as long as Rachel deemed her assistance necessary. He admired the way she'd stick up her chin and take on every challenge that came her way, but being a single mom was going to be difficult—and expensive. He'd have been happy to dock his own pay to keep her on, but that wasn't discreet. And there was no way Jess would agree to it.

Deacon realized he'd finished his bland meal while he thought about Jess. He thought about her too much. She was staying in Cupid's Crossing, and he needed to remember he wasn't.

His phone ringing was a welcome distraction. He saw his cousin's name on the display and was smiling as he answered.

"Meredith! How lovely to hear from you." Deacon had a lot of distant cousins, people like Meredith. His family was proud of their ancestry and kept close tabs on everyone located somewhere on the family tree. All those branches specialized in overachieving, whether it was in academics, careers or marriages. Deacon never felt that he measured up, and neither did his family. His parents were the only ones who put it in words, but it was impossible to miss.

He didn't graduate top of his class. He hadn't made the connections others had in school and didn't bring in new clients with deep pockets. He did good work, but it wasn't splashy. Even his golf handicap was the highest at the family tournaments and was only going to get worse, since there wasn't any golfing in the area or indoor ranges to practice his drive during the winter.

Meredith was the only one of those vaguely related cousins working in the family law firm. The people wanting to make big money in a family business worked instead in the investment firm or the real estate company. He had one cousin who'd already made a fortune in tech, and a couple more looked to be doing the same. Meredith was much better than him at dealing with clients and networking with important people, as well as being an excellent lawyer. If it hadn't been for her gender, he knew she'd have been the one tapped to lead the firm in future. His father and the board expected him to do so by default, and the pressure to get him ready was stressing both Deacon and his father.

Deacon didn't want to head the firm, and he and Meredith had a plan. Once Deacon was in charge, Meredith would then be on the fast track to take over for him. He would eventually step back to give Meredith her well-deserved position as head. Deacon wasn't sure he'd even want to stay working there. This was not information he'd shared with anyone but Meredith.

Meredith was smart, beautiful, polished and perfect for the role, except for the lack of a Y chromosome and the last name of Standish. She was also the cousin who was kindest to him, and he valued that trait.

"Deacon! I was waiting for you to reach out. How are the yokels treating you?"

Deacon frowned. The residents of Cupid's Crossing weren't yokels. Some would seem unsophisticated to his family, but Gerald Van Dalton's girlfriend Abigail Carter—could you call someone who was over sixty a girlfriend?—was in charge of the town. Gerald's granddaughter lived here. But he knew Meredith didn't mean anything by her comment.

"Everyone has been very nice." Well, not Mr. Rankin, but he was an outlier.

"Well, of course they would be. You're delightful. But are you not dreadfully bored?"

Was he? Not at work, but right now, alone in the house? A little.

"Not dreadfully. I'm still getting to know people." That was a bit of a stretch. He knew Rachel and Jess. Ryker would come by the office to get Rachel after work, and of course, he was Jess's brother. He'd met clients, and had a couple of meetings with Mariah, the Van Dalton granddaughter, but he hadn't accepted any of the casual invitations that had been shared with him.

He should change that. He still had months to go here.

"Can you get down for Thanksgiving? I'd like to see you."

Deacon involuntarily flinched.

"I don't know." He didn't want to, if he was honest. But honesty was not usually the best policy with his family.

"Come on, Deacon. You know the expression out of sight, out of mind? You don't want to be forgotten."

He knew Thanksgiving in New York wouldn't involve quiet visits with family. There would be social events, dinners and dances and premieres and on and on. Most of them were for charities, and those causes were good, but he never enjoyed the social part. He could make polite conversation, but he felt like he was boring people when he talked. He could dance when needed, but he always thought his partners wished the dance would soon be over.

That was probably his own insecurity and not how the people truly felt, but it made evenings out at these events anything but a good time for him.

"I don't think I'm wanted, not yet. Not after…" Not after he'd inadvertently managed to get a client in legal trouble.

Meredith sighed. "You might be right. Schofields are still a little testy. Though, just so you know, I've been one of the associates tasked with checking out Wiseman's employment contracts. You caught a big hole in those."

He had. He just hadn't realized he was finding a hole in his firm's work when he'd tried to help someone at Legal Services. Schofields Inc. had had to pay out a large settlement for wrongful dismissal, and they hadn't been pleased that a Standish, even unwittingly, had been behind it.

"Not only that, but now we're looking

through Wiseman's NDAs. Seems he was a little more invested in finding tee time with clients than in making sure his work was up to scratch."

Deacon wasn't surprised. He'd thought the work was sloppy, but when he'd pointed that out to his father, he'd been shut down.

"It's still early days, Deacon, but they're going to recognize that this was a good thing. Fixing these mistakes is going to save Schofields and other clients money in the long run. You might not have to stay the full year in Cupid's Town."

"Crossing," He corrected automatically.

"What?"

"It's Cupid's Crossing."

"How cute." From Meredith's tone, she thought it anything but. "Still, I think the board are going to come around on you. Sure, you might not have been class valedictorian or have a scary low golf handicap, but you're smart and you notice details. They're going to see that, and eventually—you know, decades down the road—realize you're a good lawyer."

That would be nice. And a change.

"And then we'll have our chance to change the firm."

Deacon understood how frustrating it was

for Meredith, who had been close to being valedictorian and had an excellent golf handicap. She was good at tennis, always knew the right kind of small talk to make and was able to fit in in every situation. Everything that the firm needed in a leader.

He called her cousin, but they were several steps removed. Removed enough that Meredith couldn't push through the glass ceiling based on her parents' connections to the family. If she'd been a first cousin, she might have been close enough to become partner without any assistance from Deacon. Or if her last name had been Standish.

Deacon would have liked that.

"That's still the plan, right?"

Deacon must have been lost in his thoughts for long enough that Meredith suspected he wasn't agreeing with her.

"Oh, that's still the plan."

"Good. I've talked to some of the other women at the firm, and they're feeling frustrated. I've been encouraging them to hang on, and that things will get better. Especially with this wrongful dismissal that Wiseman messed up. I mean, he does such terrible work and still gets to be partner while the rest of us work harder and do better and get nothing."

Deacon knew that Meredith made a comfortable living, and she was part of the Standish family, even if on the outskirts. But her point was valid. He thought his father and the other partners were afraid of what might happen if they opened to the possibility that a firm with people just like them at the top might not be the best way to ensure long-term success.

Change could be scary. But sometimes it could also be liberating.

"We're going to improve things. We need to." Deacon seriously believed that if the firm didn't adapt going forward, they'd be left behind, or find themselves on the wrong side of an affirmative action case. He'd been raised to believe that it was his duty to his family and the family's firm, to keep it alive and healthy until he passed it on to his descendants.

It might be better to leave that to Meredith's descendants. He didn't think he wanted to place that kind of burden on any children he might have.

Meredith, assured that their plans were still in sync, proceeded to catch him up on all the firm and family news. Some of it he was aware of from his weekly calls to his mother.

One of his male cousins had just become engaged to an ambassador's daughter. There was talk about a presidential bid for another. Deacon was resigned to standing up in another large and elaborate wedding next summer but hoped he could avoid the political events.

Finally, Meredith said she had to go, and they ended the call. Deacon managed to avoid any promises about a visit later in the month. He washed the few dishes he'd dirtied and decided the next day he was going to the diner for lunch. He didn't care if he accumulated some excess calories. He wanted taste.

Then, after locking up the doors and checking that the window coverings were all carefully drawn, he sat down to enjoy his guilty pleasure.

He wasn't going to impress anyone in the firm, or their clients, with his abilities in role-playing video games, but for a while he could enjoy being someone else.

JESS DROPPED HER bombshell at the table. Rachel was as excited about the news as Jess had predicted. Benny would have heard Rachel's squeals if he'd still been on the premises, but he was safely away at his father's, so his eardrums were intact.

Ryker tensed, knuckles white on his spoon, and Jess knew he was worried for her. She promised him she'd reach out for help when she needed it. After all, the reason she'd returned to Cupid's Crossing was because he was here.

He was going to be the best uncle.

Jess hadn't really considered telling Deacon. She wouldn't be working at the law office much longer, so she didn't think she had to tell him for professional reasons, and she didn't consider him a friend who would want to know. But Rachel couldn't stop asking questions, all the things she'd forgotten to ask last night, and Deacon walked out of his space just as Rachel asked if they'd been able to tell if Jess was having identical or fraternal twins.

Deacon's eyes had bugged out, and his gaze fell to her belly. Jess's morning sickness had eased, but her clothes were still loose on her, and he wouldn't see an actual bump. Jess could tell, but she didn't think anyone else could yet.

That bump was going to be huge, she realized.

"I didn't know you were expecting twins."

Jess shrugged. "I didn't, either, until yesterday, but I don't have any reason to doubt the people at the clinic."

Deacon glanced around the office. "Do you

need anything? More time to rest? Sit down more often?"

Jess waved her hand at him. "I'm fine. Don't worry. They're pretty small right now, so I'm good."

"This is so exciting!" Rachel said.

Jess wondered if Rachel would be as excited if it was her body handling this whole process, but she didn't say anything. She was glad Rachel was invested in this and would be a help with these babies once they arrived. But right now, Jess didn't want to dwell on what was becoming an overwhelming reality. She didn't want to talk about baby names and plans. Right now, she just wanted to focus on her work.

"Don't you have some documents to file at the courthouse in Oak Hill?" she asked Rachel.

Rachel took a glance at the time. "Right. I'd better get going. You're going to serve that guy about the divorce, right?"

Jess nodded. They didn't have any appointments scheduled today, so it was fine to leave Deacon by himself. Not that the guy couldn't handle legal matters on his own, but he wasn't used to doing his job without a lot of support. Jess had never mentioned it, but she'd seen him working at his desk, reaching out for an intercom or telephone that wasn't there to contact Rachel. Or stepping out and looking around the office space, file in hand, seeing Rachel on the phone and then pausing, as if unsure what to do with it.

He was trying. She'd come back from lunch before Rachel one time and found him in the file room, looking for documents but with no clue how to locate them. Jess had asked what he wanted and shooed him out of the room as quickly as she could before he messed up her work. Then she'd dropped the file on his desk, picking up a couple of others he'd made notes on.

Still, the legal stuff he knew. Rachel had told her how he'd improved contracts her uncle had written up. Jess had seen him looking over legal texts, but when clients came in, he could rattle off case numbers or rulings or whatever without needing to check again.

Yeah, he was smart, and he would soon figure out how to do the things he wasn't used to. Meanwhile, Jess would serve the scumbag out in the hills with his divorce papers while Rachel handled the courthouse in Oak Hill and Deacon checked on a contract for the hotel being built on her family's old property.

Jess wanted to finish her filing before heading out. She'd grown up in chaos and moved a lot, so it was important to her that everything was in its proper place now, whether in her home or her workspace. Rachel was driving over to Oak Hill with Ryker. He was going to visit a client, and depending on how things went at the courthouse, the two of them might go out for dinner—a date night. They'd invited Jess, but she preferred a quiet evening at home. She needed to rework her budget for twins.

Twins. She shook her head.

Once the office was again organized, nothing piled up on either her or Rachel's desk, she switched the phone over to the answering service and picked up the documents she was taking with her.

Deacon stepped out of his office, reading glasses on the bottom of his nose. Jess would never tell him, but she thought they made him look cute.

"You're heading out now, Jess?"

She hoisted her purse over her shoulder. "Yep."

He frowned. "There's no chance the man will get violent, is there?"

Jess shook her head. "Nah. Apparently the husband of the latest woman he was cheating with caught up to him and worked him over.

He's gonna be pretty sore. And I might look skinny, but I've learned some moves."

Deacon removed his glasses. "I'm not sure I'm comfortable with you serving papers to someone violent. Not on your own."

Jess cocked a hip. She seriously doubted that he was more capable in a situation like this than she was. He'd want to be sure that everything was fair and aboveboard and would follow whatever rules people like him had set up for physical fights. Whereas Jess would be quick and dirty. And win.

Deacon held up a finger.

"Just a moment."

Jess frowned. What was he doing? Did he have a gun? Dagger? Blackjack? Some kind of weapon for her? She could take that along if he wanted, to make him happy. He didn't know she had a baseball bat and some bear spray in her van, just in case she got in trouble.

Next thing, Deacon was standing beside her, car keys in hand.

"What? You want to serve the papers instead?"

Deacon shook his head. "I'd get lost finding the place. I heard those directions—'left at someone's farm and past the old graveyard, not the Baptist one.' But I can come with you, make sure this man doesn't get upset."

Jess took a moment to confirm that he really meant what it sounded like.

"You want to drive me out there?"

Deacon walked toward the office door. "Yes. You can tell me when we get to the correct graveyard."

# CHAPTER EIGHT

JESS OPENED HER mouth to argue but then changed her mind, following him out of the office and standing by while he turned the lock. She hadn't forgotten how well he'd stood up to the chain saw–wielding Rankin. It wouldn't be bad to have him on hand.

He looked around. "It's a lovely day for a drive. I'm looking forward to seeing more of the area."

Jess kept her eye rolling to herself. It was November, the leaves had fallen and all that was left to see on the hillsides were evergreens and bare trunks. But driving in Deacon's Audi would be much more comfortable than her van. The speedometer had stopped working, so once she was out of town, her speed was an educated guess, based on how hard the engine was whining.

Deacon's seats were comfortable, the warmth of the seat heaters a luxury on a cold day, his speedometer working, and he drove well. Not fast, but not too carefully. Jess was able to relax and keep an eye on the directions. The GPS couldn't take them the whole way, since this was another section where cell coverage was spotty, but Rachel had left precise instructions.

Jess was familiar with the area around Cupid's Crossing, but things had changed a lot in the years since she'd left. Buildings had grown over and disappeared and new ones had shown up. She did know which cemetery was which, so she did better than Deacon would have on his own.

Deacon asked about places they passed, and Jess answered as best she could. When they ran out of anything but trees, she asked him if he'd always wanted to be a lawyer.

His lips compressed. "Not always. But sometimes it's tremendously satisfying."

Jess considered him. She'd assumed he'd happily followed the route to success that guys like him had presented to them. Private schools, Ivy League colleges, big-money jobs. Deacon was a bit of a puzzle, though. He was here, in Cupid's Crossing, instead of where guys like him would normally hang out, and he didn't seem anxious to get back to the city. But when she wanted to probe a little further, he asked an unnecessary question about their next turn, so she let it go.

They followed the last direction and

bumped up a long, tree-lined driveway. Jess cringed as she heard the underbody of the car hitting a rock. She hoped it didn't cause any damage, but another thump and she worried the car might not make it. A somewhat decrepit house appeared at the end of the drive, and a man stepped out of the door as they pulled up.

"What you want?"

He remained in his doorway, and Jess would have bet that he kept a rifle inside the door. He had a black eye and one arm wrapped around what might be cracked ribs. Jess hoped the guy who'd hit him hadn't done the same to the woman involved.

"Let me," she told Deacon. The guy wouldn't think of her as a threat. He wouldn't need to posture and put up his guard.

She stepped out of the car, envelope in her hand. "Dwayne Hawkins?"

His eyes narrowed. "Who's asking."

Jess smiled. "I'm Jess Slade."

"Branson's sister?"

This guy knew the twins. Figured.

"One of them, yeah."

"You girls all took off, didn't you?"

"Wasn't much to stay around for."

The man squinted as he looked her up and down. "I'm a good friend of the twins."

*Great*, Jess thought. Maybe he went to visit them in prison. At least he didn't claim to know their father as well.

"So does that mean you're Dwayne Hawkins?"

The man had relaxed his pose, leaning against the door frame. Hopefully not closer to a gun or baseball bat.

"Yeah. Do you have a message from Branson?"

"Sure." Jess walked up to him and slapped the envelope against his chest. "You've been served. And I don't deliver messages for my brother."

She pivoted on her heel and walked back to the still-open door of the car, hoping Dwayne wasn't reaching for his gun. She made it to the car and slid into the seat, slamming the door behind her.

"Let's get out of here."

Jess looked at Dwayne, who stood with his jaw hanging open, frowning at the envelope. Deacon did a quick three-point turn and headed back down the drive at a quick but not frantic pace. The potholes wouldn't allow for it in any case.

"Did you know him?" Deacon asked as they turned onto the paved county road. Jess would have liked to be offended, but the man knew her brother. Not impossible for her to have met him.

"Don't remember seeing him, but he said he was a friend of my brother. Branson, the oldest twin."

"In prison?"

Jess twisted her lips. "Yeah."

"I'm glad you didn't come on your own." Deacon kept his tone neutral, but Jess could hear the concern behind his statement.

"Me, too."

She'd have been fine, she knew. It wasn't like Deacon had had to do anything to protect her. But it was nice to have the support. And she might have left part of her van on that driveway.

The Audi's engine started to sputter.

DEACON HEARD HIS engine make a strange noise and looked down to see if his gauges could explain the sound. At first, he couldn't interpret what he saw. The gas gauge was below empty.

No, it couldn't be. Could it?

He'd filled up the car last week. He'd only had to put in a quarter of a tank since he walked to work and rarely needed to drive.

"I think you're outta gas," Jess said beside him.

Deacon steered the car off the road. He reached for his phone, ready to call AAA to help him out. But just like when he'd first met Jess, there was no reception.

Deacon closed his eyes, mortified that he'd managed to find himself in this predicament again. He wanted to beat his head on the steering wheel.

Stupid!

He had Jess with him, so he'd better not bang his head or try to bargain with the car. He was reluctant to face her, sure she'd be upset with him.

"If we were teenagers and this was a Friday night, I'd think you'd done this on purpose."

Her voice was teasing, and he knew she was trying to make him feel better, but it didn't silence the voice in his head.

"I'm sorry, Jess. I don't know how we can be out of gas. I filled up last week."

"Hey." He felt Jess's hand on his arm, and he forced himself to open his eyes and look at her.

There was no anger in her expression, or frustration or disappointment.

"It's okay. I don't think you forgot to get gas—I think one of those bangs when you were on that driveway might have nicked your fuel line."

"But we're stuck. You can't change an empty gas tank. The closest house I can think of is the guy you just served, and I don't think we should go ask him for help."

Jess chuckled. "Yeah, if he's figured out what that paperwork is, he's not going to help us at all."

"So what do we do?"

"For now, we wait. The sun's out, and we've got some heat in the car. Someone might drive by, and we can flag them down for help. Also, Rachel knows where we are. She'll come looking for us after she gets back, if no one else comes by."

"But your van is back in town. She doesn't know I came with you."

"She'll figure it out. Believe me, Ryker has been like a mother hen since I came back. They'll check on me, and when I don't answer the phone, they'll come back to check the apartment and the office, and they'll work it out."

"And if no one comes by and Rachel and your brother don't track us down tonight?"

Jess reached for the lever and let the seat fall back farther, settling in with her hands on her abdomen. "Then we'll have to walk. But honestly, I'm tired and willing to wait a couple of hours before we have to do that."

"I can walk and you can wait in the car."

Jess shot him a teasing grin. "I'm not sure

you'd find your way back on your own. I promise, someone is likely to come. We're safe here for now."

Deacon wasn't sure, but then, when he'd had a flat tire, he'd thought no one would come by and Jess had shown up. He just had no experience with traffic patterns on these rural roads. He'd been raised in the city, where there were always people and vehicles around. If he'd run out of gas on a New York City street, angry drivers would probably have pushed him to a gas station to get him out of the way.

Deacon pushed his seat farther back. "Might as well be comfortable, right?"

"Right. Give it an hour, and then we'll figure out if we need to start walking," Jess agreed.

"Did you have plans tonight, something I've interrupted?"

Jess snorted. "Hardly. This pregnancy is kicking my butt. I'm tired all the time. Plus, I don't know many people here anymore. I've been away a long time."

Deacon had never pried into Jess's life. As her employer, it would be intrusive and cross some ethical boundaries, and it could upset the balance in the office. But they were stuck here, and sitting in awkward silence didn't sound appealing.

"You left Cupid's Crossing because of your home situation, correct?"

Jess nodded, eyes on the road ahead.

"Why did you come back?"

She turned toward him with a lazy smile. "Because of the peanut." She moved her hands. "Or peanuts, I guess. If I was keeping the babies, I knew I'd need help."

Jess didn't accept a lot of help, he knew.

"Did you expect your family to still be here?"

"Hardly. I looked up Ryker, since he was the best of my siblings. I read an article about him and Rachel getting married here, and it talked about this romance thing they've got going in Cupid's Crossing. I figured I'd be able to find work, and Ryker and Rachel are good people. They're the ones I'd want in my corner."

He didn't know Ryker very well, but Rachel was a lovely person.

"How old were you when you left?"

"Sixteen."

That was young.

"Sixteen? Where did you go? Who helped you?"

Jess raised an eyebrow. "Help? There was no one to help. Ryker had been the only one who helped us at home, and he was gone. I hitchhiked to Albany. Was able to find a home-less shelter there, got a job washing dishes in a kitchen. Worked my way up to waitress and hung on to my tips. Then I moved on to Syra-cuse. Was there for a while. Got my GED, got bored and moved on again."

Deacon shook his head. How had this hap-pened? Had no one realized what the family situation was like for Jess and her siblings and tried to help out? It had to be bad if running off on her own was better. He tried to imag-ine leaving his home at sixteen with nothing. He had no idea what he would have done. The risks Jess had taken...

"Were you safe?"

There was a faraway look in her eyes. "Probably not all the time. Maybe not most of the time. But someone was looking out for me, because nothing very bad happened."

Deacon would have categorized the things she'd dealt with—living with an alcoholic and abusive parent, running away from home and hitchhiking to the city, being on her own all this time—as very bad, but they obviously had vastly different frames of reference.

"I'm glad nothing very bad happened to you," he said, using her terminology. "And I admire what you were able to do on your own."

She sat up and stared at him. "Are you serious?"

"Absolutely. I couldn't have taken off by myself at sixteen."

"Sure you could have, if things were bad enough. When you don't have much choice, you'd be surprised at what you can do."

She'd been through tough times, but she had an inner strength that he didn't think he had. He just wondered what that had cost her.

"I hope the worst is behind you, Jess, and that life goes well in the future."

"Me, too."

She settled back in her seat. There was a moment of silence as he contemplated what she must have had to deal with. Jess broke it.

"Can I ask you something?"

"As long as I can decide if I want to answer."

Jess grinned. "That sounds like such a lawyer thing to say. So, do you hate being a lawyer?"

Deacon looked at the road. That was a question he'd been trying to avoid for a while.

"You don't have to answer." He heard the shrug in her voice. He'd asked personal questions, and she'd answered. Did some part of him feel that his privileged upbringing meant he didn't need to do the same?

He moved his gaze back to her. "It's not necessarily that I don't want to be a lawyer. It's a question I've been struggling with, and I'm not sure I have an answer. There are some parts that I enjoy. Other parts, not as much."

"Cherry trees and chain saws are probably the parts you don't like."

His lips curled up. "Actually, that wasn't so bad."

Jess pressed her hand to her chest. "No, you didn't just admit that. What could be the bad parts if that qualifies as a good part?"

"As you pointed out, we did save some cherry trees, so that makes it good. Doing something and seeing the benefit from what you've done is very rewarding. But that's not the kind of law I've been practicing. Our firm deals more with contracts and business law. Mergers and acquisitions. Most of the work I've been doing involves long legal documents that seem designed more to confuse people than to help them."

He looked across at her, saw her frown as she thought over what he'd said.

"Is that why you came here, to Cupid's Crossing? To get a break from the boring, confusing stuff?"

Deacon debated how he should answer. *Yes* would be a partially truthful answer and wouldn't reveal anything. It would protect his reputation here.

But Jess wouldn't spread the story around. She was blunt and impulsive, but she'd been discreet enough at the office. He felt an unusual desire to unburden himself. He was curious how she'd respond to his story.

"You remember when you first started, you were worried that I'd fire you because you were pregnant? Or rather, not hire you?"

"Yeah. I didn't know you then."

That made something inside him feel warm. Because it meant that Jess thought he was one of the good people now.

"Back in New York, I did some pro bono work for an organization called Legal Services. One woman came into the office because she'd been fired, and she was sure it was because her employer had discovered she was pregnant."

One of Jess's shoulders moved up and fell back down. "It happens a lot."

Deacon nodded. "I checked over her employment agreement. We weren't able to prove that she'd been let go because of her pregnancy, but I did discover a loophole in her contract. It allowed her to sue her employer for a substantial sum."

Jess held out her fist to him, and he realized

she wanted to fist bump. He was a little awkward but managed to touch her fist with his.

"That's good, right?"

"Except that her employer was a subsidiary of a rather important client of our firm. It was a subsidiary another partner dealt with exclusively, so I'd never come across the name before, and my pro bono client didn't know the corporate structure. I didn't find out the connection until I'd already given her the information she needed to sue. It made our firm look bad."

"Ah. *Your* firm?"

"Exactly. It's a family firm."

"And that's why you're a lawyer."

He nodded. He'd never considered any other career, not once he'd grown past the stage of wanting to be an astronaut or a cowboy. "This suit was a problem for our client, and when they discovered that I'd been the cause of it, the client was not very happy."

"But it wasn't your fault!"

"My family wasn't very pleased with my choice of pro bono work anyway."

"Coming here was your punishment?"

She sounded incredulous.

"Gerald Van Dalton does work with our firm, and having someone in the office here, at least until the town can find another lawyer who wants to stay permanently, is a favor to him. And this way I'm not visible for a while until all this settles down."

"It's not fair."

Jess was upset on his behalf. Another warm thing.

"I actually didn't mind coming here. This is like the pro bono work I'd been doing, which I found enjoyable. I've resigned from Legal Services, of course."

That had been a decree, with no option of arguing back. Deacon returned his gaze to the road, empty ahead of them, the sky growing darker. He was embarrassed, explaining this to Jess. But it wasn't as simple as someone might think, looking from the outside.

"Do you want to go back?" Jess's voice was quiet. "I mean, it's not my business, obvs, and I don't believe that everyone gets to do the job they want, but you don't sound like it's where you want to be. And you have choices, right?"

Yes, he did have choices. He was fortunate to be in a position where he did. He was sure that Jess, as a sixteen-year-old runaway, had had very little choice. But his were tangled up with other people and he wanted to do what was best for as many as possible, not just for him.

"I do have choices, yes, but my choices impact other people, and I need to think about what is going to benefit them as well as myself."

"Does going back benefit people that are worth it?"

Deacon turned to her. "It does."

Her nose crinkled. "Are those people the ones who thought you had to disappear for a while because you found a mistake they made?"

Deacon smiled. "They *think* they are the ones who will benefit."

Jess smiled back. "Oh, you've got a plan. Excellent! And devious, which I didn't think was your thing."

Her eyes were sparkling as she enjoyed the shared joke.

"It's not, you're right. My sort-of cousin is more the instigator than me. Our firm is not the most progressive when it comes to hiring and promoting people of diverse cultures and genders. Because I'm a Standish, it's expected that I'll be in charge of the firm one day, and when that happens, I can make changes to improve the situation."

"Is your cousin someone of diverse culture or gender?"

"*She* is."

"Does she work for the same firm?"

"Yes. She'd be a much better head of the firm than I would, but because she's not a first or even second cousin, is female and not a Standish, they won't seriously consider her for that role."

Jess was quiet. "You're a good guy, Deacon Standish. I'm sorry I judged you wrong when I met you."

Warmth moved through his chest again when he heard that. "We all tend to make snap judgments."

"Yeah, you're right. I thought you'd be like my ex, the one who got me pregnant."

Deacon stilled. He'd wondered about this missing man. But he couldn't push.

Jess sighed and rubbed her finger on the door handle.

"His family had money, so he had money. He didn't really do anything, not after he'd graduated from college, but he wanted to make a difference, do something different than he was expected to, you know?"

Deacon knew, all too well.

"I was working in a diner outside Seattle, and he came in every day—that's how we met. He was kinda lost, and I wanted to help him and—well. We spent time together, and more time, and things heated up. He asked me to move in with him, and he got a job working in a bookstore, but it was hard for him to adjust to not being able to do everything he wanted. He had no idea how to keep a budget or to pick up after himself, but we were doing okay.

"His family wanted him to come home for his grandfather's eightieth birthday, and he said he had to, but he'd be back. Just before that, he took me to Vegas for a weekend. He said he wanted to do something for me, so we went to a chapel and got married.

"I thought he was pushing back at his family and wasn't even sure if the marriage was legal. After we got back, he went to the birthday party. It wasn't a total shock when he didn't return. I found the marriage paperwork after he left. He left a note to explain why he'd changed his mind and taken all the documents back from the wedding chapel, so his family couldn't find out. He found out that the information about Vegas weddings was public and was afraid they might hassle me about a pre-nup, or the press might come after me. I think he meant well, but it was a lot easier to just do what his family wanted. Living without all the stuff he was used to was hard. Too hard, I guess."

Jess had a tough exterior, and Deacon understood where it came from. But when someone listened, like he had just now, they could hear the hurt underneath. Because this guy hadn't just left a more challenging life behind him—he'd left Jess behind. She hadn't been enough for him to return.

"I'm sorry Jess. I'm sorry he did that to you. You're being very kind to him. I think he lost more than you did, in the end."

Deacon didn't think a lot of people had found Jess of value in their lives. Despite their different circumstances, he felt some empathy with her.

He had value, but it wasn't based on himself. He had value to his family because he could take over the firm and keep the family name going for another generation. He was expected to marry and have children who would then be part of the firm as well. He had value to Meredith because he could change her future in the firm.

Meredith did like him as well, as a person, didn't she?

He was pretty sure if his surname was Smith, he could have taken this position in Cupid's Crossing permanently and his absence would never have been noticed in the firm.

Before he let himself get too sorry for himself, he considered the differences between his position and Jess's. He had money to support himself even if he wasn't working. He had a profession that meant he would be able to work as much as he wanted. He'd never worried about his next meal or where he would stay.

He really didn't know what it was like to be her.

"This is the family you don't want to have involved in raising your children, correct?"

She flashed him a wary glance. "You think they'd be better, don't you?"

Part of him wanted to promise to be on her side, no matter what. But did he really believe that, or just want to?

"I don't know, Jess. There's something to be said for having the security of money to handle the things in life that come up—medical expenses, education, etc."

Those gray eyes of Jess's seemed to be looking into his deepest held feelings.

"Money isn't everything, you know. Thom—my ex hated the way he was raised, and he swore he'd never do that to his own kids."

"Do you think your ex would want to know about his children, and do you think your children would want to know him and his family?"

Jess frowned at him and then turned away to rub her finger on the car door again.

"He complained a lot about his family. That

he and his siblings were always pawned off on nannies and boarding schools and that the family wasn't affectionate. They're also very controlling. He said the pressure was so bad that sometimes he'd be sick to his stomach and lie that he had the flu, just to cope. He had to take off to get a break from them. He ran away to Seattle and put up with a pokey little apartment to get some space for himself.

"I think…" Jess's voice trailed off before she collected her thoughts and continued. "I think he'd rather not have to make a decision. And if the kids want to know him, sometime, then I could reach out, through lawyers or something, right?"

"Absolutely. It's going to be more difficult for you without his support, especially financially."

Jess jutted out her chin. "I don't mind hard work. Plus, I have Rachel and Ryker to help. We'll be okay."

Deacon found himself wanting to offer his help as well, which was absurd. Jess wouldn't accept money from him, and what else could he provide? He wasn't going to be in Cupid's Crossing for more than a year. He had his own path, a different one.

He'd been curious about Jess's story, how she ended up pregnant and alone and unwilling to reach out to the father of her children. But now that he knew some of her story, he wanted to know more—and wanted to help. It was going to blur the lines between employer and employee.

How much longer were they going to be stuck here on the side of the road?

## CHAPTER NINE

JESS WAS RELIEVED when Deacon stopped asking questions about her ex and they moved away from serious topics. They covered favorite movies and TV shows from when they were kids and by the time help arrived were comparing foods they liked and didn't like. Jess was right. A car came by and gave them a lift to a gas station a few miles down the road.

They arranged a tow and called Rachel and Ryker. The garage was quiet, and the car was towed before Rachel and Ryker came to pick them up. It turned out that something *had* put a hole in the Audi's fuel line. Obviously, based on the timing, it was from the driveway they'd had to bump their way down. Deacon's car would need to be repaired, and then he could come and pick it up. Meanwhile, Rachel and Ryker brought them back to Cupid's Crossing.

Jess dropped onto the couch with an exhausted sigh. It had been a long day. She'd acted confident for Deacon, but she'd been afraid they might have to walk a long distance to get some help. Now, she needed to make something for dinner, but she was leaning heavily toward warming up some canned soup. She didn't have energy for more.

But maybe, maybe she'd make up some biscuits to go with it. She'd told Deacon she'd learned how to make some really good ones at a diner she'd worked at that had been spotlighted on a TV series for its biscuits and gravy.

Maybe she could bake some of those to go with the soup and take the extras into the office to share with Rachel and Deacon.

Deacon had said he liked biscuits.

THE BISCUITS WERE a success—Rachel demanded Jess make some for Ryker as well. Deacon didn't say a lot, but Jess noticed that he ate the last one. She was happy to make something for her brother, but it was Deacon's pleasure in the biscuits that was the most rewarding.

Jess was enjoying her stint at the law office. She knew Deacon cringed sometimes when she didn't talk super politely with some of the customers—no, *clients*—who called into the office. She was blunt and not especially tactful, but even if she didn't always say the right thing, she made sure she never revealed anyone's business, and she did the rest of her job well. Rachel would always say something kind, but Jess could tell when she'd really impressed her.

She wouldn't be here much longer, but it was a good thing to have on her résumé.

One morning, a week before Thanksgiving, Deacon came in with a bandage on his thumb. Rachel was out of the office again, so Jess was the one who noticed the bandage he'd wrapped clumsily around his right thumb.

"What happened to you?"

Deacon was trying to balance the cup of coffee he'd picked up at the diner. Jess felt bad that she couldn't make coffee in the office, but it still sent her stomach tumbling.

"Ah, I was doing some DIY and had a slip."

Jess frowned at the bulky bandage. "Did you slice it on a blade?"

Deacon sighed. "No, I was putting an ottoman together and… I'm not exactly sure what I did wrong, but suddenly I was bleeding. I just hope I can work with this."

Jess shook her head and got to her feet. "Sit down at my desk."

She pulled out the drawer in Rachel's desk that held the office first aid kit.

"I know it's hard to put a bandage on the

hand you use most, but that is way too much stuff on there unless maybe you need stitches." She sat on the edge of her desk and reached for his hand. His fingers were long, his nails well cared for and his hand felt good in her grasp. She pulled off the wad and found a moderate sized cut, nothing needing a trip to the hospital.

Jess snipped off some gauze and a piece of surgical tape. She protected the cut with the gauze, wrapping the tape around it in quick, efficient movements, making it as smooth as possible.

"There."

She held his hand for an awkward moment before he rose to his feet, pulling his hand free. "Thank you, Jess. That's much better." Deacon smiled down at her, and she realized they were standing close. Too close. She shifted sideways and snapped the kit shut.

"Okay, go do your lawyering now."

Rachel returned and the office got busy, but Jess worried about Deacon. He was super smart, but he didn't know how to do some of the more blue-collar stuff. Jess had been doing things like that all her life, and she'd still struggled with those instruction puzzles for furniture you bought unassembled. They appeared to have gone through an internet translator about five times and always left out a key step.

At the end of the day, when Rachel had left to set up something at the church for her dad, the minister, and Deacon was lost in some file on his desk, Jess closed her laptop and then knocked on his door frame.

Deacon looked up, blinking.

"Oh, Jess. Yes, what is it?"

Jess grinned. "It's closing time. Last call. Time to stop working."

Deacon looked back at his file.

"It'll still be there waiting for you in the morning. I wondered if you wanted some help with that ottoman thing you were putting together."

They both looked at Deacon's thumb.

"It shouldn't be that difficult. I'm sure I just read something wrong."

"Hey, boss man, I know you're smart, but honestly, that stuff isn't something you can read your way through. I've put things like that together before. I figure if I help you, you're not going to come in with your arm in a sling next, 'cause if that happens, people are going to think this place is cursed."

A corner of Deacon's mouth quirked up, and Jess knew she'd gotten him. She wasn't sure why this was important to her, but she wanted to help him. Which wasn't the smartest thing for her to do, but she was here now.

Deacon insisted if she was going to help him, he was going to provide some food. They called an order into the diner and picked it up on the way to Deacon's place.

Deacon was staying in one of the smaller homes in the downtown area of Cupid's Crossing. Jess admitted she was curious about what his place was like. She'd imagined it— tidy. Lots of books. She pictured a leather chair behind a desk and a pipe and realized she was projecting TV lawyer onto him.

They walked over in the dusk. Christmas decorations were shining from lampposts, and most of the homes, stately Victorians in this part of town, had Christmas lights hanging from eaves and verandas. The town Christmas tree wasn't set up in the park yet, and they were still waiting for the first snow, but there was a festive atmosphere, enhanced by the crisp bite of cold in the air.

Jess wondered when her winter coat would no longer fit.

Deacon's rental was on a side street, and not as large as some. It also wasn't as tidy as she'd imagined, and the piles of books played a part in that. Her fingers itched to put his place in order. If this had been a sci-fi movie, with the books taking on the humans, the books would be winning.

The pieces he'd been trying to assemble were scattered around his living room, probably where he'd left them once he started bleeding. There were also parts of a game console. So, Deacon liked to play video games?

He set down the bag of food and smoothed his tie. "Sorry, it's a bit of a mess."

Jess nudged him with her elbow. "Nah. I've cleaned hotel rooms. This is nothing."

Deacon shook his head. "You've done almost everything."

He made it sound like a compliment, something to be proud of, not something she'd been forced into out of necessity. It warmed Jess inside, in places her coat didn't reach.

"Well, let's eat and then we'll see what's up with your ottoman."

Deacon pulled out plates and cutlery, where Jess would have eaten from the diner boxes. But once they were seated at the table, eating, conversation was easy.

Jess told him some stories of the work she'd done.

"You really dressed up like a lobster?"

She nodded. "Yep. Waved the claws around to entice people to eat at a seafood restaurant."

Deacon fought a smile.

"Go ahead, you can laugh. It was funny. Hot and pretty smelly, but yeah, funny."

He let some of the smile escape. "Did you enjoy it?"

"It wasn't as bad as some jobs."

He cocked his head.

"What jobs did you like best?"

Jess considered, fork suspended over her pasta. "You asked me that before."

Deacon set his own fork down. "Maybe it's part of the privilege I've had in my life, but enjoyment of one's work has always been considered an important element in choosing a career."

She wasn't sure that was totally true.

"But not for you."

Deacon straightened up. "I— No, of course for me as well as anyone."

"I dunno." Jess set her own fork down. "When we were stuck in the car, it sounded like you didn't really choose to be a lawyer because you wanted to, but because it was expected of you."

Deacon smoothed his tie again. Did he know how revealing that was?

"I do enjoy my job. Not all of it, of course. No job is perfect."

Jess had never imagined any job would be.

"Okay, you like being a lawyer, but there's different kinds. And you like what you're doing here more than what you did back with your family, right?"

"Yes, that's what I told you. And you've made a good point. But it seems like you're deflecting. You haven't told me either time I asked what work you like to do."

Jess huffed out a breath. "I've never sat down and thought about the perfect job. It was just if the people I worked for weren't jerks and if the pay was good. If my coworkers were good people and the environment was nice."

He seemed to consider her words. Parse them for deeper meaning. "Did you ever find a job you wanted to stay at?"

Jess shrugged. Had she? She'd never stayed in one place, but was that because she didn't like the job, or because she wanted something better?

"I never found a place I wanted to stay, no. But it wasn't just the job. I always moved on."

Jess waited for Deacon to ask her why. He didn't. But she did wonder what she would have answered. Was there a reason she'd never settled down? What had she been looking for that always kept her on the move?

Fortunately, their meals were mostly done,

and Deacon took the dishes and put everything in the dishwasher. When he turned down Jess's offer of assistance with the rest of the cleanup, she went over to the living room to see how Deacon had done.

She sat down, cross-legged, and picked up the instructions. She ignored the narrated sections and instead looked at the drawings. She worked better with those.

By the time Deacon joined her, she'd taken apart one of the pieces and replaced it with a similar-looking but different piece.

"I messed up?"

Jess looked up. There was something in his expression and posture. A tiredness, like this had happened before.

"You tried to follow the words. I think the pictures are clearer."

He sat down beside her. "Show me."

So she did. Once Jess had, in a sense, explained the code to him, he was able to make better sense of the task.

"But doesn't that mean this part goes in here?"

Jess shook her head. "They're trying to get you with that part. What they really mean is to put this thing in between those two parts."

Deacon looked closely at the diagram and then at the pieces in front of them.

"It makes sense when you show me, but that is absolutely not what the diagram shows."

Jess chuckled. "It's cute that you think this is gonna make sense."

Deacon frowned at the part in his hand. "Are they trying to make this an impossible job?"

"Well, you can pay extra for them to put it together for you."

"I think it might be worth it."

Jess put a hand to her chest, overplaying the shock.

"No, no, you can't let them win."

Deacon laughed. "They have already beaten me."

"No, we're doing this. Have you got that white thingy? With the—"

Jess waved her hand, words failing her as she tried to describe something she could picture in her head but couldn't name.

Deacon put down the part he'd been holding. "Is 'thingy' a technical term?"

She held up the two parts she was trying to join in her hand. "It's for here."

Deacon looked from her hands to the pieces remaining on the floor. He moved the box aside and grabbed a white plastic part.

"This?"

"Yes!" Jess held out the join, and he held her hand as he carefully twisted the plastic in.

Jess froze, his skin warm on hers as he focused on his task. His hands were soft and smooth, not roughened with calluses. Firm and warm, and a little shiver rushed up her arm. Once the thingy was in its place, she quickly pulled back her hand.

"Put that on that side." She hoped her voice sounded normal.

Deacon got up on his knees and carefully attached the part.

"There. I think if we just put these in place now..."

Jess scooched back to let him work. Once he put the last parts of the bottom together, suddenly the whole thing made sense. Jess let Deacon finish up. He made quick work of it once he understood what he was doing.

She helped him settle it in front of the couch.

Deacon smiled at her. No, it wasn't a smile, it was a grin. Something she'd never thought to see on his face.

"We did it!"

"We did."

"So what are you going to hide in here?"

Deacon's cheeks flushed. "Um, the gaming stuff. It's my guilty pleasure, but right now it's kind of taking over."

Jess didn't think he needed to feel guilty about playing a video game to unwind. He worked hard. Totally reasonable.

"I won't tell anyone if you don't want, but it doesn't seem that horrible to me."

"Thank you for this, Jess. I really appreciate it. And now I won't be showing up at the office with further do-it-yourself injuries."

There was something warm happening inside Jess. At the pride he showed in a simple accomplishment, in the way he acknowledged her help, in the grin he didn't often show. And that warm was all kinds of trouble.

She'd done this kind of thing before, bought the T-shirt and now was about to stretch it out of shape with her twin-pregnancy belly. She in no way needed to go through this again.

"Glad we avoided that terrible fate. So, um, I'm gonna go now, okay? I'll let you put your stuff in it."

The ottoman had a cushioned top that lifted, providing storage inside. Deacon needed that if this place wasn't going to trip up anyone who walked through.

A tiny crease appeared on Deacon's forehead. "I didn't mean to keep you, Jess. I'm sorry, I didn't think to ask if you had other things to do tonight."

"No, just a little tired, and remember, I offered to help. See you at the office."

"Wait, just a moment. Let me walk you back to your place."

Jess stepped back. "What? No, you don't have to do that. I'm fine."

Deacon moved toward the door, where their coats were. "I'm sure you are, but I'm going to escort you anyway." When she still stood for a moment, not moving, he sighed. "It's good exercise for me. Will that make it all right?"

Jess flushed. "Sorry, I didn't mean—" What did she mean? Deacon waited, so she had to come up with something. "I didn't mean to put you out."

"It's okay, Jess. Sometimes it's okay to put people out."

# CHAPTER TEN

JESS PULLED HER coat back on and wrapped a scarf around her neck. Deacon grabbed his coat and, after consideration, a hat and gloves. He closed and locked the door behind them, almost expecting Jess to have taken off down the sidewalk without him. Deacon wasn't sure what had changed Jess's mood, but he wasn't going to let her walk around after dark on her own. He'd hoped walking her home like this wouldn't be too awkward. Was she afraid he would somehow take advantage of knowing where she lived?

He cast about for an innocuous topic of conversation and asked her how the town had changed from when she'd been living here as a child. And as soon as he did, he worried he'd be raising bad memories for her.

It seemed the bad memories were from her home life, not the town as a whole, or perhaps enough time had passed that she didn't mind talking about the place. As they made their way by the park in the center of town, she had stories about school outings and hanging out with friends, but other than a couple of names, she didn't know the people who'd lived in the big houses around the park. As they got farther away from the downtown area, the homes got smaller; the holiday decorations were less elaborate and were often missing. Those people she knew better: children who'd been in her classes.

The large lawns surrounding the small homes were foreign to Deacon's experience. He'd grown up in a condo in New York. Green space was found in parks or in country homes, and those spaces had been large and well-manicured, not filled with rusty play structures.

Deacon was out of place. Should he even be here?

Jess stopped. "Are you okay?" Her breath puffed in the cold air.

Deacon looked around them, the streetlights casting the world into monochrome shades. "This is just so…different from anything I grew up with."

Jess frowned. "It seems pretty normal to me. But we grew up a lot different."

"Can I actually do any good here? I can't relate to how so many of the people in this town were raised and how they live. I'm an outsider."

Jess started walking, so Deacon moved to keep up with her. He had promised to escort her home.

"What did you think you were gonna do here? Come and show us the error of our ways? How thingsare supposed to be done?"

Deacon sighed. "I was escaping. People were upset with me, and I was getting away. I thought I'd have a chance to do some easier, more interesting work. I hadn't considered the people I wanted to help and if I could actually be of benefit to them."

Jess patted his arm. "I'll give you points for honesty. And, for what it's worth, I think you are helping people. I mean, you listen to them, and I know Rachel thinks you're doing a good job."

"Rachel is good—not just in her skills, but in the way she is concerned for people."

Jess sighed. "She is. And maybe it's okay to just try to do a good job."

Their footsteps were loud in the cold air. No one else was walking the streets at this time. An occasional car passed by, but otherwise they were alone.

"You know how I asked you about what kind of job you wanted, and how enjoying a job was important, at least to the people I know? I'd never considered whether I was actually good at what I do—good enough, I mean."

Jess took a moment before replying. "You went to law school, right? Passed the bar? Wouldn't that mean you're good at it?"

Deacon stopped. "I'm not good at all parts of it. And those parts are the ones I need for the family firm. Maybe I'm not the person they need there."

Jess had her head cocked in the light of a streetlamp. "Then maybe it's the wrong job, or maybe you need to get better."

"There's been a Standish heading the firm for generations, and I'm it for this one."

"Is it really *that* important?"

"I think if that was all, I could step down." Deacon hadn't considered that before. But despite his name, he'd never felt like he was the right person, even if he enjoyed the work more than he did.

"So what else is there?"

"I'll be in a position to make some changes to the firm if I'm heading it up."

"I know you talked about making it better for some people, but can you do that much if the others don't want to do it?"

"Not totally on my own. But most of the

partners are getting older. Once Meredith is with me, things can start to open up. She makes things happen."

"That sounds like someone good to have on your side."

"She is. It's why she's a better successor to my father than I am, but the partners haven't been willing to consider her. I've suggested it before, but my father won't entertain the idea."

Jess moved ahead again. "Benny's place is just up ahead."

"Ah, right..Sorry, I didn't mean to hold you up."

"No, it's okay. For what it's worth, it sounds like you do have something important to do at your law firm. I mean, being able to see what the needs are is a big part of that, right? And if you know there's stuff you can't do, you can get the people who can do it to help you. That seems a lot smarter than thinking you can do it all yourself."

Deacon smiled in the dark. He'd considered a lot of factors when it came to stepping up in the firm. Responsibility, duty, what others would think. He'd always noted the qualities he was lacking when it came to assuming his father's role.

Maybe that was actually an asset, in a

twisted way. By recognizing his own weaknesses, but seeing those of the firm as well, maybe he could find the right way to initiate change, even if he wasn't the person who could do that. A variation on what he planned with Meredith. He didn't need to concentrate on being the one to fix the problems in the office. His role could be to note those problems and find the right person to deal with them.

"Thank you, Jess."

They'd arrived at Gifford's Repair Shop. Jess stopped at the foot of an outdoor stairway, leading, presumably, to the apartment she was living in.

"For the ottoman?" she asked, doubtfully.

"No, for your insight."

Jess crossed her arms. "You're making fun of me, aren't you?"

"Absolutely not. You're totally right, that I don't have to be able to fix every problem— I just need to *find* someone who can fix each problem as it arises. I might not be the best at networking, but I can give the people who do that well a chance to assume greater responsibility."

"Well, if you find that to be amazing insight, you're welcome. I just thought it was common sense."

"It is, except that sense is often not very common."

Jess shook her head at him. "I'm gonna say thanks for the compliment and let it be. Glad if I could help."

"This is your place?" It didn't look bad, but it also looked very…utilitarian, without any of the charm of the house where he was staying.

Jess looked up the steps. "Yep. Nicer than a lot of places I've stayed."

Deacon smiled. Jess was so different from the people he'd known. What did it say about him that he was more at ease with her than with those people?

"I'm glad you're comfortable there. See you in the morning?"

"Yeah. Thanks for walking me home. Sure you'll be safe going back on your own?"

Deacon held back a grin. "Guess we'll see if I show up in the office in the morning."

DEACON SHOWED UP at the office in the morning, quite safe after his solitary walk home in the dark. Despite his doubts from the evening before, or maybe because of Jess's reassurance, he was looking forward to his workday.

He did most of the time. It had only been a matter of weeks, but once he'd gotten over his nerves in the first few days, he enjoyed going to the office. The work was often surprising and unexpected, but he liked it. He felt a greater sense of accomplishment when he left the office than he had at Standish Legal. A part of him wished his name wasn't Standish so that this was what his life could be.

Then Rachel dropped the bombshell over morning coffee. Jess had gotten over her violent reaction to the smell, and they'd been able to enjoy coffee in the office the past week. Jess still wasn't drinking it, but she made very good coffee on the office machine.

"I've got an appointment next week to get my cast off." Rachel looked down at the plaster on her arm with dislike.

"That's awesome," Jess said. "You can get back to doing all the things you've missed."

"Excellent," Deacon said, but despite the fact that it really was good news, it made his mood dive.

Rachel having use of her dominant hand again would be more than helpful, but it meant they would soon be a two-person office. Deacon wasn't used to that. Jess had started almost as soon as he arrived, and he'd liked having her around. He didn't want anything to change.

"You'll need some therapy, though, won't you? To get your muscles working properly again?" Deacon was sure he'd had to do some of that when he'd broken his leg as a child.

Rachel nodded. "I'll have to see someone and do some exercises, but the tendons weren't affected. Nothing is guaranteed, but the doctor expects I should be mostly back to normal in a couple of weeks."

Jess grinned at Rachel. "Then Ryker won't have to do all the cooking?"

Rachel laughed. "He's actually a pretty good cook, so we've split that job anyway."

Deacon thought that sounded nice, and Jess did, too, based on the expression on her face.

"He's a good guy," Jess said, looking serious.

"I know. He's the best. Oh, before I forget, Jess, Mariah wanted to talk to you. She needs some help for a new project she's working on. I told her about you but wouldn't let her try to poach you until I could handle things here."

"Awesome," Jess responded. "You have any idea what she's got in mind?"

Rachel reached out to grasp Jess's hand. "I do, and I think this will work really well for you. We've never had a childcare here. Kids were looked after by their mothers or grandmothers or a friend down the street. It worked, but that was different. Now we've got new people coming, more women are working, and having a proper daycare is something we need.

"Mariah's started the ball rolling and has someone with early childhood education experience hired for when we open the daycare, but they'll need more staff. And she wants someone to work on the site before it opens as well—setting it up, maybe painting, handling some of the paperwork. I thought, if you were working there, you could have your twins with you."

Jess was wiping at her eyes with the heels of her hands. "Stupid hormones. That sounds so awesome, Rachel. Childcare, especially for two babies, was going to be a thing. But if we could swing that, yeah. I've done my share of babysitting and nannying, so I have some idea of what I'm getting into."

Deacon admitted that sounded good for Jess. She was going to have a lot of responsibility on her shoulders, with two babies and no partner or guaranteed financial aid. He wished she'd let him reach out to the twins' father, but he had to respect her wishes.

Even if he didn't, he had no way of finding out who the man was, so moot point.

"I'll let Mariah know. She'll want to meet with you and figure out the details."

"You're the best, Rachel. And I'll be happy

to help out here as long as you need me to. Benny might have some stuff for me to do as well."

Deacon wanted her to keep working here, but he also worried she was taking on too much.

"Make sure you don't overdo it."

Both women looked at him as if they'd forgotten he was there.

"I'll be careful, don't worry." Jess's hand rested on her belly, now noticeable when her clothes pulled tight against her body. "But I have to get as ready as I can."

"Good." Deacon wanted to say more, but he couldn't. "I'll get to work, then—let me know when Mr. Jones arrives, please."

They always did inform him when someone arrived in the office, though most of the time Deacon could see for himself, but it seemed the easiest way to segue out of that conversation that he wasn't truly a part of.

It was a good thing for Jess, and it was one of the things he and Meredith wanted to change in the firm. To provide an on-site daycare for staff. With the hours people often worked, it would make the firm more attractive for women—or men. He had to remember not to stereotype. But daycare wasn't considered necessary by his father and his cronies. To them, it was just another indication that promoting women came with a risk and cost.

They didn't hear him when Deacon talked about house husbands and two working parents, or single moms. They were in their privileged, insulated world and refused to recognize that they were fortunate more than deserving.

Rachel stopped in his doorway to say Mr. Jones was there, and he pushed those thoughts aside.

DEACON SPENT THANKSGIVING weekend with his family. The family dinner included more than twenty people, and no one asked more than perfunctory questions about what Deacon was doing.

He was fine with that. He claimed an early meeting and left Sunday afternoon to get back to Cupid's Crossing. He felt more comfortable in his rental space than he had in his parents' condo, and he played video games for the evening, feet resting on the ottoman Jess had helped him put together.

The day Rachel got her cast off, Jess brought in a cake she'd made and sang an off-key rendition of "Happy Cast Removal Day to You." Deacon admired her confidence in singing when she clearly was unable to do it well.

Rachel was noticeably touched. "Thank you, Jess. Did you make this?"

Jess looked down and twitched a shoulder. "It's not a big deal. Gave me something to do last night."

Jess pulled out some plates, since Rachel had to get her arm back to strength and cut pieces for the three of them.

"Thank you, Jess." The cake was clearly homemade, a little taller on one side than the other, but Deacon understood why Rachel was moved by the gesture. It wasn't something he was used to. He was accustomed to perfect cakes, made by a professional, purchased and brought in without a single flaw. That was on the rare occasions that they had a cake. But this tasted good and had the added benefit that someone had labored over it for Rachel.

"This is really good, Jess. Can I take some for Ryker?"

"Take all of it." Jess glanced at Deacon. "Unless you want some, Deacon?"

The polite thing to do would be to let Rachel take it all with her. It was sweet, extra calories and wasn't really meant for him. He'd been an overweight child, and sweets had been removed from his diet. He still was careful with what he ate in order to keep his weight under control. Yet Deacon found himself saying, "I'd love to have some, if Rachel doesn't mind."

"No, I don't mind at all. There's way more than we can eat on our own."

Jess looked pleased, and Deacon decided every extra calorie was worth it.

"Oh, Jess." Rachel had put her plate in the sink and started to run the water. Jess hustled over and bumped her aside with one hip.

"I'm doing those before you drop and break something. What's up?"

"Mariah wants to meet you. Are you free tonight?"

Jess nodded. "Absolutely. Tell me where and when. And thanks again."

"What are sisters for? Now, let me wash the forks. I won't break them, and I want this hand to do something now that I'm finally rid of that cast. Then we're getting out the Christmas decorations."

Deacon realized he was standing there, plate in hand, listening in with no good reason to be doing nothing. He took over his plate and then returned to his office.

Jess was a little nervous about this meeting with Mariah Carter, née Van Dalton. She'd been introduced to the woman. Mariah was scarily competent, married to a Carter and the granddaughter of a very rich man. Those weren't the circles Jess was used to.

Mariah had asked her to come to the diner to talk over coffee (or, for Jess, tea), after the dinner rush was over. Mariah was already there when Jess arrived, appearing both well-dressed and organized. Jess stiffened her back and walked over to meet her, doing her best to look like this wasn't a big deal.

"Thanks for meeting me, Jess. How are you doing?"

"I'm fine." She wasn't going to tell Mariah that she had any problems that would interfere with the job. Thankfully the upchucking was over, but there were leg cramps and heartburn to make up for that. She could manage, though. It wouldn't prevent her working.

"Rachel tells me that she'll be able to take over a lot of her usual office work in a couple of weeks and that you might be available then."

Jess nodded. "Whenever they don't need me at the law office, I'm free. I could probably do some stuff before then on evenings or weekends."

Mariah opened her tablet. "The space we've made available is having some renovations done to bring it up to code, so while I appreciate the offer, we probably won't be ready to do any work on the inside until the New Year.

"I've been in touch with the director, Dinah, who'll be taking charge of the daycare. She has some ideas about how she'd like the place set up. We've made up an order for decals and murals, things like that. I was hoping you could do some of that work."

Jess nodded again. "Definitely."

"Your brother has set up the website, but I don't have the time to oversee that, answer queries and respond to phone calls. Do you think you could? If you could liaise with Dinah, we could work out the number of children we can expect and the ages."

"Sure." Jess could handle all that.

Mariah pinned her with a look. "There is something else. To work there, you need to take an online orientation, apply to Children and Family Services and attend fifteen hours of health and safety training. Can you do that?"

Jess pulled out her phone and started to make notes. "Absolutely."

Mariah smiled at her. "I don't know how this will go, as far as number of children and staff, but if you decide you'd like to take more training and become more than just an assistant, we can probably work something out.

I know Rachel is impressed with the work you've done for her. I don't apologize for snapping up people I can trust to do their jobs well."

Jess looked down. "Thanks. I'm going to be handling babies in any case, so I might as well be paid for it."

Mariah made a note. "I'll email you and Dinah and let the two of you handle most of this. Let me know if you have any problems, either with her or with any of the suppliers or contractors. I'll send you a link to the list of legal requirements to get a daycare set up. Most of it has been dealt with, but if you notice anything missing or being done wrong, let us know."

Jess squinted one eye. "That's it? You don't have more questions?"

"I think I'm a pretty good judge of character. I've talked to Rachel. And, to be blunt, this is a small town, so there are only so many people available."

Jess appreciated the honesty. She'd rather know exactly where she stood. She wasn't the most qualified person, but she'd do, as long as she didn't mess up. Therefore, she just had to be sure not to mess up.

"That works for me, so I'm not complaining. Just let me know when you need me."

Mariah raised a finger. "I almost forgot. We have to do a background check—will that be a problem?"

Jess quirked a smile. "Nope. Unlike others in my family, I've never had any problems with the law."

"Excellent. If I need any information that's not on your résumé, I'll let you know."

Mariah stood. "Thanks for meeting me, Jess. I'll pay for the drinks."

Jess took a look at the almost untouched coffee in Mariah's cup. Had Mariah even wanted it?

"Thanks." Jess was going to stay and finish her peppermint tea.

Then Mariah was gone, and Jess had another job lined up. She should have kept some of the cake for her own celebration.

When she finished her drink, Jess walked back to her place. There was no sign of Benny—he had a more exciting social life than she did. Jess wasn't interested in going out or partying, not anymore. She was watching what she ate and drank and was tired most evenings by nine. Growing babies took a lot of energy.

She let herself into her quiet apartment.

She wasn't going to feel sorry for herself that there was no one here. Soon enough she'd have her twins. In the meantime, this place was all hers. There were times when this had been the sum total of her dreams, and she wouldn't take it for granted.

She grabbed an apple instead of the cake she hadn't brought home and looked up the orientation she'd need to do to work in the daycare. She could take care of that this weekend. She'd do her best to cover all this training before she started working at the space where the daycare would be. It would be a good thing to have on her résumé when she might have to look for another job.

She forced down the feeling of loneliness.

She'd spent Thanksgiving with Rachel and Ryker, and that had been the best Thanksgiving she could remember. She was spending Christmas with them and Rachel's father, and next year, she'd have her babies.

She wondered what Deacon's holiday would be like before reminding herself that wasn't her problem. After she was done at the law office, she might not ever see him again, and that thought bothering her was good reason to take warning.

She was used to being alone. Now she had a place to stay, enough to eat and twins on the way. There was no point in dreaming of more.

## CHAPTER ELEVEN

ON JESS'S LAST day at the law office, Rachel brought in a cake. She'd been thrilled that she had enough movement in her arm to manage baking again. Deacon insisted on taking them out for lunch to Moonstone's rather than the diner. He called it the office's holiday lunch, since it was just a week till Christmas.

Jess appreciated the send-off, since she hadn't actually worked at the office that long. But Deacon was a decent guy and Rachel was her sister-in-law, so they were generous and kind.

She was sad to be done. She hadn't looked at the job as more than a way to make some money till she found something else, but she was going to miss it. Not necessarily the job. Jess preferred to be more active than office work, but the work environment was nicer than any other place she'd earned her pay.

She had the holidays off before she could start in the daycare space, so this was her chance to catch up on things she'd been too busy or too tired to do before. She drove into Albany to do the health and safety requirements for the daycare job and some Christmas shopping. Afterward, she looked at some secondhand places to see what was available for baby furniture.

She'd done research on the safety issues for cribs and couldn't find anything secondhand she thought was safe enough. She wasn't going to take risks with her babies. As she drove back to Cupid's Crossing, she reviewed her finances in her head. She knew exactly how much money she had, all the time. With that, and keeping things tidy, she exerted some control over her life, after having none while she was growing up.

She'd been well paid at the law office and might be called in to help again if things got busy. Mariah was going to pay her pretty well to work in the daycare. Benny had threatened to reduce her rent if she did any more work around his shop.

She spent an evening at home researching new cribs. If she couldn't find what she wanted secondhand, she'd buy the most affordable new ones she could. After some searching, she found a place to buy an unassembled crib. She wasn't going to pay the store people to do it for her.

Jess spent Christmas with Rachel and Ryker and Rachel's dad, one of the local pastors. She'd helped Rachel make the traditional meal in the parsonage kitchen. Rachel worked smoothly, wrist back to normal, obviously having done this countless times. Her mother had died when she was young as well, but Rachel, an only child, had had her pastor father instead of a drunk parent and six siblings, three following in their father's footprints.

"Does Ryker get along with your dad?" Jess asked.

Rachel paused in the middle of mashing the potatoes. Jess was whisking the pan drippings with flour to make gravy.

"Dad knows I love your brother, and he loves me. And my dad always looks for the best in people. But their conversations are awkward because they have nothing in common."

Rachel resumed her work on the potatoes. "I remember last year when they tried a discussion about football. My dad's understanding of football starts and ends with the high school team, and Ryker only watches when his friends do, so that was an excruciating effort. But I appreciate that they try."

Jess's heart gave a pang. To have people love you, to try so hard, just because they wanted to make you happy? That was a gift. She knew Rachel appreciated it, but she couldn't help envying her.

"And next year it'll be easier."

Jess stopped the whisk. "How come?"

Rachel grinned at her. "You'll have two babies then. They can look after them while we work. They'll have something to do and talk about while you get a break from childcare for a bit. Win/win."

Jess moved the whisk some more, though she didn't really see the gravy forming in front of her. She hadn't thought of what the holidays would be like. She hadn't thought much beyond the arrival of the babies. But Rachel would help her give her children Christmas memories of the good kind. The kind Rachel had experienced growing up.

Coming back to Cupid's Crossing was the right choice, she was sure of that. She was determined to stay and make a life for herself and her children here. She dropped the whisk and grabbed Rachel in a hug.

"I'm so glad you and Ryker got together."

Rachel hugged her back. "And I'm so glad you came here. But you're about to burn the gravy."

Jess blinked her eyes and pulled the pan

from the heat. Pregnancy hormones again. Except she was pretty sure it was more than that.

She was back to herself when they all sat around the table, enjoying the best Christmas Jess could remember. It was difficult to believe that she could have more memories like this. But she would. She'd fight for them for her babies.

She wasn't fighting alone.

EARLY IN THE new year, when she was in Albany running some errands for Mariah and the daycare, Jess stopped to pick up the kits for the cribs. The guys at the store helped her wrestle them into the back of her van. She wasn't sure how she'd get them up the stairs to her place. Benny couldn't help with that, and she wasn't sure if Ryker was free. They wouldn't fit in the lift. If worse came to worst, she'd take the parts out of the boxes and carry them up in manageable amounts. Jess usually found if she was determined enough, she'd find a way to get things done.

She pulled into the lot at Benny's and parked the van near the bottom of her stairs. She opened the back doors of the van and eyed the two boxes.

They weren't all that heavy. They weren't light, but she could handle the weight. She just couldn't handle the weight and the unwieldy shape together. She wasn't going to make the attempt and risk a fall.

Could she do it if she wrapped a rope around each one and dragged them up the steps one at a time? It was worth a try.

She had some line in her van, so she managed to pull out and tie up one box. She gave a tug. It would be a struggle, but it was worth making at least one attempt before taking the package apart.

She managed to drag it over to the bottom of the stairs. Then she heard a vehicle pulling into the lot. She expected Benny, but when she turned around, it was an Audi, not Benny's van.

Deacon parked beside her.

"Do you need some help?"

Jess didn't like admitting that she wasn't capable on her own. But this was a task that would go much more smoothly with two people.

And she was happy to see him. She pushed through the initial discomfort she always felt when saying yes to the offer of help. "I'd appreciate it if you could give me a hand with this."

He smiled when she said that, so she thought he must like being the helper for a change. Not that this was new for him. He helped people all day long. But she'd helped change his tire and put together his furniture, and she expected he'd like to do something for her this time.

He got out of his car, still in his suit. She wondered where he'd been, since he normally walked to work, but it wasn't her place to ask. He crossed to the foot of the stairs where she had the rope tied around the unwieldy box.

"What is this, if I might ask?"

She grinned at his way of asking. "You might ask, if you wanted. These are a couple of cribs."

His brows pulled together. "Some assembly is required, isn't it?"

She nodded. "A lot of assembly is required. But I got a deal on these, since they were the last two they had, and secondhand ones aren't as safe."

He smiled at her, and she grinned back.

"Then you definitely made the right choice. What do you need me to do?"

Jess considered. "If I pick up the front, you could take the back, and hopefully we can get it up the steps without either of us falling down or the crib sliding back."

Deacon looked at the box, and the stairs, and then at her. "I'll do my best, but I've never tried this before. Are cribs difficult to wrangle?"

"Dunno. We'll find out, won't we?"

Jess grabbed the rope at one end and lifted. Deacon reached his hands under the box at his end and raised it up. Jess went up a step, and Deacon supported the weight, so she took another step. He then took one step as well.

They were slow, but soon they'd maneuvered it up the stairs, resting it on the landing while Jess unlocked the door. It was much easier to drag it into the living room.

"We did it!"

Deacon wiped his hands together. "What would you have done if no one came by like I did? Called Ryker?"

"I could have opened the box and taken the parts out. Carried them up separately."

Deacon nodded. "That would work, but it would be terrible to lose a screw or some other tiny piece."

Jess nudged him. "I was really happy you stopped to help."

Hauling up the second box was also a slow process, but they knew what they were doing now, and both boxes got to the living room without any people or parts falling. There weren't any pinched fingers or even swearing. Jess called that a success.

"Thanks." She untied the rope from the second box. "Do you want something to drink?"

Deacon paused, and Jess was sure he was going to make some polite apology. It wasn't like her apartment was the nicest place to be in Cupid's Crossing. Deacon's place was a lot more attractive and comfortable. But why did she care about that? His opinion didn't play a part in her future.

"Why don't you let me get that for you? You must be tired."

Jess's eyes opened wide. She wasn't used to this. "Oh, it's okay. I'm fine."

Deacon shook his head. "If you're not tired, I'm sure you want to take a look at what's in those boxes."

Jess bit her lip. She *was* curious about how difficult this might be.

"Go on, open one of them up and tell me what you want to drink."

Jess caved. While Deacon started boiling water for the peppermint tea that Jess had become fond of since she'd been pregnant, she grabbed a box cutter to open the package.

There were instructions on top. Jess sat down on the floor and took a look at what they expected. She spread the paper out and checked for the list of items that should be inside.

She twisted, set the paper on the couch and began to take the pieces out. She'd set aside the last package of screws when Deacon put a cup of tea on the coffee table beside her.

"Thanks."

"No problem. Have you got everything?"

"Not sure yet."

Deacon sat down beside her while she started to tick off the items against the list.

"This one looks okay." Which was good news. She wouldn't want to have to drag this back to the store again. Deacon leaned over the instructions, a frown crossing his face.

"That looks complicated. When are you going to put them together?"

Jess rubbed her finger under the first step on the sheet of paper. "I'd like to start now, but it would be smarter to wait till I don't have anything else to do. I'm supposed to check out the daycare space to see how the painting is going tomorrow. So maybe Saturday."

"Would you like some help?"

Jess looked at him, but he was still frowning at the directions. "Are you volunteering?"

"I thought I could return the favor, since you helped me."

Didn't he have something better to do with his time? He wasn't even her boss anymore, so why was he being so nice?

"Are you sure? This isn't the most fun way to spend a Saturday."

"I'd be happy to."

Those were some extra manners. He sounded like he meant it. Jess considered. She couldn't get used to having his help, but then, when would she be assembling cribs again?

"Okay, then. I can feed you some lunch in return?"

Now Deacon looked at her. "That would be lovely. Thank you."

Jess gave a snort laugh and clapped a hand over her mouth.

Deacon's eyes crinkled, as if they wanted to laugh. "What was that about?"

"You were thanking me for coming over to help me!"

"I understand that, but what was that sound?"

Jess felt her cheeks heating up. "I may have a weird laugh."

Deacon's brows went up. "That was a laugh?"

Jess made a fake frowny face. "Do you want to come help and get a meal or not?"

Deacon stood, hands raised. "I won't say a thing. What time on Saturday?"

After he left, Jess stared at the mess scattered around her living room, and then at the door. Had he really just volunteered to help her? And she'd agreed?

She had, because she liked Deacon. He was from a totally different background than she was, but he didn't act like he thought that made him better. That scored him a lot of points in her book. It wasn't just that, though.

He didn't rush in and try to take over like so many guys did. She liked that as well. And she liked that they could talk, despite the differences in their backgrounds and life experiences.

It was nice to have some help, and someone to talk to while she was home. Jess hadn't had that since her ex had left.

This wasn't something she could rely on, obviously. Jess had no hold on Deacon, and no expectations. He was probably a little lonely himself, in a new town. As long as she didn't decide it was her responsibility to make sure he learned to fit in here, or didn't expect anything from him, it should be okay to take the help he offered and enjoy his company.

Jess had been on her own for a long time. She'd made her share of mistakes, but she'd always been smart enough to learn from them. She didn't make the same mistake twice. And she wouldn't now. She'd opened herself up to a guy who was from a whole different world from hers, and she'd been hurt. Not heartbroken. She hadn't been that open.

But knowing how easily she'd been left behind, again… Well, courting that feeling was not on her list of things to repeat.

With a sigh, she shoved to her feet, leaving the crib parts scattered around her. She didn't like the mess, but she was tired, and it would wait till tomorrow. She took her tea mug over to the sink and rubbed her back.

It was early, but she needed to rest. *They* needed to rest, she and the two peanuts.

She made her way to the bedroom, still surprised that she'd relaxed enough to let her snort laugh out. And grateful that Deacon hadn't made too much fun of her for it.

DEACON KNOCKED ON Jess's door at 9:00 a.m. on Saturday. He'd debated if this was too early and decided to risk it. The law office opened up at nine, so he hoped it was a reasonable time.

He'd picked up some baking from the diner: doughnuts and muffins. They'd had those at the office a few times while Jess had been working, and she had enjoyed them. He wasn't certain if the foods her stomach reacted to changed over her pregnancy. The coffee smell had gone from a vomiting trigger to something she was able to handle, but he'd yet to see her drink any of it.

Jess answered almost immediately, so he hadn't wakened her. That was one concern gone.

"Hey, Deacon. Come on in. Wait, are those muffins?"

They did make nice muffins at the diner, and these were fresh out of the oven. The aroma had been teasing his own taste buds for a while.

"And doughnuts."

Jess stood back and waved him in. "A man with baked goods is always welcome. In fact, you can just sit back and watch if you want. You've done your quota."

Deacon smiled, relieved that his idea had been successful. "I'm glad you still like them. I wasn't sure."

Jess had taken the bag from him and was already looking inside.

"I think the morning sickness has worked itself out. Thank goodness. I'm not sure how I'd survive not being able to enjoy muffins." She pulled one out and took a bite.

"Mmm-hmm. That's great." She looked up guiltily. "I'm sorry, I just wolfed into this. Can I get you something to drink? Tea? Water?"

"I'm good for now. I had some coffee on the way over."

Jess passed him the bag. "Good plan. Still

have problems sometimes with that one. Get yourself something to eat, and we can get started."

Deacon looked in the bag, as if he wasn't the one who'd just bought the treats. His family had always taken care to eat properly, so he hadn't had that many doughnuts or muffins. Being overweight as a child had left a mark. He grabbed a doughnut, telling himself it was because they were less messy to eat, when he knew he just liked them better.

Jess finished her muffin, grabbed a cup with peppermint tea in it and sat on the floor in her living room. She set the tea down and picked up the instructions.

Deacon followed her. "How was the daycare when you stopped by yesterday?"

Jess looked surprised. "Pretty good. It's been a few different things over time—was a barbershop when I was growing up, but it's a good size, with a big yard around it, and some parking. They're redoing the fence, and then there's some play structures coming in. I told Mariah I could probably stay on-site to check on the crew assembling them if needed."

Deacon looked at the parts on the floor and wondered how long this would take, even with two of them working together.

It took three hours. Jess took charge, and

Deacon provided extra hands when needed and searched for parts. He refilled Jess's tea and gathered the refuse left behind. When they had the first crib ready, Deacon felt uncomfortable taking any credit.

Jess put her hands on her hips. "I know now why I got such a good deal on these things. That was…just stupid the way they expect you to put them together."

Deacon gave the crib a tug. "Are you worried they aren't safe?"

She shook her head. "Their safety rating is good. I looked them up. The comments were all about how difficult they were to put together, not that they weren't good when you got them assembled. I thought, you know, if people haven't put together furniture, it seems difficult. But I misjudged them."

Jess looked up to the ceiling. "I'm sorry, reviewers! You were right!"

Deacon laughed. "I'm sure they feel much better now. Where do you want this?"

"In the spare room. It's kinda small, but that's gonna be the nursery. It's empty now, because I don't have any guests coming, but there's no reason not to put things in there."

He wondered if Jess had friends who might come, at some point, to visit her. She gave an impression of being a very solitary, self-contained person. He didn't think many people got close to her.

Deacon was relieved that none of his family had come to stay with him as guests. His visit home for Christmas had been uncomfortable enough. He and his parents had been out for Christmas Eve with family and then hosted a catered Christmas dinner with more of the extended family. Everyone thought he was doing penance in Cupid's Crossing, and he'd been the recipient of either sympathetic or disappointed looks and comments. He hadn't been able to talk to Meredith in private, but he'd heard enough to know that the firm was not in danger of becoming progressive while he'd been gone.

Very few people asked about what had happened with him over the fall, and everyone assumed he was bored and frustrated. He'd responded as little as possible. He'd been in Cupid's Crossing for less than three months, but he felt protective of it. He was afraid his family would see the flaws and mock the place, missing the charm and warmth he'd found here.

"I can move the crib for you."

Jess started to shake her head but stilled and closed her eyes.

"Thank you, Deacon. That would be nice."

She huffed a breath. "I'm really bad at accepting help, but right now the chance to sit with my feet up and rest is good."

"I don't think I was really much help in making the crib, but I can do this for you."

"Go be manly, then, and I'll sit right here and rest up for the next one."

Deacon picked up the crib, more awkward than heavy, and started down the only hallway. He liked being told to be manly. He mostly impressed people with his brain, not his brawn.

"Last door on the left."

Deacon passed a bathroom and, after a quick glance, refused to invade Jess's privacy by looking into what was obviously her bedroom. He set the crib down outside the last room and rearranged his grip to get it through the narrow doorway.

For a moment he'd wondered if they'd miscalculated and the doorway wouldn't be wide enough, but Jess was either lucky or, more likely, smart enough to have made sure of her measurements before she started the project. The room would have very little space after the two cribs were in place.

Jess had said the room was empty, and sure enough, there wasn't any furniture. But the walls were painted a fresh, light, springy green, and there were clean yellow window coverings on the one window. The closet was open, and a few folded scraps of clothing were piled on the shelves. Deacon wondered if these might be some old family things she'd carried with her, or if she'd been starting to collect supplies for her twins.

He could only imagine how much she would need. Everything a baby would require times two. He admired her strength and determination and wished he could do something to help. But Jess had had a difficult time letting him bring this crib in. It wasn't going to be easy to assist her.

He wondered why she was so resistant to help but wasn't sure he'd ever know. Instead, he pushed the crib into one corner and returned to Jess. She pursed her lips.

"I think I'm going to eat before I try the second one. You can join me if you want, but if you have something else you need to do…"

Deacon shook his head. "I'm committed to getting both of these cribs done, and I'd be happy to join you, but why don't you let me do whatever preparation is needed?"

Jess grinned at him. "Not a lot of preparation involved. I made some bread and was going to have sandwiches."

Deacon had turned in the direction of the

kitchen, but he twisted around to look at her. "You made bread?"

Jess laughed. "Yeah, I had some time yesterday, and the pregnancy hormones are really pushing me into homemaker mode. I watched some videos, and it didn't look that hard. But to be honest, I wasn't totally successful. I mean, it tastes good, but it's a little flat."

"I'm still impressed." Deacon examined what he could see in her kitchen. "Where is your bread?"

Jess pointed at a cupboard. "In there. I've got cold cuts and some fixings in the fridge. Nothing fancy, but—"

Deacon pulled open the fridge. The contents were sparse, so it wasn't hard to find what Jess had ready for sandwiches.

"I'm not really a cook, but I'm pretty sure I can put sandwiches together. Can I get you a drink first?"

Jess accepted water, and Deacon poured himself a glass. Then he prepared the sandwiches.

The loaf of bread wasn't very tall, and when he sliced it, it was very dense. But the aroma of freshly made bread was enough to make his mouth water. He checked what Jess wanted on her sandwich and made the same for himself and then brought them over.

"Thanks. Sometimes I just run out of energy."

He set her sandwich down beside her and settled on the floor not far from where she had slouched into the corner of the couch. She watched him sit and frowned.

"Are you comfortable there? I can sit up."

Deacon put a hand on her shin, stretched out beside him. "Jess, it's fine. Tell me how the sandwich is."

Jess rolled her eyes but took a bite. "Hmm. Good, even mustard application. Nice layering of the meat. Now, the cheese…"

"Okay, I get it. Sandwich making isn't really a challenge."

Jess took another bite. "The bread isn't right, but I like the flavor."

Deacon swallowed his mouthful. "It's really good. Much better than the store product I've been using."

Jess looked at her sandwich. "Maybe. But the store stuff is a lot prettier."

"Since I'm not taking pictures to post on social media, this is great."

Jess sighed. "You're a nice guy, Deacon Standish."

Deacon felt his face heat and looked away. His gaze caught on her TV. "Do you watch a lot of TV? Or play video games?"

Jess looked over as well. "No to the games—never had the time or money for that. Sometimes I watch TV. I wasn't going to bother, but Benny fixed up an old one for me. I have it on when I'm here on my own in the evenings, for company, or I watch things on my computer."

Not wanting to return to a discussion of his niceness, Deacon pursued this line of conversation. The shows they'd talked about when they'd been stranded in the car hadn't been current ones. "What do you like to watch?"

"I used to watch a lot of home renovation shows. Still do sometimes." She waved her hand around the room. "Not that I do much of it."

Deacon considered that tidbit of information. Maybe when you moved as much as Jess had, the idea of a place of one's own to renovate had appeal. Or maybe he was reading too much into this.

"You're good at putting furniture together, so I bet you'd be good at that kind of thing."

"Nah. I can do the easy stuff, like painting and refinishing, but the plumbing and electric I couldn't even start."

Deacon set down his plate. "I wouldn't have tried even what you call the easy stuff."

"You wouldn't need to." Jess was blunt but truthful. Still, it made him uncomfortable. If life was fair, he'd have had less privilege and Jess and her siblings would have had more.

Jess must have picked up on his discomfort and changed the topic. "What do you watch?" she asked, sitting up and reaching for his now-empty plate.

Deacon intercepted her and stood, plate in hand. He requested hers with a gesture, then answered her question as he returned to the kitchen. "I don't watch a lot of TV."

"Are you busy going to museums and the opera?" Deacon turned and saw Jess was grinning at him, clearly making a joke. She hit closer to the truth than he wanted to share.

"I read a lot."

"That explains all the books at your place."

Deacon put the dishes in the sink and ran some water. "Most of the books are for work. I just brought some favorites with me. Usually I use a digital reader. My mother complains that otherwise my books take over the place."

Jess sighed, and Deacon turned to see what had caused that. She was looking down the hallway. "I'd like these kids to be readers, but since I don't read much, that probably won't happen, will it?"

"Do you not like reading?" Deacon knew

that lots of people didn't like to read, but he'd never been able to fully understand why.

"I don't hate it. But we didn't have books growing up, and I didn't have room for them in the van. Some of the places I've worked or stayed at would have books left around that I could read, but sometimes I was just too tired to bother reading. TV was easier."

Deacon was fully behind her desire to raise kids who read, and he was going to make sure that there was reading material available for these children. Jess might resist his assistance, but this was important, and he knew she'd give in if it was good for the twins. Maybe, instead of his first urge to mass order online, he could visit a secondhand bookstore in Oak Hill, or even Albany.

Then he wondered if Jess would like to read now as well. "I could lend you some of my books, if you wanted. I don't know if you have time, but I'd be happy to share them."

Jess blinked at him. "Not your law books, right?"

Deacon held in a grin. "No, I'd only recommend those if you were suffering from insomnia. But I have novels. What do you like to read?"

Jess twisted her lips as she considered.

"Why don't you pick one, and I'll give it a try and let you know."

Deacon wasn't sure why this idea pleased him so much. He hoped he wasn't imagining himself as Pygmalion. He didn't want to make Jess think he felt superior. He just wanted to share his love of reading, didn't he?

He came back to the living room, where Jess had slid back onto the floor and was pulling out the pieces for the second crib. Did he want to educate Jess? Make her into what some might consider a better person?

No, he didn't want to do that. He liked her the way she was. But if he was going to lend her a book, they'd need to meet up later to return it. Maybe they could get together to discuss it.

Deacon wasn't an outgoing person, and he hadn't made many acquaintances in Cupid's Crossing so far. He wasn't here for long, so it didn't seem worthwhile to push out of his comfort zone when there would be a minimal return on the investment of time. But he did know Jess, and he liked spending time with her.

Reassured, he promised to pick out a book for her to read and drop it off. While he held pieces for her to assemble or found her a missing screw, he mentally reviewed the books he had with him and tried to figure out which would be the best one to lend her first. Because he definitely hoped there would be more than one.

# CHAPTER TWELVE

ONCE THE SECOND crib was put together, Deacon carried it to the nursery. He told Jess to sit with her feet up while he gathered the leftover papers and cardboard and plastic. He'd put everything in a garbage bag, ready to take it down to the bins at the edge of the parking area, when there was a knock on the door.

"I'll get it for you, if you don't mind. You can stay there."

Jess rested her head on the back of the couch. "Sure."

He opened the door and found Rachel on the other side. Her mouth fell open when she saw who was answering the door.

"Deacon?"

Deacon reminded himself that he wasn't doing anything wrong.

"Good afternoon, Rachel." He looked down and then up. "Um, I was helping Jess put the cribs together."

Her face relaxed. "Oh, that's so kind of you. I didn't know Jess even had cribs yet."

"Come on in, Rachel!" Jess called out.

Jess had risen to her feet, and Rachel gave her a warm hug. "Ryker wanted to stop by and talk to Benny, so I came up to invite you to dinner."

"That sounds great, Rachel. Deacon and I have spent most of the day putting the cribs together, so I hadn't even thought about dinner yet."

Deacon had. He'd intended to offer to pick something up for them. Well, for Jess, but he thought she'd ask him to stay, and he'd been counting on that.

Rachel turned to Deacon. "You're welcome, too, Deacon. It's the least we can do after you've spent a day helping Jess."

Jess laughed. "Yeah, since all I fed him was some of the bread I made, which wasn't that great."

"It tasted good."

Jess grinned. She was a happy person, despite the obstacles she faced. "But it only rose about half as much as it was supposed to. I'll do better next time. Come look at the cribs. Deacon took them down to the nursery, so I haven't seen them in place yet."

Rachel and Jess headed to the bedroom, so Deacon opened the door again and took the garbage out.

He heard footsteps and saw Ryker heading around the corner of the building. Ryker paused when he saw Deacon.

"Hello." Ryker sounded wary.

Deacon nodded. "Rachel is upstairs with Jess. I helped her put her cribs together today, so they're looking at them."

Ryker was quiet for a moment. "That was nice of you. I didn't know she was doing that. We'd have offered to help."

Was Ryker upset that Deacon had been the crib assistant instead of her brother?

"I was driving by Thursday when she was trying to get the boxes up the stairs, so I stopped and helped with that. It was the least I could do. Then I offered to assist again today."

Ryker nodded. "Jess doesn't like to ask for help."

"She's very independent," Deacon agreed. "But since she helped me change my tire, and then rescued my ottoman when I couldn't get it together, she may believe I owe her. And honestly, I wasn't that much help. Just extra hands when she needed them."

"We were going to invite Jess over to dinner. Maybe you'd like to come as well?"

Deacon tried to read Ryker's tone of voice and expression. "Rachel extended the invitation, but if you want to have some time, just family, I'll excuse myself."

Ryker smiled, perhaps the first smile Deacon had seen on the man's face. "I have a feeling there's going to be a lot of baby talk, so don't worry about the family thing. Feel free to come if you like. Rachel wants to cook again, since she couldn't for a while with her cast on."

"Then I'd like that." Deacon hesitated, the winter air reaching through his sweater. His coat and keys were upstairs, but maybe Jess would bring them down?

"Ryker! Come see the cribs—they're beautiful. And Jess and Deacon put them together themselves!"

"We're coming." Ryker started up the stairs, and Deacon followed. They all stood admiring the new furniture. Deacon stayed back in the hallway, partly because there was no space in the room with two cribs and three adults. He deflected compliments that Rachel sent his way, since Jess had done most of the work. But as they headed out the door, he accepted Jess's quiet thanks with pleasure.

JESS FROWNED AT the book.

It was one of the greats, she knew that. And

Deacon had lent her his own copy, so it meant he liked it. But honestly, she didn't.

It wasn't because she didn't get it. It wasn't full of words she didn't know or filled with tangled sentences that were impossible to understand. She had no problems following the plot, and it hadn't been precisely boring. She just didn't like any of the people. Not because of what they did: she could understand Daisy wanting security instead of risking love, though if Jess had been in her shoes, she'd have gotten a job and taken care of her own security instead of marrying someone wealthy. It was set a hundred years ago, so not as many jobs for women, but Jess was sure, if she'd been determined…

But these people didn't feel like real people to her. Just dolls Mr. F. Scott Fitzgerald was pushing through their actions. She'd felt more connected to characters she'd found in romance novels and thrillers she'd picked up to read in her travels.

She huffed a breath and set the book down on her coffee table. Deacon was coming over with something he'd found at a secondhand store for her nursery. If it was something big, she was going to have to say no. She wasn't Daisy. But he also wanted to know what she thought of his book.

She didn't want to tell him what she really thought of it, because she didn't want to hurt him. As if her opinion on a book could do that.

She'd looked up some online reviews so she could understand what people liked about it, and so she could fake some comments for Deacon, but that didn't feel right. There was no good reason for her to lie about what she thought of the book unless she was trying to earn his good opinion. And the fact that she wanted to made her more determined to be honest.

Her ex, Thomas, hadn't been into reading, but he liked movies. Black-and-white ones, arty ones that made little sense to her (really, bunnies raining into a trench?) and Jess had sat through a lot. She'd pretended to like them more than she did, which meant she got to sit through even more. When she finally admitted her real opinion on the bunny film, he'd been offended and told her she didn't understand. She'd at least understood that he thought she was either too stupid or too uneducated to get it.

Not doing that again. When the urge came up, to do what she thought Deacon would like instead of what was real, she'd immediately stopped and decided on honesty. She didn't want to spend more of her time with things she didn't like and that made her feel less than. Maybe Deacon wouldn't want to lend her more books once he heard what she thought, and maybe he'd think she was stupid, but better now than later.

She heard steps coming up the stairs outside, so pushed herself upright and was almost at the door by the time Deacon knocked.

She pulled the door open and had to smile.

Her first meeting with Deacon, he'd been wearing a suit. Every day in the office after that, he'd been in another suit. And he looked good in them. But seeing Deacon in jeans and a sweater under his coat felt like a glimpse into a part of him others didn't see. It was kinda cute.

Plus, he was carrying two bulging canvas bags that looked to be full of books. Kids' books.

"Come on in." She led the way down the hall and into the kitchen, where she switched on the kettle. She didn't have any coffee around, but she'd discovered a green tea that Deacon liked.

When she turned around, he put the two bags on the countertop. Then he looked at her, really looked, like she was something he enjoyed seeing.

"Hello, Jess. You look lovely this morning."

She was annoyed to feel the flush in her cheeks. "Thanks. You look different when you're not in your suit." Rats. That had sounded much better in her head before she wrestled the thought into words.

Deacon ignored her silly comment and tapped one of the bags.

"This is what I found for you and the twins."

She didn't need to feel mushy because he phrased it that way, like her babies were people he already knew and liked.

"It looks like books."

A smile split his face. "I went to a second-hand bookstore in Albany and found some great titles." Jess tried to count the number of books in just one of the bags, and her eyebrows flew up.

His smile faded. "I may have gone a bit overboard."

Jess didn't want him to second-guess a nice gesture, so she poked him in the ribs with her elbow. "Of course you did. You're you, and these are books."

The smile returned. "You're right—I love books. Some of these I remember from when I was a kid, and some I wasn't familiar with, but I found them quite interesting."

Jess looked at the two big bags. "You read them all?"

He looked at the floor. "Well, they *are* children's books. They don't take long to read. I'm a fast reader." Was he embarrassed to have read kids' books? Or did he think she was making fun of him?

"Hey, Deacon, it's okay. It's nice that you did that. Why don't I bring the tea over to the couch, and you can bring the books and show me?"

Deacon looked up, again with the happy expression, and grabbed the books.

"I'D NEVER CONSIDERED THAT." Deacon was staring at the copy of *The Great Gatsby* as if he could pull information out of it with his mind.

They'd gone through the books for the twins. There were a lot of them, but they ranged from a few with nothing but pictures to books that would take maybe fifteen minutes to read. It would cover the twins' increasing comprehension skills as they grew older. Then, over a second cup of tea, Deacon asked her about *The Great Gatsby*, and Jess had ripped up his story with her own, unpopular opinions.

"Hey, I only have a high school education. What do I know, right?"

Deacon turned his attention to Jess. "I didn't mean that. I think it's a valid point. We've always looked at the themes, the writing, the commentary on the American dream, but I didn't consider the characters as people, so much. Do they not act believably?"

Jess shrugged. "People do weird things all the time. And of course, a hundred years ago, things were different, especially for women. But I just didn't feel this amazing connection between Daisy and Jay."

"The next book, I'll be sure to pick something where the characters should work better for you."

Jess liked the sound of a *next book*. And she liked that Deacon didn't dismiss her opinion. Maybe he was just being polite, but he sounded like he thought her opinion had value.

"First I'm rereading this with your comments in mind. It's an interesting view I hadn't considered. A word of warning, though. If you take a lit class someday, make sure you have a lot of support for your position, because there are people who are really committed to this book."

Jess snorted. "I've got two babies coming.

I don't think I need to worry about taking any classes."

Deacon shifted to look at her. "Would you want to? If you had time?"

Jess blinked. "I just finished what I had to take for the daycare job. I never thought about taking more classes."

"There are fairly inexpensive or free online classes you can take in almost any subject. If you wanted to. Maybe, when the twins are older, you could look at doing something for yourself—classes or something else."

Jess opened her mouth, but nothing came out. She was afraid if she tried to speak, her voice would quaver. When had anyone suggested she do something for herself, something frivolous like a literature course? Never. That's when.

Deacon ran a hand through his hair, mussing it up in a very un-Deacon-like way. "If I was staying here, I'd offer to do something with your kids—maybe reading—so you could have some time for something like that." He tapped a book. "But you'll have friends. You can work something out if you choose to. Or not. I didn't mean to be pushy."

Jess swallowed. "No, that's not pushy. I'd just never thought of it before. It was a nice idea. Maybe someday I will."

She had no idea when that would happen, but when Deacon spoke like it was a totally reasonable thing for her to do, she believed him.

"I hope you get the chance, Jess. But now I should probably put these books someplace for you. You won't want them scattered around the living room."

"Yeah, that's not the best place. We'll have to stack them up on the floor in the nursery until I can get a bookshelf."

Deacon paused, an armful of books in his hand. "I didn't think of that."

Jess picked up a load of books. "No reason you should."

"Maybe…" Deacon was staring toward the door.

"Deacon Standish, you are not buying me a bookshelf."

He headed to the nursery. "What if we went to a secondhand store to find one?"

Jess followed him into the room and passed him her books.

"I can do that."

Deacon carefully stacked a pile of books by size, largest on the bottom. "I should help. I caused the problem, after all."

Jess passed him another armful. "You think so?"

"We could go now, if you don't have plans."

Jess froze. He wanted to go now? Spend more time with her?

"But I'm sure you do." He stood, brushing his hands on his jeans.

Jess wanted to go. More than she should, probably. But she wasn't going to make the same mistake she had with Thomas, was she? She knew better than to get invested, or dependent.

Maybe Deacon was a bit lonely. He'd been spending time with her, and she had no illusions that he was attracted to her pregnant, high school–educated self. But he didn't seem to know a lot of people, and he was a quiet guy. Not one to put himself out there.

"Nah. No plans. But we'll have to take the van if we're bringing back a bookshelf."

Deacon's hand smoothed the place where his tie would hang when he was wearing a suit. "Um, is your van reliable?"

Jess rolled her eyes. "Who's had the flat tire and fuel leak, hunh?"

"Okay." He still looked uncomfortable.

"And this way the inside of your car won't get messed up."

"I said okay." But he smiled at her, and she grinned back. It was nice to have a friend, even one as unlikely as Deacon.

DEACON WASN'T TOTALLY comfortable in Jess's van. He was used to his Audi, which sounded much quieter. Jess wasn't disturbed by the various noises, but he kept looking at the gauges on the dashboard, sure that something was wrong.

Despite that, they made it safely to Albany. Jess had looked up secondhand stores online, and she followed her phone's directions to get to the first of them.

Deacon had never been to a secondhand store other than a used-bookstore. He'd gone with his mother to antique stores, but this was a totally different experience. The place was cluttered, organized in a way that presumably made sense to the owner, but none at all to Deacon. Some of the pieces were so decrepit he couldn't understand why anyone would purchase them. Others were painted garish colors or were in a fashion that was no longer in style, for which he was grateful.

Jess went through the store quickly but deliberately. She knew what she was looking for and was able to spot some bookcases behind a moth-eaten sofa and a coatrack large enough to hold a couple of dozen coats.

Jess knelt on the sofa, checking over her prize.

They were white, made of cheap-looking particle board.

"Hmm." She nudged the shelf with her hand, and it wobbled.

"That seems likely to fall over," Deacon cautioned.

Jess gave it a slightly stronger shove. It moved again.

"I could always attach it to the wall, but something that can stay up on its own would be better." She pulled out her phone and took a photo. "In case I don't find anything else."

Deacon opened his mouth to protest that he'd buy her something new if this was the best she could find, but he held the words in. Jess didn't want him buying her things.

They didn't find anything better in that store and got back in the van to find the next one on Jess's list.

This one wasn't any better smelling, or organized, but it was bigger, as well as colder. Secondhand stores didn't appear to invest a lot in fighting the January cold. Jess was slower checking it out, since there were more pieces to look through.

She stopped in front of a hutch and ran a hand over it.

It looked more solidly made than many of the things in the store, but it wasn't a bookshelf. Deacon wasn't sure why Jess was examining it so closely. She opened every drawer on the bottom and every door on top.

"Are you looking for a hutch?" He had no idea where she'd put it.

"No, but I thought maybe I could separate it into two. The bottom could be a dresser, and if I added a kind of rim around the top, it would be a changing table, too. And the other half, if I took off the doors, could hold books and some toys, too."

When Jess described it, Deacon could see it. He nodded and began his own inspection. "It's solid oak, so it's heavy, but that should make it stable. Would it be difficult to adapt it? And it needs to be refinished."

The hutch had experienced a difficult life, based on its current appearance.

"It won't be that hard. I did something like this before. Not as a changing table, but I could put something together on top of the base and taking off the doors is easy."

Jess climbed around the back of the hutch. "It was either taken apart before, or it broke, because they've got plates screwed in to keep the top and bottom together." Deacon followed her to the back of the hutch and winced at the sight of the ugly attachment.

"That's a terrible thing to do to a lovely piece of furniture."

"I'm not complaining—it'll make what I want to do with it easier."

Deacon tried to imagine what Jess would need to do. "Isn't that a big project?"

"Maybe, but I've got time. It won't cost much, and it's going cheap because of these plates on the back."

Deacon checked the price on the tag she pointed out and yes, it was going cheap.

"And it won't be as big a project as trying to restore something like that."

Jess jerked her head toward a dusty, beaten-up object on the television cabinet next to her find.

Deacon looked, and then looked again. He left Jess examining her hutch and ran a hand over the remains of a writing desk.

It was old, since no one used these anymore, but not old enough to be of value. Rubbing the dust from the top exposed the mahogany. He raised the lid, and it came off in his hand, the hinges missing. The felt inside was partially gone, and what remained was stained. The tiny drawers were all there, but when he pulled them out, some were lacking the backs.

"What's that?" Jess asked over his shoulder.

"An old laptop writing desk."

Jess ran her hand over it. "You mean, like a computer laptop?" She sounded puzzled.

"No, old-fashioned writing on a lap."

"Hunh. Do you put it on a table, or only your lap?"

"Either." It was a pretty piece, but not of great use now.

Jess looked behind it. "It doesn't cost much. Why don't you get it and fix it up?"

Deacon shook his head. "I couldn't."

Jess examined it closely. "Sure you could. You could get new hinges at a hardware store or go to the restoration place and find some old ones to match. Some wood, and glue to fix the drawers, felt from a sewing or craft store, and a bit of muscle, and it would be almost good as new."

"I don't need a writing desk."

Jess had a smile on her face. "But you want it, don't you? You're looking at that the same way you do your first cup of coffee at the office."

Deacon stepped back. "What would I even do with it?"

"Write letters? Keep papers? Look at it and fondle it sometimes?"

Deacon caught the teasing note in her voice.

"Well…" It was silly and pointless, but she was right—he did want it. He wanted it enough to start writing letters by hand just to have an excuse to get it. With a fountain pen.

"Tell you what." Jess patted the desk gently. "You get this, I'll get the hutch and we can work on them together."

Deacon looked from the hutch to the writing desk. Jess nudged him in the ribs again. He didn't know if she realized how often she did it. He wasn't going to tell her.

"It's not a lot of money, and I can show you how to fix it."

The desk had once been a thing of beauty. Refinishing furniture wasn't anything he'd done before, but why shouldn't he? The piece deserved some love and attention.

"Okay, you've got a deal. It's a good thing it's not any bigger, because the hutch is going to take up a lot of space in your van."

Jess sighed. "I hope it's not too hard to take it apart, because even that way it's gonna be a bear to get in."

She was right. It was. But they managed, with help from the store staff. Deacon sat in the passenger seat with his desk on his lap, carefully wrapped in a towel Jess had in the back of her van. She drove them to a restoration store to get some parts for the desk. The hinges were missing altogether, and the lock had no key. Fortunately, a bit of searching found two hinges that were almost the exact size of the missing ones, and a lock and key set that Jess swore he could install.

Another stop at a home store to get the restoration supplies they needed meant the van was crowded as they made their way back to Cupid's Crossing. Jess called her brother before they left Albany to come help them get the furniture into a part of the garage Benny used for larger repairs.

Benny watched them struggle with the pieces, a smirk on his face. "This almost makes me grateful for the chair."

Jess stood beside him. "I helped get it into the van, so I don't know why Ryker won't let me help them get it out."

Benny rolled his eyes. "Sure you don't."

"I'm pregnant, not consumptive."

Ryker slammed the doors on the back of her van.

"Call me if you need any more help." He looked at Deacon as he spoke. Jess was the one who answered, giving her brother a hug to thank him.

"I'll let you know when it's done. I should be fine till then."

Ryker nodded and left them with their

finds. Jess waved him off and turned back to Deacon and Benny.

"So, when do you want to get started?"

Deacon rubbed his hand over the desk. "Tomorrow's Sunday. I've got time."

"Bright and early?"

"Don't call on me!" Benny rolled back to his shop.

Deacon smiled at Jess. "I'll bring muffins."

## CHAPTER THIRTEEN

DEACON SPENT THE next few weekends learning about restoring furniture. Jess had a lot of experience in the basic techniques of stripping and refinishing, and what she didn't know, she looked up online. Deacon had done his own research for his desk, since he wanted to keep as much of the original character as he could.

He found the whole process surprisingly enjoyable. He liked seeing the piece come back to life as he worked on it. He liked knowing he'd done that himself. He enjoyed helping Jess and chatting with her. He helped her move the furniture around the garage space as needed and did his share of sanding on the large pieces.

He was enjoying his time in Cupid's Crossing more than his father would have guessed or wanted.

Deacon brought Jess another book. This time he'd gone with a female writer, suspecting Jess would like those characters much better. He'd wondered what she would think of the meddling Emma.

This time, instead of waiting till she finished the book, she'd shared her opinions on it as she read through. Deacon enjoyed experiencing the book through her fresh eyes. Jess thought Emma was more like people she'd known, even if the character was from Regency England.

Deacon was comfortable with female friends. Meredith was probably his closest friend of the people he knew in the city, so he had no qualms about enjoying Jess's companionship. A couple of evenings a week, either he'd bring food to her place or she'd prepare something herself, and they'd share opinions on the book while they ate. Then Jess gave him an introduction into reality TV, claiming he also needed to broaden his horizons.

He'd heard of the Kardashians but had never watched their show and had no idea why someone would want to watch them, even after he'd seen a couple of episodes. They dipped into *Survivor* (why were all these people so unpleasant to each other?) and touched on a cooking show with *Nailed It!*

Deacon wasn't a fan till Jess showed him *The Great British Baking Show*, and that he enjoyed immensely. The people appeared to like each other, for one thing, and he was impressed with what they could do as amateur bakers. He and Jess had their own competition, making baby cookies.

Deacon found the days passing in a pleasant round of work and helping Jess, with time to walk and read that he hadn't been able to enjoy in years. It was so pleasant that the cold heart of winter started to melt as February waned into March, and the message about the annual golf tournament from his mother was a jolt to remind him of his real life, waiting in New York. It was easy to forget to call her back.

"THE PLACE LOOKS GREAT, JESS."

Jess simply shrugged, but she agreed with Mariah's assessment. The rooms of the daycare were bright, freshly painted, with cheerful murals on the walls. There were toys and books and dress-up materials. Outside were play structures, and inside, seats and tables and puffy cushions to sit on, as well as cribs and beds for naptimes.

The woman who'd be running the daycare, Dinah, was expected soon. Jess had been in touch with her online and finished the spaces as per Dinah's specifications. It looked ready for children.

"I know Dinah's been pleased with the pictures she's seen so far. How many children are on the list for when we open?"

"Ten."

The ten were mostly younger. In this town, the kids who were old enough were expected to be at a friend's or at home on their own when school was over for the day. Jess and her siblings had never been to daycare or a babysitter's. After her mother's death, the older kids had been expected to take care of the younger ones, but that care had been sporadic or missing altogether.

Jess tried to imagine growing up with a place like this for her non-school time. It would have been a safe place and could have changed so much for her family. It was a contrast to the house she'd grown up in, and the thought of her own kids being here was satisfying.

"That's good to hear. This is going to be the next step to bringing businesses to this town. So far, we've focused on adults. I wonder if we should offer childcare for visitors. If they'd be happier coming here if they could bring their children but have a place to leave them so they could have time on their own." Mariah was staring into the distance, pen tapping her chin.

Jess wrinkled her nose. She wasn't sure that was the best idea.

Mariah must have caught her reaction. "You're not a fan of that idea?"

"Doesn't matter. I'm not the one you're trying to make happy."

Mariah crossed her arms. "I'd still like to hear your thoughts."

Jess rested her hands on her belly, a place they landed on frequently these days. It was convenient, now that the babies were large enough that people had started to ask when Jess was due, and she could feel them moving around under her skin, something that was both creepy and amazing. Kind of like the whole pregnancy experience.

"Okay. It depends on what kind of people come here. Some parents are too attached to their kids. So, if say, Mom was a helicopter mom, and Dad brought her here to have some alone time, if the kids were this close, she'd still be distracted by them. She would come by, decide to do stuff with the kids, and Dad doesn't get his romantic time.

"Or you might get some real brats. I mean, the local people, we tell them that if their kid doesn't shape up he's gonna get kicked out, and the parents will do something about it because they need the daycare. Visitors won't care because they're leaving anyway. And then there's the whole staffing issue if the numbers go up."

Mariah looked around the space.

"But we might get people who wouldn't come without their kids."

"Do you want this to be a family place or a romance place? In my opinion, kids might be the result of romance, but they don't really help it."

Mariah made a note. "So, are you giving up on romance when your children arrive?"

"I gave up on romance before I got here."

Mariah shot a keen glance her way.

"But word is you're spending a lot of time with our lawyer, who's single…"

Jess hoped her cheeks weren't flushing. She wasn't surprised there was talk about her and Deacon. It was a small town, and it had always been gossipy.

"He's a nice guy and doesn't know many people. But it's not dating or anything. He's only here for a short time, and we're from very different worlds."

Mariah started tapping her pen again. "He's rather reserved, isn't he?"

Jess nodded.

"We should be making him more welcome. Nelson's been tied up with the house and some new rescue horses, and I've been keeping an eye on my grandfather's build, so we've been remiss. Do you think he'd like an invitation to join us for darts, or trivia at the Goat?"

Part of Jess wanted to argue that Mariah should leave well enough alone. She didn't want to give up the time she was spending with Deacon. But that wasn't good. She was going to have to give up all of it when he left. And once the twins were born, she'd be on her own and needed to be used to it.

"You should ask him and see if he says yes. I don't know if he plays darts, but he's smart enough for trivia."

Mariah made another note. "I could ask Rachel to invite him to trivia night, but she's been staying away from the Goat because of Ryker."

Jess frowned and then nodded. "Right. He's avoiding the bars. Well, I could ask him, if you want."

Mariah tapped her tablet. "You haven't been out for darts or trivia, either."

Jess fought to keep her eyes from rolling. "Yeah, the pregnant woman doesn't hang out at the pub a lot. But I could take him, introduce him to you and the others, and then he could go back on his own if he wanted."

Mariah nodded. "That could work. He'd

probably prefer to come with someone he knows. I've only dealt with him on business. Do you know Dave and Jaycee? They're some of the locals who play trivia and darts with Nelson."

"I know who they are. I didn't hang out with them in high school, but I can pick them out in a crowd." Rachel was almost the only town kid who made time for the Slades. Well, the only nice one. The twins had known people in town.

"If that works for you, that should be good. Give him a chance to meet some people outside of legal issues. And we should definitely have you two over."

Jess eyed her warily. "You don't have to invite me."

"I'd like to. I'm hoping you might have some stories about my husband. Rachel and Delaney are too nice to spill the good stuff, and Dave is Nelson's friend first, so I'm sure I'm missing something."

Jess grinned, wishing she could help Mariah. Her memories of Nelson were of a confident, fortunate guy who didn't appear to have any problems. "I'm sorry to disappoint you, but I never knew much about Nelson. He was a couple of grades ahead of me, and our lives didn't overlap much."

Mariah shrugged. "Then just come so I can get to know you."

Jess felt her cheeks grow warm. "Sure, if you want."

"I do." Mariah touched her arm. "You seem like the kind of person who gets things done, and those are the people I want to know and exploit for Cupid's Crossing. Fair warning."

Jess had a feeling Mariah was playing her. That she was being nice but hiding it as something work-related. It reminded her of Deacon. Jess wondered how Mariah knew that was the way to get to Jess.

She needed to watch Mariah. And be sure not to underestimate her.

"YOU'VE BEEN BUYING more books." Jess tried to sound upset when she spoke to Deacon, but there was no heat behind it.

If he'd bought things for her, or even some of the big-ticket items for the babies, she'd have starched up and told him no. But books? That she couldn't be annoyed about. It made her believe that she could raise her twins to be more than she was. That she could give them a good start in life, and they could dream big things. At least bigger things than she'd ever had a chance at.

Deacon lifted his hands in surrender before returning to work.

He was helping her now with a stroller she'd been able to buy secondhand, one of the double-wide ones designed for two babies. She'd taken off the worn fabric, refreshed it and was stitching up a couple of places where it had frayed, while Deacon washed down the frame.

They'd also started reading another Jane Austen novel, after experimenting with some other of Deacon's favorites. Jess had seen the movie and TV adaptions of *Pride and Prejudice*, but she liked reading Jane's words, some of which weren't in the movies.

"I can't resist books."

"These are going to be the best-read kids I've ever known."

Deacon set down his scrubber. "Then my work here is done. I think that's the best thing you can do for your children."

"Well, I can't afford private school for them, so this will have to do."

"Private school isn't without its own drawbacks."

Jess set down the fabric she'd been stitching.

"You went to private school, right?"

Deacon nodded.

"Would you send your own kids to one?"

Deacon's mouth dropped open and then closed. He swallowed. "I don't know."

Jess leaned back. "That says a lot. You didn't like it."

Deacon's hand smoothed over his shirt. Jess bit back a smile. Someone was nervous, talking about this.

"The instructors were excellent. And it looked good on college applications."

"But you hated it."

A sigh. "No, not all of it, but I didn't enjoy it as much as some. I didn't like boarding away from home."

"Aren't there good schools with excellent instructors that look good on applications that aren't boarding schools?"

"Yes, but my father and grandfather and great-grandfather had all gone to this school."

Jess stood, stretching out the stiff places in her back. "I dunno. That's not the best reason to go there."

"What is the best reason?"

"That it's where you want to go, and it can help get you to where you want to be in life."

Deacon put his scrubber back in the bucket. "I wasn't asked if I wanted to go, and I'm not sure I could have honestly said I didn't want to, not at first. And I always knew where I was going to be and needed the tools to succeed there."

Jess cocked her head. "It was where your family wanted you to be, not where you wanted, right?"

"It's—it's complicated. Maybe it's not exactly what I'd have chosen, but we have a history. That tradition and continuity is special. It's worth sacrificing for."

"It's a good thing I wasn't born into a family like yours, because my ideas of what's worth sacrificing for are a lot different."

Deacon tilted his own head. "What would you sacrifice? And for what?"

Jess patted her belly. "For these two, I'll sacrifice a lot. I don't care if I have to work two or three jobs, or if I don't have some things, as long as they have what they need. I won't sacrifice what they want for what looks good to someone else.

"I could get the good things, like fancy schools and money, if I told their father. But he wasn't happy growing up with that stuff, and I don't think you were happy."

Deacon protested, "I didn't say I wasn't happy."

"Yeah, and you didn't say you were. That missing bit was actually pretty obvious. And that you don't want to do the same to your kids?"

"I didn't say I wouldn't."

"I think if you'd really liked it, if you'd been happy, you wouldn't have hesitated. If I thought that kind of thing would make my kids happy—and not just happy, but good people, not jerks—I'd sacrifice raising them myself. I hope I would, anyway. It hurts to think of doing that, but I know it's gonna be hard if they have medical issues and I don't have enough money."

"You don't think the father could add more than money to your children's lives?"

Jess's lips tightened. "I get what you're saying. But you don't know what it was like for him, what he told me. You think these kids might miss a father in their lives, and family and stuff?"

"It's a consideration."

"My ex? Swore he was never having kids. He didn't have a father figure, he had a drill sergeant, someone telling him what he had to do and how he fell short. He never got to be a kid and have fun. It was always a performance, always people watching. And he hated it. Really, really hated it.

"He ran away at thirty to try to finally have some kind of life for himself, but I guess it was too late. He couldn't say no to them, not even when he wanted to." Jess paused, thinking about the man who'd left her. "He said he wanted to, but…" She shrugged. "I don't think he could stand up for his kids if he couldn't stand up for himself."

Deacon smiled down at Jess and rubbed her arm. "You're going to be a great mother."

She blinked and looked down. "You don't know that. It's not like I had great parenting models."

Deacon's voice was soft. "But you want what's best for your children, not for you. I think that's going to make the difference."

Jess wiped her skirt. "Well, enough maudlin thoughts. How would you like to go to the Goat on Thursday?"

Deacon blinked. "The Goat?"

"The Goat and Barley. It's a pub, halfway between here and Oak Hill. They have trivia nights on Thursdays."

Deacon frowned. "You want to go to a pub for trivia night?"

"Mariah suggested it. It's a chance for you to get to meet some people. I mean, you shouldn't be stuck with just me all the time."

Deacon flushed. "I—I'm not stuck. And I like spending time with you."

Jess grinned. "I like spending time with

you, too. But we are a pretty unlikely pair. Like, we have nothing in common."

Deacon considered the time they'd spent together. Fixing up the furniture, discussing books, watching TV shows. He had enjoyed those times, a lot more than he had the time he'd spent with family and friends in the city.

"Maybe we don't on a surface level. But the fact that we get along so well must mean we have more in common below the surface."

"Still, you should get to know people outside of being a lawyer in this town. And I bet you're great at trivia."

Deacon looked doubtful. "I'm not so sure about that. I don't know a lot about sports or popular culture."

Jess nudged him. "You know more now that I've introduced you to reality TV. And you'd be good at all the history and literature questions. Come on, you can show how excellent your instructors were."

"If that's what you want, to go out, then we can do that."

Part of Jess wanted to say no. She liked these quiet evenings they spent together, whether working on things for the nursery, discussing the latest book Deacon had brought her to read or watching one of the TV shows she insisted he needed to know about.

Mariah had reminded her that Deacon wasn't really like Jess. He had his fancy family and law firm back in New York City. He must be bored if he was spending so much time with her. And while she wanted to enjoy all the time she could with him, it would be wrong to get too dependent on it. Because at the end of the day, Jess only had herself to rely on.

If you didn't expect people to help you, or to stick around, then it didn't hurt as much when they bailed on you.

DEACON GUESSED, CORRECTLY, that the dress code at the Goat and Barley would be casual. He tried to convince Jess to let him drive in his Audi, but she argued that she'd be the designated driver, since she wouldn't be drinking. He'd still offered his car, since he thought it was more reliable, but she said she was more confident driving her own vehicle.

They arrived at the Goat in the old van, Deacon in jeans and a sweater under his winter coat and Jess in cheerful maternity overalls peeping out from under hers, brightening the dark winter night. She looked much healthier and happier than the woman who'd rescued him from his flat tire. Now, with her shiny dark hair and her light gray eyes clear and sparkling, she was more than pretty.

Deacon drew in a long breath. He didn't need to notice how pretty she was.

The pub was crowded and busy. Jess gripped his hand, and it felt good, having that support as he was dragged into a mass of people, most of whom he didn't know. The pub was warm, a contrast to the winter air outside, and people were packed together. Despite being shorter than he was, she managed to spot where she wanted to go, and he was soon facing a table of people about his own age, some of whom he vaguely recognized and some complete strangers.

Mariah was one of the people he recognized.

"Hey, Mariah. I brought him." Rather as if he was a package she'd needed to hand over. Jess didn't hand him over, though. She stood by him as he was introduced to Mariah's husband, Nelson Carter.

Nelson Carter, whose grandmother was involved with Gerald Van Dalton, Mariah's grandfather. These were the people his family would want him to spend time with.

There were others as well. Dave and Jaycee, another married couple. Jaycee, he recognized from eating at Moonstone's, where she was the hostess. Her husband was Nelson's best friend. There were two men from Oak Hill whose names he never quite heard, but it didn't seem to matter. He and Jess were pulled into the group around the table, and just like that, they were part of the trivia team.

A beer appeared in front of Deacon, one Nelson assured him he'd enjoy. Jess got some sparkling water, and bowls of fries and onion rings and other finger foods followed soon after. Nelson apologized for not making an effort to get to know him earlier. He was a veterinarian and rescued horses, and he said that and building a house had been keeping him occupied.

Deacon made polite responses. He was out of the habit of making new friends. His social circle in the city consisted of friends of the family and people he'd met at school or other lawyers at the firm.

Jaycee leaned across the table, interrupting Nelson.

"What are you smart at?"

"Um, legal issues?"

Jess leaned forward as well so that Jaycee could hear her. "He's being modest. He's super smart—went to Harvard."

Deacon put a hand over his face. He hated bragging about his alma mater.

Nelson smirked. "Don't you mean you went to school in Boston?"

Deacon dropped his hand. "That's just as bad. I promise, I don't really bring that up in conversation."

"Why not?" Jess asked.

"People have assumptions about Harvard graduates. And often very strong opinions about the school. I'd rather they didn't judge me by that before they know me."

"Huh." Jess's nose wrinkled up. "If it was me, I'd be bragging to everyone."

"That's one of the things people assume about Harvard graduates."

Jaycee ignored the byplay. "So, if you went to Harvard, you know a lot, right?"

Deacon sighed, while Nelson laughed. "Do you know a lot, Deacon?"

Deacon narrowed his eyes at Nelson. "Where did you go?"

"University of California."

"That's a pretty good veterinary college."

Nelson's eyes sparkled. "Not too shabby."

Deacon wasn't giving ground. UC was one of the top ranked vet schools in the world. "So, do you know a lot, Nelson?"

"About animals. And veterinary medicine."

"Well, I can tell you a lot about legal precedents, if that comes up."

Jess elbowed him. "You know a lot more than that. He's got tons of books, and no, not all law books."

Jaycee slapped the table to regain everyone's attention. "Come on, Jess and Deacon. Tell me what you're good at."

"He knows literature. And things like classical music, right? He goes to museums and places like that. Are there questions about that kind of thing?"

Jaycee shrugged. "Depends on the night."

Deacon wasn't going to let Jess be left out. "And Jess knows television and movies. And refinishing furniture. And she's worked in a lot of different places, so has great practical knowledge."

Jess's cheeks flushed, and Deacon felt good. Jess undervalued herself.

"Okay, Deacon can pick up the slack for Trevor, since he and Andie aren't here. And we'll see if we need pop culture tonight."

Jaycee went up to get the papers for the trivia challenge.

"Do you not want people to know about the Harvard thing?" Jess asked him as the others debated who was the best at sports trivia.

"I don't want people to think I brag about it all the time."

Jess pursed her lips. "Okay, I get that, but

for something like this, people want to know you're smart, right?"

Deacon looked around. "I also wasn't at the top of my class. Much closer to the bottom, so…"

Jess came to some conclusion, but he wasn't sure what. "Okay, I'll let you be the one to bring it up another time. Like, I don't want people to judge me by the fact that I lived in my car for a while."

"You're much more than that, Jess." Maybe he shouldn't admit that to her, but he'd noticed that she often used bravado to cover when she felt insecure.

"And you're more than a stuffy lawyer," Jess said, which made him feel good. Sometimes he felt like "lawyer" and "Standish" were all that people saw in him, and that he didn't live up to the hype.

Jaycee returned with the challenge paperwork. There wasn't a section on law, or veterinary medicine, or cooking shows. But Jess and Deacon did carry their share.

Jess had been working in Syracuse during March Madness one year, so she was able to answer a question about that particular season that had stumped some of the supposed sports experts. And Deacon's knowledge of literature and foreign countries gave the team enough of a boost to propel them into first place.

As a result, their bar tab was covered for the night, and everyone left in a good mood.

"Come out again," Nelson said to Deacon as they made their way out of the pub. "If you're any good at darts, we do that on Tuesday nights."

Deacon shook his head. "Sorry. The only sport I have some skill in is golf, and I don't think you play that at the pub."

"We don't have a lot of golf courses around here. The terrain makes it difficult, and this part of the state has hit some bad economic times. Golf isn't much of a thing for most people."

Deacon didn't really mind. Golf hadn't been about the fun of the game lately, but about networking. His dad, and even Meredith, were much better at that. Wherever the sales gene was carried on the family DNA, it had skipped him.

"Maybe I'll need to pick up darts, then."

Nelson leaned in. "Come and learn anytime. The only people around here who are really good at darts are Mariah and Trevor, and Mariah usually doesn't play. Without her, we always lose, but it's more about getting together than winning."

"You're sure about that?"

"If I've had a tough day at work, I just want to unwind. I don't need the pressure of winning."

Deacon looked around. "What about trivia?"

"Jaycee is competitive, but we don't usually do that well. Just be aware, if you show up at Moonstone's again, Jaycee will try to get your promise to come back to help the team."

Jess appeared at his side. "You ready? Or do you want to talk some more?"

Deacon could see the signs of fatigue on her face, shadows under her eyes and a droop to her mouth.

"I'm ready. Thanks, Nelson. I just might be back."

Nelson looked at the two of them, Jess digging for keys while Deacon waited for her.

"Are you two…"

Deacon didn't know what to say. Nelson thought they might be a couple? They'd been spending a lot of time together, but they'd never crossed the line from friends, had they?

Jess fished out her keys and shook her head. "Are you kidding? I barely have a high school diploma, and he graduated from Harvard. We have nothing in common."

Deacon winced. Was that how Jess saw them? "Jess, don't put yourself down like that."

Nelson raised his brows and waved a farewell as he headed for Mariah.

"That's not a putdown, it's a fact."

"You're using it to put yourself down. Just because you didn't go to college doesn't mean you're not intelligent, and I think we have a lot in common." Deacon had thought about this since she'd last mentioned it.

Jess paused by the van.

"Yeah? Like what?"

"We both like to read. And you have good insight into what you read."

Was that a flush on her cheeks under the yellow parking lot lights?

"You're kind, which is something I try to be. You put others first, which is something I believe I do as well."

"But I'm nothing like the people you're used to hanging out with."

Deacon crossed to his side of the van. "Don't say that like it's a bad thing. In case you haven't noticed, I enjoy spending time with you."

JESS STOPPED, the van door open, while that thought sank into her brain.

"Jess?"

Deacon was already in the passenger seat, and she was standing there staring at nothing.

"Sorry. You like being with me?"

Deacon smiled, that sweet smile that made her feel so good. "Why do you think I'm at your place so often?"

"Because you like helping people. And I need a lot of help."

"Because I enjoy being with you, and while I can try to help you, you're helping me even more."

"How?"

Deacon let out a long sigh.

"You give me the chance to be myself, without expectations. And a window into your life, your world, that's so different from mine, but without judgment."

Jess put the van in gear. She wasn't sure how to respond to what he'd said.

Of course, she didn't have expectations of him or judge him. She was surprised he got that from other people. His family, she guessed. Maybe that was what Thomas had seen in her, too. She'd let him be himself. But in the end, it hadn't been enough for him to stay.

She hadn't had those kinds of expectations of Thomas, anyway. She didn't do that. She was the rolling stone, the one who always moved on. She hadn't moved on soon enough from Thomas, and she hadn't liked that feel-

ing of being left behind. Maybe that was because of the Vegas not-quite wedding, but
she'd promised herself she wouldn't be left
behind again.

So even while she warmed to the words
Deacon said, and while something inside her
wanted to grab on and keep those, she knew
better. Her head was fully aware that he was
leaving, going back to his family, where he
might not be happy but he could help people.
That was the way he'd found to connect with
people, since he'd never met his family's expectations.

"I like that you don't judge me, either, Deacon. And I like spending time with you, too."

She could give him that much. That he'd
accept. That didn't risk anything to admit. He
wouldn't want more, not from her, because
while he might not care that she didn't have
a college education, or that she was pregnant
with someone else's kids, she wasn't enough
for him to stay.

She never was. That was just the way it was.

## CHAPTER FOURTEEN

"It's the annual tournament. We expect you to be here."

Deacon resisted the easy response, of saying of course he would be there. And wished he'd been able to postpone this call indefinitely.

He didn't want to fly down to Florida for the charity golf weekend. It was scheduled in April, a chance to hit up the greens there before the clubs opened up here in the north. Those who had the time and resources to golf in the winter in warmer climates did better than those who couldn't afford to get away. It was a petty way to draw lines between the haves and the have-mores.

Deacon had never truly enjoyed it. He didn't mind a round of golf, even if he didn't have an impressively low handicap, but this wasn't about golfing. It was about networking, forging connections, making contacts. Establishing who was in and who was out. It was an extension of the job, and he was taking a break from it. A respite. He'd hoped to avoid it a little while longer.

"When you banished me, you didn't say anything about coming back for the tournament."

"It was implied."

Deacon shook his head, though his mother couldn't see. It hadn't been implied at Christmas, when his father had mostly ignored him. He wasn't sure what she was doing, but she'd never have told him he was expected unless his father was onboard. He knew that while they talked, she was commuting, waiting for someone or taking her daily walk. Never just talking to him. Multitasking at its finest.

"No, I don't think it was. If I was an embarrassment in the office in New York, why would it be any different on the golf course in Florida?"

His mother sighed. "Your…mistake is no longer the topic of conversation."

He was tired of what he'd done being called a mistake. "I didn't make a mistake, Mother. I *found* a mistake someone else had made. I didn't know it was made by someone in our office, so I understand how it was embarrassing for it to be revealed in a way that cost one of our clients money, but what I did wasn't a mistake."

"I don't want to argue with you, Deacon. We expect you to be there, representing the family."

His hand smoothed his tie. "Is Dad going to be there?"

"Of course."

"Then the family is represented. I have commitments here that I need to meet."

He heard the long indrawn breath. "Commitments that are more important than your family?"

"Mother, the tournament is connected to the firm. I'm on leave from the firm, working somewhere else. Therefore, I didn't assume I was going to the tournament, and I have work I need to do here. When I'm working for the firm again, I will of course prioritize going to the tournament."

"Deacon, are you feeling well?"

Confused by the change in topic, Deacon responded. "I'm feeling quite well. Why do you ask?"

"Because you're not usually this contrary."

Hmm. She was right. But he meant what he said. Before he'd left he always did what was expected. He didn't argue or make a fuss, even when the requirements for social events and work events were so interwoven that family events became work.

This year in Cupid's Crossing was his escape. He didn't want to miss any of it. And he really didn't want to spend the time driving to New York, packing for a golf tournament and flying to Florida, only to spend a weekend being made aware of his shortcomings.

Maybe his father wanted to test the waters by parading him around at the tournament. If so, he should have given Deacon some notice.

"Tell Dad I'm working hard and doing what he asked. Here in Cupid's Crossing." He pulled out a card he'd been saving for an occasion like this. "I've met Gerald Van Dalton's granddaughter and her husband." He wouldn't mention that their social interactions had begun at a pub trivia night and that Deacon had only gone a couple of times. "When Dad wants me to return, I'll need some notice to wrap projects up here, including the hotel Van Dalton is constructing. But Florida is out this year."

He was pleased with himself when he finally ended the call. He didn't usually stand up for what he wanted. This time in Cupid's Crossing was changing him, and he thought it was for the better.

He'd need to be able to stand up to the entrenched culture at the firm to make the changes he wanted to implement. It wouldn't be just Meredith who would take on the old boy network. He could, too.

"I LIKE THAT he admitted he'd been a jerk."

Jess was animated as they discussed Jane Austen on their drive to dinner. He'd convinced Jess that it was his turn to provide food and that way had coaxed her out to Oak Hill. She'd been hesitant at first, but he'd thrown in a chance to look at the secondhand bookstore, and she'd caved. She wanted more Jane Austen books, and she wanted her own copies, to keep. Deacon could have bought her some new versions, but it was important to Jess to feel independent and self-sufficient. Since he planned to pay for dinner, this was a workable compromise.

They'd left the bookstore with some musty-smelling books for Jess. Deacon had barely restrained himself from buying more baby books. Jess had given him a look, and he'd walked away, but he might come back.

"Do you think he was a jerk?"

Jess snapped her head toward him. "Are you kidding me? Telling her he loved her in spite of a huge list of problems? And assuming that of course she'd marry him because he was rich?"

Deacon wanted to distract her before she

noticed that he'd picked a nice restaurant. An expensive one. He wanted to treat her, and he didn't want her to argue. Though, unless he could convince her not to look at the menu and the prices, he knew he was going to get a lot of resistance.

"But he had to love her a lot to want to marry her in spite of her mother and father and sisters."

Jess waved a hand. "If someone comes up to me and says they love me *in spite* of the fact that I'm a single mom with a high school education, they'd better duck."

Deacon had no problems believing that. Jess did have reason to see herself in Elizabeth Bennet, less accomplished in the world of polite society of the time, and poor, with embarrassing relations. Was Deacon similar to the hero, proud and aloof? Darcy was reserved in part because he was shy, and Deacon could identify with that.

Was he really comparing the two of them to the characters in *Pride and Prejudice*? He'd best control thoughts like that.

He pulled up in front of the restaurant, where a valet came to collect the keys.

Jess stared at the valet. "What's going on, Deacon?"

"I'm spoiling you. And you're not going to

argue." There was no chance she'd do that, but he had to start from a position of strength.

Jess turned to look at the restaurant. He saw her eyes blinking.

The valet was looking impatient, but Deacon ignored him.

"Jess, are you okay? I didn't want to upset you—I just wanted you to have a nice time."

There was an undignified sniff. Then she nodded, and he relaxed.

He let the valet open the door and passed him the keys. Jess waited in the car and let Deacon open it and hand her out. Her hands smoothed her puffy coat as she looked around, the fabric stretched tight over her expanding tummy.

"You look lovely, Jess, don't worry."

He held out his arm, and she wrapped her hands around it, and he led her into the restaurant.

He gave his name to the hostess and checked Jess's coat. The hostess waited and then led them to a table near a fireplace. Deacon asked for a bottle of sparkling water and watched Jess examine the room.

"I thought you'd give me a hard time about this."

She focused on him again. "I don't mean to act like a jerk."

He shook his head. "You aren't. But I know being independent is important to you."

She ran her fingers over the salad fork. "It is. I've learned a few things—if you rely too much on someone, they go away, and then you're stuck. If you do everything yourself, then you know where you are."

Dean nodded. "And sometimes, when you get something from someone else, it comes with strings."

Jess caught his eye again. "Yeah."

"No strings tonight, Jess. I just wanted to see you have an evening to relax and enjoy yourself. I am fortunate to have a lot of material things and sharing with you—it makes me feel good."

She drew in a long breath. "I'm trying to be nice about it. But it's not easy, you know?"

He did know. He knew a lot about her. "Would you be okay if I ordered?"

She narrowed her eyes. "Are you going to order something weird like caviar?"

"I'll check everything with you. I know there are some things pregnant women shouldn't eat. But then you don't have to see the prices and you can pretend it doesn't cost any more than the diner."

Jess passed her menu to him. "You are too smart for your own good, Deacon Standish.

You go ahead and order, and I'll pretend I'm getting soup and French fries."

A smile escaped him. "You can pretend, but I'm definitely going to do better than that."

He did do better. He skipped the wine, since Jess wasn't drinking and he was driving. He ordered an appetizer for them to share and chicken for Jess, beef for himself. He watched Jess as he ordered, careful to check for the wrinkled nose that would tell him he'd made a mistake in what he'd chosen.

"We can decide on dessert later, if that's all right with you."

Jess nodded, and their server left. Jess sat stiffly in her seat, still glancing at the other diners.

"Can you relax and just enjoy yourself, Jess?"

She drew in a breath. "I'll try."

Once Jess stopped worrying about the prices and what the people around her were doing, they had a wonderful time. They talked about what kinds of food they liked in restaurants, and that segued into places they'd traveled again. Jess had funny stories about things that had happened on her trek across the country. Deacon noted what most interested her in the places he'd been.

He'd love to see her reactions to those places.

When it came time to choose a dessert, they shared a chocolate lava cake, because Jess loved to see the "lava" flowing out. Deacon let her finish most of it. He was enjoying her pleasure more than the food.

Then it was time to go, and he wanted to stretch out the evening. He wasn't sure she'd let him spoil her like this again. And he wanted to—more than he should.

JESS COULDN'T REMEMBER an evening when she'd enjoyed herself more or felt more like she was special. Deacon's manners were perfect, and he watched and listened to her as if she was the most interesting person in the world.

She was not.

When they'd finished dessert, which he'd let her eat most of, he'd sent off a black credit card with their waiter to cover the cost. He saw her looking at it and held up a finger.

"Soup and French fries, remember?"

She rolled her eyes. "Right. That was the best soup and French fries I've ever had."

He smiled, even his eyes lighting up. "I'm glad."

Once the waiter had returned with the credit card machine, and Deacon had probably added a ridiculous tip (she was guessing that from the waiter's facial expression as he took back the machine), he helped her up from her chair. She needed that now that she was in the last trimester. The twins were active and getting much bigger.

She wasn't sure what she'd be able to wear if she got any larger. This coat was so big it stuck out at her shoulders and was baggy everywhere but around her abdomen. She couldn't afford more clothes she'd never wear again, not with her due date approaching fast.

Deacon helped her into the passenger seat once the valet brought the car around. Jess relaxed into the seat, belly full and mind contented.

This was not her usual, and she knew it wouldn't happen again, but it was nice to pretend this was her life, just for a few minutes. That she had a partner who took her out and treated her and who'd be there to help when the kids arrived. Someone she could talk to about anything she wanted. Someone who would stay.

Someone who thought she was worth staying for.

She sighed.

"Is something wrong?" Deacon asked.

The night was dark, the moon late to rise. The car's headlights showed the road in front of them, but there were no other vehicles, and where they sat in the Audi was a bubble. One out of time.

"No, nothing wrong. Just…"

"Just?"

"This is like a magical thing. Like it's not really me. A life that isn't mine, but for one night, it is."

He shot a glance at her before turning his attention back to the road. "And that made you sigh, because?"

"Because it ends. Which is stupid, because of course it does, but sometimes I wish it didn't."

Deacon nodded. "I wish it didn't as well."

Jess turned to look at him.

"You really don't like working for your family, do you?"

Deacon's head moved. "No. I've enjoyed the law I practice here much more. But I also know that I have responsibilities I can't ignore, not forever, back in the city, and in the firm."

Jess wished his family could see this part of him and not judge him for being different from them. Different was good and necessary. But she understood that he wanted to change things so others didn't feel out of place. And if that's where he felt he had to be, she admired him for following through.

"I get it. I'm sure these kids are going to make me want to walk away sometimes." The twins were moving, taking it out on her ribs. She knew having two babies was going to be difficult. "But I won't."

She'd never walk away from them. They'd know they were worth it. That someone would stick around. Jess knew her mother hadn't chosen to die, but it still felt like she'd left them to the drinking and violence of their father. Not her babies. Hopefully they'd grow up to be good people, without issues that made them prickly and difficult like she was.

Because people did stay—just not for her. She suspected that growing up with her dad and brothers—not Ryker, but the others—had made her the way she was, and that was why no one stuck around. Rachel was staying for Ryker, and she was so happy for him. Just, maybe, a little envious.

Deacon put his hand on hers where it was resting on the armrest between them. "I know you won't, Jess. You're going to be a good mom. These babies are going to be very lucky."

Warmth moved up her arm and over her skin at the touch of his hand and the comfort of his words. A lot of people would look at her and say she had no business raising these kids, not when they could be brought up with so much more money if she just reached out to their father.

But Thomas didn't think money made up for the demands of his family. Deacon was the same.

"You're right, they are. I might not have all the money, but I'm not going to force them into something they don't want."

She considered. "Unless it's bed when it's late."

Deacon chuckled and moved his hand as they approached the turn. She missed the touch, but she knew that was as temporary as the night.

Eventually, they arrived back in Cupid's Crossing. Deacon pulled into the parking lot at Benny's. It was dark except for the light outside Jess's door at the top of the stairs. She hadn't been out this late in forever.

Deacon put the car in Park and stayed her with a touch on her arm when she moved to open the door. He walked around and opened it for her, helping her leave the comfy seat.

"Thanks." But when she headed to her stairs, he followed.

"You don't have to walk me to the door."

"I want to."

Jess shook her head. "You're acting like this is a date."

There was a pause, as if she'd somehow thrown them off balance by saying that.

Jess could feel her cheeks warming as she climbed the stairs. Such a stupid thing to say. It wasn't a date, and she knew that. Even if he felt something for her in a romantic way, she wasn't the right person for him. He needed someone who could fit in with his family, help him try to make this company the family owned into a better place. Jess couldn't do any of that.

She stood in front of the door, digging into her purse to find her keys. Was there something wrong with her tonight? She couldn't find them. Finally, she was able to grab the slippery metal in her fingers and wiggle them out of her bag.

She slid them into the lock and twisted, the click loud in the night.

She turned around to tell Deacon good night. "Thanks, a lot. And sorry for making it weird."

"Making it weird?"

"When I talked about it being like a date. I mean, I know it's not, so I don't know why I said that."

Deacon raised a hand and gently brushed a loose lock of her hair back.

"Do you wish it was?"

Jess swallowed down the *yes* that wanted to come out. "Do you?"

"If it was, I could…"

"Could what?" Her voice was soft and breathy.

"This." He leaned down and brushed her lips with his.

Jess gulped in a breath, filled with his scent and the warmth of his exhale. She couldn't think of a single thing to say. After a minute…or ten, he drew back.

"Good night, Jess."

Then Deacon was moving down the steps, and she reminded herself to open her door.

She stepped in and closed the door behind her. She leaned against it, listening as the Audi drove out of the lot and down the road.

She rubbed her fingers lightly over her lips. Had that really happened? Was it just part of the bubble she'd been in all night?

Maybe, maybe he liked her. As more than a friend. Maybe, if they'd been different people, in different situations, this might have been the start of something. Maybe he would have fallen in love with her—

Oh, no. No, no, no. She couldn't think thoughts like that. Falling for a guy who was leaving? Who she'd always known was leaving?

She ran her fingers over her lips one more

time. Maybe she wanted to do something stupid. It wasn't the first time, and it wouldn't be the last. But now there was more at stake. She'd just do what she always did—work hard and keep moving.

For a moment, she wished that's what she really could do. Pack up, hop in the van and drive till she was someplace new. She'd been doing it since she left this town as a teenager.

She dropped her hand to her belly and rubbed, feeling the bump of a knee or elbow or foot. She couldn't pack up and go this time. She was going to put down roots here, to make a family with her babies and Ryker and Rachel and their kids someday, if they had them.

She couldn't run, but she could prepare for when Deacon was gone. She went down the hall in the dark to her room, switching on the bedside lamp. It lit up the book she'd last borrowed from Deacon.

There was her first step. Give Deacon back his book. She was almost done. She'd have to finish it, or when he asked what she thought about it, she'd have to lie, and she didn't want to. But it would have to be the last book.

She should join the library, because borrowed books were all she was getting.

## CHAPTER FIFTEEN

DEACON WAS IMMERSED in the sheaf of documents in front of him, trying to figure out what was niggling in the back of his brain. Somewhere in here…he'd seen something… Part of him was aware of Rachel greeting a new arrival in the office, but he kept his focus on what was in front of him. It was right there—

Then the voice broke his concentration.

"I'm here to see Deacon."

Deacon's head popped up at the familiar tone. Rachel started to ask about an appointment when he saw his almost cousin and pushed to his feet.

"Meredith!"

Both women turned to look at him, Rachel questioning, Meredith smiling confidently.

He stepped out to meet her, hugging her warmly.

"You didn't tell me you were coming!"

Meredith pulled back. "No, I didn't. Does that mean you don't have time for me?"

"Of course not." Deacon turned to Rachel. "This is my cousin Meredith Morrison. Meredith, this is Rachel Slade, the backbone of this place."

"Nice to meet you." Meredith immediately turned back to Deacon after that short greeting. "Can we talk?"

Deacon frowned. Meredith didn't need to be that abrupt with Rachel. That was what things were like back at the firm. One of the many things that frustrated him there. "Rachel, when is my next appointment? I got a little lost in that case file."

Rachel smiled at him. "You've got an hour. I'll hold your calls. Do you want coffee?"

"Thank you, Rachel, that sounds splendid. Come on in, Meredith."

Meredith walked into his office, looking around with a smirk on her face. "This looks like the set of a small-town lawyer on a TV show."

Deacon bit back the words he was about to blurt out, defending the room. He took a fresh look at his office. He liked it and was comfortable here, but he'd forgotten his own first impressions. He kept his voice level.

"It *is* a small-town law office, so that makes sense."

Meredith sat down and looked at him quizzically. "Do you not find it…frustrating? Is she the only support you have?"

Rachel came in with a tray with two mugs, the coffeepot and milk and sugar. She must have heard that. "Thank you, Rachel."

Meredith gave Rachel a polite smile and then ignored her again. Rachel closed the door behind her as she left.

"I couldn't have handled this place without Rachel, and if I thought there was a chance she'd be willing to move, I'd ask her to come back to New York with me."

Meredith looked surprised. "Really? If she's that good, why is she staying in this place?"

Meredith had been spending too much time with the partners at the firm, Deacon concluded. Just because it was a small office in a small town didn't mean it wasn't a perfectly feasible option for work. There were a lot of advantages to the smallness of both the office and town, and Deacon had come to appreciate them.

But there was no point getting into a debate with Meredith.

"She likes it here and has friends and family."

Meredith shrugged. "She could make new friends and visit family on holidays."

"Not everyone wants to work in the city."

Deacon took a sip of his coffee, hoping Meredith would get to the reason for her surprise arrival.

She hadn't touched her own cup. "Is that your way of saying you don't want to come back?"

Deacon blinked at her. "I never said that."

"No, but you aren't coming to the charity golf tournament, either."

Deacon shook his head. "Ah. That's why you're here."

Meredith took one sip of the coffee, then set it down. "Everyone was…surprised when you said you weren't coming."

"Everyone was, were they? I was supposed to keep a low profile. I have. That doesn't include flying to Florida to play in a very visible golf game."

"It's time to start raising that profile." Meredith settled in her chair. "Wiseman's work has been checked, as I told you, and he got a little sloppy. And Schofields was hit with another wrongful dismissal suit, from the same kind of contract you found the hole in. Now they're feeling fortunate that we've already started changing their contracts, preventing similar problems popping up in the future. You're not the thorn in their backsides that they thought you were."

"Oh." Deacon knew he should be happy about this, but he was mostly frustrated that no one had appreciated his finding when it happened, and instead had berated him and sent him off like yesterday's newspaper.

He wasn't upset to have come to Cupid's Crossing, not now, but he shouldn't have needed to.

Meredith rapped the desk in front of him. It was something his father liked to do. "Come on, Deac, this is what you've been waiting for, right? And that's not all."

Deacon knew he should be more curious than he was. "What else?"

"It's my dad. There's good news and bad news."

Deacon focused his attention on Meredith, not on what had happened months ago. He'd always liked her father, who wasn't a lawyer but a professor of political theory. They'd had some interesting discussions. "Is your father okay?"

"That's the bad news. My dad has a heart condition."

"I'm so sorry, Meredith. That's terrible."

She nodded. "Yes, it's not great news, but they've caught it, he's on medication and he should be fine as long as he takes care of himself. He's retiring early, and he and my mom are going to travel and play golf."

"So that's the good news?"

"Not exactly. But it's got the whole family pondering their mortality, especially the men older than my dad."

Deacon caught on to what she was hinting at.

"Like my father."

"Exactly. At the last family dinner, he started talking about cutting back his hours. You know what that means."

Deacon relaxed. "A lot of golf."

Meredith slapped her hand on the desk again, and he flinched. "No, Deacon, it means someone else has to step up and lead the firm."

Of course. Meredith had her eye on the prize. To her this was good news.

Not to Deacon. He was glad his father was prioritizing his health, but Deacon wasn't ready to lead the firm. His father certainly wouldn't consider him ready at this point. Any suggestions Deacon had made, especially in regard to changes in the firm, had been brushed aside. Father hadn't discussed anything related to work over Christmas. And now, after Deacon had spent the last several months working on the kind of law that had no bearing on what the firm specialized in?

This could upset the plan he and Meredith had prepared. They had assumed a few more years of preparation before Deacon as managing partner became more than a vague possibility.

"I don't think he's going to want me in that role. Not now. I was in trouble, and I've been away. There are people he'll consider better suited." Deacon didn't mind that. He might think he had a better idea of how the firm should handle hires and promotions of underrepresented legal faces, but that didn't mean he was ready to lead the way when it came to the business as a whole. He wasn't.

Meredith was leaning forward, eyes intent on him. "That's why you need to get back to the city. We can spin this. You've been heading up a practice on your own. You've acquired more experience, and this wrongful dismissal just shows that they've undervalued what you can do. We can make a case for you, but you have to be there, ready to fight for your place."

Deacon smoothed his tie. "Meredith, you know me. I'm not about to lead a coup at the office."

She let out a sigh. "I know. But if we work as a team, I think we can do it. We make sense that way. I'm good at leading a coup and facing down the partners and schmoozing new clients. You're good at the details and understanding the fallout and consequences. Together, we're a perfect team."

She made a good point. A happy thought hit Deacon—maybe if he just supported Meredith, she could be the one to lead the practice. Maybe she was enough to prove to the partners a woman could do it. She was family, even if a third cousin. The partners had always ignored him when he'd brought up the idea, but maybe they'd all be feeling less omnipotent now.

"Do you think, if I was supporting you, we could convince them you're the right person from the beginning?"

Meredith's expression fell. "No. I've put out feelers, but I'm not even on their radar."

Deacon could sense her frustration. "I'm sorry. Meredith. That's shortsighted of them. You'd be perfect."

Meredith sat up straighter. "I would be. And I will be. But I think the best bet is for us to face them as a team."

Deacon held back a sigh. The idea of being out of the whole competition, and instead having Meredith wade in with him only providing support had been nice, but it wasn't realistic. They had to change entrenched beliefs, and the partners weren't there yet.

"Okay, so we work as a team. It will take a bit of time to get things ready here, but maybe by the end of May? That gives me time to wrap things up and find a replacement."

It was perhaps a little silly, or sad, but he'd really like to still be in Cupid's Crossing when Jess had her babies. She'd need help getting settled and used to dealing with two newborns.

Meredith frowned. "I guess you do need to leave things in good shape here—show that you're committed and finish what you started. That's good. But we can't leave it that long. We need to make a move earlier."

Deacon was relieved she wasn't pushing him to leave immediately, but he wasn't sure what kind of move she was talking about.

"Make a move?"

Color rose in Meredith's cheeks. Deacon was surprised, because not much embarrassed Meredith.

"I think we should announce our engagement at the tournament. You come for that, we'll tell them we're getting married, and that's going to put you on the fast track to being the next managing partner."

Deacon knew his jaw had dropped open,

but he was speechless. Married? He and Meredith? He had never considered her like that. He'd never even considered dating her. He didn't have feelings like that for her—did she think she felt something for him?

He finally managed to close his mouth and swallow.

"Did you say *married*?"

Meredith was fussing with her skirt, pressing out nonexistent wrinkles. "It would be the best way to show we're a unit. Together. And then my name will be Standish, which will help."

"But I don't... We don't..." He was floundering, unsure how to express how uncomfortable he was with this idea without insulting her.

"No, we don't. We're not in love, and we won't be. And if you find someone, someday that you want to marry, we can divorce amicably, but by then we've settled our futures and the firm's future."

It sounded so clinical, and calculated —not the least bit romantic. Jess's face popped into his head, and he firmly banished her.

"But, I mean, we haven't even dated."

Meredith looked up at him. "This is a business marriage. Our family will understand that much better than thinking that we fell in love suddenly. They'll respect that."

Deacon would have liked to deny it, but he couldn't. His father would probably commend it as a smart move. But Deacon didn't want to marry Meredith. He didn't want a business marriage. Before he could find a way to explain it to Meredith, there was movement in the office, and he saw Jess had stopped by.

There, his reprieve. He leaped to his feet. "Oh, here's Jess. I have something to give her. You should come and meet her."

He pulled open the office door, needing some space from Meredith and this idea. He needed to escape before it happened without his agreement.

Rachel was in the file room, and Jess was standing by Rachel's desk. Jess looked from him to Meredith, who had followed him out. She smiled at him, a tight movement of her lips that didn't reach her eyes. "I'm bringing back your book."

Deacon was grateful she'd interrupted his cousin and didn't even ask why she'd come to the office instead of waiting till they met up. "What did you think of this one?"

"Not as good as the last couple."

Deacon felt a warmth inside. Jess never

held back what she thought. "No? What was the problem?"

Jess shook her head. "Those people acted like idiots. I mean, really—"

"Who's this?"

It was Meredith, interrupting. He turned and saw her staring at Jess. Right, he should have introduced them.

"This is Jess Slade. Jess, this is Meredith, my...." He couldn't call her cousin the way he used to, not when she was talking about marriage.

Jess's smile was a polite curve of her lips. "Nice to meet you. Deacon's talked about you."

Meredith also wore a polite smile, but her eyes were cold. "Interesting. Are you related to Deacon's paralegal?"

Again, Deacon didn't like the way Meredith referred to Rachel. And he wasn't imagining the tension between Jess and Meredith.

"Yes, Rachel is my sister-in-law. And I worked here as a temp for a bit."

Jess's chin was in the air.

"You're married to her brother? Are you due soon?"

Deacon opened his mouth to interject, but Jess beat him to it.

"No, I'm not married. Rachel is married to

*my* brother. I'm doing the single mom thing. Due in May. Twins. Any other questions?"

"Not at all," Meredith responded. "Congratulations, and I hope everything goes well for you."

Deacon forced himself into the conversation. "Meredith surprised me with a visit, Jess. We'll have to talk about the book later."

"Don't worry. I know you're busy. I gotta go. See you later, Rachel?"

Rachel had stepped out of the file room and nodded, casting worried glances between the other three. Jess left as quickly as she came. Deacon braced himself for questions from Meredith, but she didn't say a thing. She asked where she might find a place to stay for the night, and he agreed to meet her at Moonstone's for dinner.

THERE WAS A knock on Jess's door. She checked her phone, but there were no messages from anyone she expected letting her know they were coming so she could be prepared. Being prepared mostly meant being upright, since getting up from the couch took a while.

There was another knock. Jess sighed, then yelled "Coming" and started her getting-up maneuvers. One baby kicked her ribs, and now Jess was getting annoyed with whoever was still knocking.

She finally made her way to the door and threw it open with a testy "What is it?"

It was Deacon's almost cousin, Meredith. Jess rubbed her back. She had a good idea what this was about now.

"I wanted to talk to you, Jessalyn."

Right. The full first name, letting her know Meredith had looked her up. That must have been fun.

"Yeah, yeah. Come on in and say your piece."

Jess waddled back to the kitchen, and stood, leaning on the counter. She didn't offer Meredith a drink or a seat. She was sure the other woman would turn them down, and she wasn't feeling hospitable.

Meredith's heels clipped the floor as she followed Jess in. She took a moment to examine Jess's place. It was undoubtedly meant to make Jess feel bad, but Jess refused to let a stranger have any effect on her self-respect.

"Were you expecting me?"

Jess crossed her arms. "No. If I had, I wouldn't have settled in on the couch where I have to wrestle to get back up. If you haven't been pregnant, you won't know what I'm talking about. I'm tired, and I figure if I let you get whatever it is off your chest, then I can lay down again. So, go ahead."

Meredith shifted her feet. She looked uncomfortable.

"It's about Deacon."

Jess rolled her eyes. "Of course it is. We don't have anything else in common."

That seemed to get Meredith going again. "Deacon doesn't belong here."

She paused, as if waiting for Jess to argue or respond. The woman seemed to think Jess was some kind of threat to the plans she had with Deacon. Jess might as well speak— maybe it would speed this up.

"I know he's not staying here. He's going back to New York. But that's his call, so not really any of my business. I don't work for him anymore."

"He's mentioned you frequently in our conversations lately. I think he feels obligated to you, and that's caused him to refuse to come back for family events."

Jess's lip curled. She knew what happened when family—Deacon's kind of family—started demanding attendance at family events.

Meredith responded to the lip curl. "You don't think he has an obligation to his family?"

"Not my call. But I haven't asked him to stay, and I'm not expecting him to. You want him back, you talk to him. I'm not going to tell him what to do."

Jess wasn't going to let Meredith see that she was getting to Jess. But it was a painful reminder that for some kinds of families, the obligations ran deep and could choke a person. Jess had been ignoring the fact that Deacon was going to leave. It had been nice to have someone around, but he wasn't staying.

Meredith frowned at Jess, and Jess made sure her expression didn't change. She didn't think Meredith was in much of a position to mess with Jess's life, but she didn't need to antagonize her, just in case. And Jess didn't want to make things any more difficult for Deacon.

"Deacon is going to do a lot of good for a lot of people when he comes back. I don't want you to lure him to stay here for your own benefit."

Jess snorted. She rubbed her hand over her large belly. "Right, me, luring men to their destruction—is that it?"

"Deacon has a soft spot for people who need help."

Which was exactly why he was going back to the family firm.

"I have help—Rachel and my brother—so don't worry. I'm not messing with Deacon's plans. But just to be clear, you're one of the people he's going to do a lot of good for, right?"

Meredith drew in a breath. "Not just me. It will mean opportunities for many people in the firm, people who deserve a fair chance to succeed."

Jess sighed, just wanting the woman to leave. "I know. Deacon talked about this. None of this is new information, and I don't know why you're here to tell me all about it again. I get it. I always got it. He's a nice guy—he helped me a bit, and I helped him, but he's leaving, and I'm staying."

Meredith relaxed her shoulders. "I guess I should apologize. I thought you were hoping he'd be your golden ticket."

"Nice to be judged a freeloader by someone who knows nothing about me," Jess retorted.

"There had to be something making him want to stay in this place. You seemed like the obvious answer. As I said, he likes to help people."

Jess almost growled at the obvious inference. That Jess was someone who needed help.

She did. Once she'd decided to keep the baby, now babies, she'd known she had something that was worth asking for assistance. But she hated the conviction in Meredith's eyes that there was nothing she could help Deacon with.

Even if it was only to make him appreciate that he had more value than his family had ever seen in him.

"I'm sure there are lots of people needing help in New York as well."

"If you need anything, Jess, please reach out to me. After Deacon is back in the city, well, call me instead of him."

Right. Like that was ever happening. "Are you offering babysitting?"

Meredith flinched. "No, of course not. But legal advice, or financial…"

"I have all the help I need. You don't need to ask me to leave Deacon alone, because first, I wouldn't bother him, and second, it's an insult to suggest that money or legal advice is all he's good for."

Meredith straightened, pulling her purse onto her shoulder more firmly.

"In different circumstances, I think we could almost be friends." She turned and headed to the door of Jess's apartment.

Jess listened to her step out the door and close it behind her.

"I can't imagine any circumstances where

we'd be friends, Cousin Meredith," Jess muttered to the empty air.

She grabbed some water, then shuffled back to the couch. She'd been ready to sleep before the interruption, but not now.

Meredith was right that she had to stop depending on Deacon. She might not take money from him, but she'd been taking his time and his friendship. And since that wasn't going to last much longer, she needed to be able to handle herself without him.

If only she'd remembered that before she started to like him so much.

## CHAPTER SIXTEEN

DEACON WAS RELIEVED when Meredith left. He knew he had to go back to New York. It was flattering that his work was being acknowledged. It was unfortunate that what he'd found had come at the expense of a client, but that was a loophole that had to be closed. He'd just hoped that he could stay in Cupid's Crossing for the whole year. But if he couldn't, he wasn't in a rush to get back to New York any sooner than he had to.

He wanted to see the hotel he'd been handling contracts for become something real. He wanted to make sure his client was able to get away from her abusive husband and see the cherry trees he'd protected when they bloomed. He wanted more time where he enjoyed going to work each day, not finding it a duty or a chore.

And he wanted to spend more time with Jess.

He wished he could stay in Cupid's Crossing indefinitely. Be around to help Jess with her babies. Explore some kind of future with her and her twins. He wouldn't say he'd fallen in love with her, but he could. So easily.

He'd have to make sure he didn't, but at least he could enjoy her company a little while longer. He couldn't kiss her again, so another dinner in Oak Hill wasn't a smart idea, as much as he'd enjoyed it. But he wanted to know what had bothered her about the people in *Sense and Sensibility*, the last book he'd lent her.

The first couple of times she didn't want to spend an evening with him didn't seem strange. She was working as much as she could, trying to ensure she had the financials covered for the births of the twins, and working at the daycare must be taxing. He'd have loved to help with her financial worries but knew better than to offer. So, the fact that a couple of times she wasn't feeling like his company was fine. He didn't like it, but it didn't alarm him.

But after a couple more refusals, made with no excuses at all, he realized there was a problem. It couldn't be a coincidence that this started after Meredith's visit.

*And the kiss*, but he pushed that thought aside.

He wouldn't stop by her place without warning. That was pushing her, and he wouldn't do that. But he did send her a message.

I'm sorry for doing something to upset you. Would you give me a chance to discuss it?

The message showed as read, but she didn't respond for several hours. Was it Meredith, or something else? Something like that kiss?

You haven't done anything, but we should talk.

When the message finally came, he read it several times, trying to work out just what it meant. First, he was relieved that the kiss hadn't been the problem. Then, after another reading, he started to worry. If he hadn't done anything, what did they need to talk about? Meredith? Something had made Jess unwilling to spend time with him, and whatever that was wouldn't be a pleasant thing.

Can I come by after work?

She sent him a thumbs-up emoji. He picked up some food from the diner to bring along. Jess hadn't told him not to, so he was going to take care of her as long as he could.

He parked at Benny's, near the garage where they'd worked on the furniture. He loved his writing desk, and every time he saw it in his home, he thought of Jess. Walking up the stairs reminded him of their struggle to get the cribs upstairs. They'd done that together. They were a good team.

He knocked and heard her footsteps approaching the door. He hoped she'd had a good day and wasn't too tired.

She swung the door open. There were shadows under her eyes, like there had been back in the first trimester when she'd been sick all the time. He had to restrain himself from taking over, making her sit down and let him take care of her till those shadows went away.

"Hey, Deacon." Only now, when her voice was flat saying his name, did he realize how warmly she used to say it.

"Hello, Jess. Are you feeling okay?"

A smile twisted the corner of her mouth. "Good enough. Incubating, you know? Come on in."

He held out the bag. "I brought some food."

Jess turned and gave him a sad smile. "Thanks, Deacon. That was nice of you."

He set the bag on the counter while Jess pulled down plates and grabbed some water from the fridge. He watched her, discreetly. She did look and move like she was tired, but he didn't see any other obvious signs of distress. She set the glasses of water on the table while he brought the plates. They'd done this before, but something was missing this time.

It was Jess. She didn't have that air of contentment that she'd had lately. Was it a pregnancy thing, or something else, something connected to him?

"So, how are things at the law office?" Jess asked.

She didn't want to talk about whatever was bothering her while they were eating. Deacon accepted that and told her about the last property dispute he'd been asked to mediate, which involved a dead skunk hidden under a pile of leaves, of which neither neighbor had wanted to claim possession.

Jess smiled at the appropriate places, but she wasn't there, not the way she normally was, and Deacon couldn't finish his dinner. He was too worried.

She was moving the food around on her plate more than eating, and Deacon didn't like that.

"Jess, why don't you just talk to me?"

She looked at him directly then, her silvery-gray eyes making something catch inside.

"Meredith came to talk to me."

"Meredith?" Anger built. Meredith could be sharp when she talked to people.

Jess shook her head at him. "No, it wasn't anything terrible. She thought I was the reason you didn't want to go back for that golf tournament, and I told her you could make up your own mind."

Jess truly believed that, whereas his family thought he must be influenced by someone when he wanted to do something different from what they wanted him to do.

"Then why have you been avoiding me?"

Now she looked down again and poked at her food.

"It reminded me that you're not staying."

He jerked, wanting to close the gap between them and tell her he would stay as long as she wanted. But that wasn't true. He couldn't.

"I think…" More moving of the food on her plate. "No, I know I can't let myself rely too much on you being around."

There was something in his throat. He couldn't swallow.

"Not that I expect you to do anything for me, but I was getting used to you coming over in the evening and helping me get things ready and talking to me. It was support—not money, but like a friend. And it's going to be hard to get used to you not being around, especially when I have two kids to take care of. I just wanted to step back a bit, so it wouldn't be such a difficult adjustment."

Deacon finally swallowed.

He wanted to argue. He wanted to promise he could always support Jess, and he'd love to do the same for her kids. But she was right. He was leaving. He hadn't thought through all the details, hadn't let himself fully realize what all would change when he went back to New York.

He wouldn't be doing the same kind of law, and he'd be living in the city again, that he'd been aware of. But he hadn't considered that he'd no longer see the people he did every day while he was here. People like Jess.

He wanted to spend every moment with her that he could until that happened. But she needed to pull back, so that she could handle being on her own once he was gone.

It felt like a fist had reached into his chest and squeezed painfully hard, but this wasn't about him. It was important that Jess be able to live her best life. And unfortunately, he wasn't part of it.

"I understand." What else could he say? Asking to see her after she admitted that she'd come to depend on him was selfish, and he didn't want that. He hadn't realized how selfish he'd been. "But we can still be friends? Just not friends who spend so much time together?"

Her smile looked forced, but she nodded. "Absolutely. Do you want to know when the babies arrive?"

"Definitely. I hope I'm still here for that. And, so you know, any way that you're willing to let me help, I want to do that."

Her smile wobbled. "Thanks. There is one thing."

His heart lifted at the thought that he could do something, no matter how trifling.

"What's that?"

"I've been thinking about what you said, about the babies' father. And the way you've been so supportive, even though these aren't your kids, and you remind me a bit of him, the kind of background you have. You'd want to know, so I thought, maybe I am being selfish. I'm afraid if his family gets involved that I'll lose them, but maybe he should know?"

"That's your decision, Jess."

"And if you were my lawyer, and I told you something, it's in confidence, right? So no one can ask you to tell what we talked about."

"You'd have to hire me, but I'm doing this

as your friend as well, so it would be just a nominal amount as a retainer."

"That's good, because a nominal amount is all I have." She huffed out a breath. "Okay. His name is Thomas Fairbanks."

Thomas Fairbanks. He only knew of one— "*The* Thomas Fairbanks?"

Jess nodded.

Deacon sucked in a breath. The Fairbanks's were a wealthy political family on the West Coast. They regularly appeared in magazines and tabloids. Thomas Fairbanks had just announced his engagement to the daughter of a tech billionaire.

No wonder Jess was afraid of losing custody of her children if she reached out for support. She had no weapons she could deploy against that kind of power and money.

His mind raced. How could he do what she wanted? He had contacts—he should be able to get the man's phone number. He would exploit client connections for all they were worth. And he'd protect Jess. He wouldn't let her lose her babies. Maybe, even, he could get her some financial support. She'd take it from the babies' father, wouldn't she?

"Would you trust me to make some inquiries, in a way that wouldn't put you at risk?"

She nodded, and that trust felt good.

"I'll start doing some research. And I'll let you go. I understand why you need to keep some distance, but if you do need anything, anything at all, just call me. I'm always available to help."

Jess smiled again, but this smile…it didn't have the same trust in it. She didn't trust that he'd be willing to help her indefinitely.

He wouldn't be around to do that.

"THANK YOU FOR taking my call, Thomas." It had taken a week and a lot of favors, but he'd managed to get a message to the man. The search had kept Deacon from dwelling on how he was feeling now that he wasn't spending time with Jess.

"It sounded important."

Deacon took a breath. "It is, and it's also complicated and private."

"You're making me a little nervous."

Deacon tried to frame this in a way that would keep Jess safe.

"Would you mind if I expressed this as a hypothetical? Something that I'm asking for your opinion on, merely."

There was a pause, and Deacon knew the man wasn't stupid. He understood the ramifications.

"If that's the most private way to handle it, sure. Give me your hypothetical."

"Imagine, hypothetically, that a young man from a prominent political family took a walkabout."

Thomas's voice was dry. "I can imagine that."

"And imagine he met a young woman, and they had a relationship together. Even went through a marriage ceremony, though the paperwork was never filed."

"Do I hypothetically imagine blackmail, Mr. Standish?" Thomas's voice was now cool and wary.

"No. If you'd let me expand on this just a bit more. Imagine that this young man told the young woman about the…nonmonetary shortcomings of his upbringing and expressed the opinion that it was not ideal for raising a child."

"I think I'd like you to get to the hypothetical point."

Deacon was reluctant. This man could pressure him. Deacon wouldn't reveal anything deliberately, but it wouldn't take a lot of work to discover where Deacon was right now and, from that, find Jess. He had to handle this very carefully.

"Would that young man rather remain in

ignorance about any child that might have unexpectedly been conceived? So that there was no chance of family involvement and a repeat of the same upbringing for this hypothetical child?"

There was a long silence. Deacon could hear the other man breathing and gave him time. It was a lot to take in.

Thomas finally spoke. "I'm not sure there is a way for this hypothetical child to be financially supported without family involvement. If that's what the hypothetical point of this call is."

Deacon imagined that money was a key issue when people interacted with Thomas. Money and power. Jess would have been a refreshing change.

"If there was no financial issue, and it was merely a question of information and perhaps some future contact?"

A long sigh.

"I think this hypothetical man would rather remain in ignorance. He would think it better that the child be raised outside the circus of the man's life. And perhaps he could set up something, whenever possible, to fund a bank account. Something that wouldn't be noticed by those who carefully scrutinize political families."

Deacon relaxed. This was what Jess wanted. It was what Deacon wanted, too, but he didn't let himself examine why that was.

"That is an interesting perspective, and I appreciate the time you've given me to express my hypothetical situation." Deacon was prepared to end the call and let Thomas go back to his life, the one he'd escaped for a short while with Jess, when Thomas spoke again.

"If there was a change in the future, an opportunity that was outside of public knowledge, perhaps the hypotheticals could meet?"

Deacon smoothed his tie. "You have my contact information. If you're in New York, we at least could meet."

"Hypothetically, this feels like an unforgivable slacking of responsibility, but I truly believe it is for the best. And maybe in the future, I can make some kind of change."

That sounded familiar.

"Hypothetically."

"Hypothetically. I wish all families only had the best interest of their members at heart, but sometimes their goals are demanding, and potent and all consuming. Things that are good on paper, but not necessarily in real life."

Deacon felt that there was a message in

there for him as well. "Again, please feel free to reach out if you're in New York City and have the freedom to do so."

"I will. And maybe you would have some hypothetical pictures?"

Deacon heard the longing in the other man's voice. Would he have pictures?

"I'll do my best to get that."

"And all my best wishes to the hypothetical woman and child in this story."

Deacon hung up. The man didn't sound like he was happy with the choice he'd made. It had been a choice, hadn't it? He could have stayed with Jess. In truth, Deacon wondered why he hadn't. It would have involved a sacrifice, but wouldn't it have been worth it?

If Deacon didn't have this responsibility back in New York... His thoughts pulled him up short. What was he thinking? That he was facing the same kind of choice as Thomas? Between a quiet, contented and happy future versus family and political obligations? Thank goodness his family wasn't involved in politics. Not yet. The obligations he already had were almost suffocating.

And this wasn't the choice he was facing. No, he wasn't making a choice. This was just following the decisions he'd already made. He'd chosen to come here to Cupid's Crossing so that his father could smooth things out at the firm for Deacon to return and work his way up to leading Standish Legal.

He'd chosen not to upset things at the firm now in order to make some necessary changes once he was in a position to do so. He had Meredith to help with that. And then he was going to make a choice to make himself happier by not leading the family firm—and possibly leaving it altogether to do the work he wanted—once Meredith was installed as head.

He'd made his choices.

He added a couple of notes into the secure folder he'd set up for Jess and Thomas on his laptop. Thomas was making a personal choice. Kind of. His connection to Jess, and the babies would obviously have repercussions on his family's political agenda as well.

Deacon was fortunate in that his family hadn't been pressuring him to find the "right" woman and settle down. He wasn't making choices about his personal life right now.

Or was he? Because if he wasn't pursuing personal goals because he'd prioritized career ones, he had made a choice. A choice to relegate those personal goals to second or third place behind his career goals.

That was a choice.

But his career choice was important. It was going to affect multiple people and continue to do so in the future. Exactly what Thomas was probably arguing. Deacon really wasn't any different. Thomas had chosen his family over Jess. Deacon was choosing his family over his own preferences. Not Jess, because she hadn't asked him to stay.

Irritably, Deacon saved and hid the folder. This train of thought was getting him nowhere. This was not the time to second-guess.

Jess would find someone who chose her first. She was amazing and deserved that. She wasn't a choice for him.

# CHAPTER SEVENTEEN

JESS FOUND HERSELF at loose ends. Once she was done working at the daycare, she was tired and didn't want to go out. The babies, they were energy drainers, for sure. The doctor had told her they were growing well and could possibly come early. She wasn't sure if she'd like them to arrive soon so she'd be able to see her feet again, or if she should wish them to stay put as long as possible.

She spent most of her evenings in her apartment. Which now felt a little lonely, since Deacon wasn't coming by. She'd tried to go downstairs and help Benny, but he insisted she sit with her feet up, and she didn't want to feel like she was imposing. Benny was a nice guy, but he tended to panic about anything related to pregnancy. One twinge in her back and he wanted to call 911. One of the twins moved around, limb poking a visible lump into her abdomen, and he almost levitated off the wheelchair.

Rachel and Ryker visited, but they had their

own things to keep them busy. Rachel helped with church events, and they'd meet with their friends sometimes. Ryker was diligent about attending his AA meetings, and Rachel went to Al-Anon in support. Too many nights Jess was left watching TV or reading.

But reading made her wonder what book Deacon would have lent her next. TV shows reminded her of the two of them watching together, and she found herself with thoughts she wanted to share with him about what she watched. She refused to let herself mope. This just proved she'd been right for them to stop spending so much time together. It was difficult enough now, though she blamed the pregnancy hormones for part of that. She wasn't going to consider anything else.

When Rachel suggested the two of them spend an afternoon getting things for the nursery in Oak Hill, Jess was relieved to agree. They booked an afternoon off, and Rachel volunteered to drive. Jess's van was bigger, but they weren't getting big items. The van was less reliable and starting to make some weird noises.

Jess went to the law office to meet Rachel. She'd almost asked Rachel to pick her up at the apartment instead, but the only reason for that was to avoid Deacon, and Jess refused to do that. She had to be strong. She had two little ones relying on her.

Rachel wasn't in the office when she got there. Of course not. Deacon came to the doorway of his office and gave her a tentative smile. She wanted to take away the awkwardness, get his real smile again, but she didn't know how. She just knew it troubled her when something upset him.

"Hello, Jess. Rachel said to tell you she'll be back as soon as she can."

"Thanks, Deacon. Mind if I wait here? It's a little cold out still. March went out like a freaking lion, and April hasn't gotten any better."

"Of course not. Make yourself at home. Or, if you wouldn't mind, there's something I'd like to discuss with you."

Jess examined his expression as best she could and didn't see anything alarming or worrisome in it. She didn't need to be nervous with Deacon. And the idea of talking to him was incredibly appealing.

"Sure."

One of the twins jabbed her ribs, so she had to pause and push her hand on her swollen abdomen to convince the baby to move back.

"Everything okay?" Worry flashed in his eyes.

Everything wasn't that okay. She was single

and pregnant with twins, with limited support. She'd been feeling lonely and sorry for herself ever since she'd told him she couldn't let herself rely on him. On the other hand, she was healthy, hardworking, and had her brother and Rachel in her corner.

"Everything's great."

Deacon beckoned her into a seat in front of his desk. She hadn't been in that position since she'd been working here. Seemed like forever ago.

Deacon closed the door and sat behind the desk. Now Jess started to worry.

"I did that research you asked me to do."

Jess frowned. Research? Then it hit her. He must have talked to Thomas. Her hands flew to her abdomen, protecting the twins out of instinct.

"Right. How did that go?"

Deacon sighed. "I wish I could say he was going to take care of all your problems."

Jess snorted but relaxed. She was safe. "No one is going to take care of all my problems but me."

"You know, you do have help."

Jess looked up at the ceiling, blowing out a breath.

"Yeah, I know. It's just hard to rely on someone else. I've had only me for a long time."

"I mean it when I tell you I'd like to be of any help that I can."

Yeah, she wasn't going to count on that. "That's nice, but you're going to be busy back in New York."

"I'll still help all I can." His chin was up, and his lips pressed together.

He meant well, Jess was sure of that. But he was about to get swept up in a different world. Meredith wasn't going to let him forget what his duty was.

"Anyway, you talked to him. He's not going to come back and offer to marry me for real, I know."

News of Thomas's engagement was splattered over all the magazines in the checkout lines at the grocery store. Jess suspected the elopement in Vegas had been in hopes of averting that, until Thomas had realized Vegas weddings were public, and anyone could find out they'd married.

"Is that what you would like?"

Jess smoothed a hand over her belly. "It would be nice for the peanuts, but... He's back in his world, and I'd never fit in. People would look down on me, which, you know, I get. I can take it. But they'd do that to the babies, too, and I wouldn't be able to sit back and let that happen."

Deacon let out a long breath. "He agreed with you about his family. That they would definitely want to step in. It wasn't what he wanted for the baby. I didn't tell him you were expecting twins. We couched it all in hypotheticals so that he had plausible deniability."

Jess swallowed. It wasn't the best circumstances, but even though Thomas had money and lots of family, she wouldn't want to trade with him. She knew her future involved a lot of hard work as a single mom. But she'd get to see her babies and love them, and she could decide for herself what their futures would be like. What hers would be.

Thomas didn't have that.

"He's going to try to find some money for you. He has to make sure no one will track it down. I'd still pursue the child support if you wanted me to. It doesn't sit well with me that he's not taking responsibility."

Jess shook her head. "This is why I never planned to tell him. I know he'd like to help, at least with money, but he's never gonna get free of his family again. And they'd hate to know he had kids with someone like me. You promised not to tell anyone, right?"

"I promise, Jess. You're my client, and I'm working for you. He can reach me through my firm when he finds a way to send some money or wants information, and that shouldn't raise any suspicions. He said he'd like to see pictures."

Jess's eyes watered, and she dashed the tears away. Stupid pregnancy hormones. But the thought that the man would only ever get to see pictures of his kids because of his family's reputation and ambition was sad.

She hoped Thomas would be able to find some kind of happiness, but she wouldn't trade his future for hers any day.

She sniffed. Deacon passed her a box of tissues.

"Thanks. These hormones are out of control sometimes. Anyway, I appreciate that you did that. I don't need to feel guilty now, that I'm keeping something from him that he'd want to know."

"I think he was happy to hear the news. Maybe, depending on how things go, he'll be able to see them sometime."

Jess didn't believe in sometimes like that. If Thomas could send some money, it could go into a fund for college, or a house or something for when the twins grew up. But she wasn't going to count on it.

They heard Rachel walking into the office. "Jess? Oh, there you are."

Jess struggled to get out of the chair. Deacon rushed around to help her.

"Thanks." It was the only help she could take from him. Then she pulled back her shoulders and went out to Rachel. Rachel was part of the Crossing, and as long as she was here, she was someone she could count on.

No need thinking about other things.

DEACON SIGHED AS he closed his laptop. This was it. He just needed to throw his golf clubs in the trunk and he'd head for New York City, ready to fly down to Florida for the stupid charity tournament. He'd arranged his calendar for the next week to allow for that. April wasn't a busy legal month. He assumed everyone was focused on taxes instead.

He hadn't wanted to fly down for the tournament, but like Meredith had said, with his father planning changes, it was time. As far as Cupid's Crossing, he wasn't sure he'd be there for much longer. His parents had been too pleased to hear he was joining them.

He would have preferred to stay in Cupid's Crossing for the full year, but not with the estrangement from Jess. He missed her—a painful amount. He hadn't realized just how much of his nonworking life was tied up with her. Despite the friends he'd made here, it was still lonely when he was no longer discussing books with Jess or helping her set up her nursery or taking her out for her prescribed walks, making sure she didn't slip on the ice or overdo it.

He found himself avoiding the places they'd been together, or where he might see her, and that kept him mostly housebound. When his mother called again, reminding him that Meredith's parents were going to be traveling after this, and touching on both her own and his father's mortality, he said he'd come for the tournament. At least there he wouldn't be both dreading and longing to see Jess around every corner.

He sent Rachel home early. There wasn't much left to do at the office, and Deacon really could have left when Rachel did, but he didn't want to putter around his place. He was postponing his departure because he didn't want to go, like a small kid dragging his heels.

The jet the firm had chartered to take the partners and their families to Florida was leaving in the morning. It would take Deacon about three hours to drive down. His parents already had their own plans for the evening. Deacon would rather drive in the dark than arrive with nothing to do but bounce around in an empty condo.

He slid his laptop into his briefcase, put his phone in his coat pocket and locked up the office. He wondered how soon he'd have to give back the key and sighed. He really needed to stop focusing on depressing topics. He'd be better going back to his true crime podcasts.

He made it home and forced himself to pack up a few essentials. He hadn't brought all his things to Cupid's Crossing—most of his warm weather clothing was still in New York City. He'd left in October, and April in Cupid's Crossing was closer to winter than summer, based on the temperature.

He put his golf clubs back in the trunk, the first time he'd had reason to handle them since he'd arrived.

He wondered what he'd been thinking, to bring those along. He'd learned more about how other people lived during this banishment, and they didn't all golf. He'd learned more about himself, as well.

He'd learned how to change his own tires and assemble an ottoman and refinish furniture. He'd learned how to mediate between clients and stand up to a chain saw. He'd learned about pop culture and reality TV and how to look at the books he loved from a different perspective.

He'd learned what the life he wanted for himself looked like. And maybe, in a few years, he could find that.

Once the car was packed, he checked that the tires were all well inflated and that his gas tank was full. He pulled out of the garage and turned to make his way out of Cupid's Crossing, deliberately calling up a podcast. He switched to the true crime one he'd been listening to when he came here.

He felt better able to handle a serial killer now.

It wasn't till he was a few hundred feet past Benny's place that he realized what he'd seen in his peripheral vision. He'd tried not to look at the place where Jess lived, but her van was there, the only vehicle in the lot. And someone was in it.

Jess, obviously. Probably heading to see Rachel and Ryker.

Except that they'd gone to Albany for a night out. Ryker had picked Rachel up from the office. Rachel had been excited at the idea of staying over, away from any demands people in town might make.

Maybe Jess was joining them? No, it was

supposed to be a romantic getaway. Jess would have avoided that.

There were lots of places she could be going. Groceries. Except the local store was closing now. Jess would have to go to Oak Hill. Which she could do. But hadn't Rachel said Jess's van was making some weird noises? It had sounded bad enough a couple of months ago when he'd been in it.

Telling himself he was being ridiculous, he turned around at the first side road. He'd either find her van empty, because she'd just gotten home and had gone up to her place, or gone altogether, after she'd driven to wherever she was going. In either case, he would turn around again and be on his way.

But he wasn't surprised when he got back to Benny's and Jess's van was still there, and she was in it. The van wasn't running, and the temperature was cold and dropping. There'd been a late frost warning.

Deacon pulled up beside the van, parking his car beside the driver door. Jess didn't notice him. He got out, walked to her door and tapped on the window.

She was bent over in the driver's seat and jerked when she heard the sound. She looked up at him, her face pale and drawn. Something was wrong.

He pulled the van door open before he realized what he was doing.

"Jess—what's the problem?"

She shivered, and he wrapped an arm around her, the best he could in the confined space.

"It's the babies. It's early, but I think maybe this is it."

Panic fluttered in his core, but he drew in a breath. Not now.

"The van won't start. I was having some pains, kinda cramps, but I figured they were the fake ones, Braxton-Hicks or whatever, but then I think my water broke, so I need to get to the hospital, and I grabbed my bag and got to the van but it wouldn't start and my phone dropped down beside the seat and I can't get it and—oooh!"

She huddled over again, knuckles white on the steering wheel.

Deacon rubbed her back with the hand that had tried to embrace her and pulled his phone out of his pocket with the other. He hit 911 while Jess shuddered and moaned, and his voice was tight when he got a response on the other end.

"I have a woman in labor, twins, about four weeks early. Her water's broken and she's got contractions—how far apart, Jess?"

Jess panted, pulling herself upright. "About five minutes, I think?"

"Five minutes apart," Deacon repeated into his phone.

The voice on the other end was concerned. "There's been an accident on the interstate, and all the ambulances are currently involved with that. Can you get her to the ER?"

Deacon wanted to swear. Jess needed help. Medical help, not legal advice. But he was all she had.

"Yes, I'll get her there."

"Has her water broken?"

"She thinks it has."

"Any blood in her discharge?"

Deacon's hand clenched on the phone. "Um, I'll ask." Jess had relaxed again, head resting on the steering wheel.

"Jess, they want to know if there's any blood...um..."

Jess lifted her head. She blinked. "No, nothing like that."

Relieved, Deacon told the woman on the phone no.

"Any urge to push?"

Jess shook her head. She must have heard. "No."

"Get to the hospital as quickly as you safely can. Call back if the situation changes."

"Right." Deacon hung up. He drew in a long breath. This was all on him now.

Jess was shivering again, but she wasn't bent over in pain. He had less than five minutes before that happened again, so he needed to get her into his car.

"Jess, we have to get you to the hospital."

"Yeah." Her voice was tight, and he knew she must be as frightened as he was.

"Can you get out of the van? My car is right here." And nice and warm. "I can drive you to the hospital."

Jess let out a long breath. "Yeah, I can do that."

Deacon wasn't sure if she could, but she'd try. He'd just have to be there to catch her if she started to fall.

Jess, with twins, was a tight fit behind the van's steering wheel. Deacon pushed the seat back as far as it would go, and Jess managed to turn herself sideways. She bit her lip and slid off the seat, landing with a wobble. Deacon wrapped an arm around her.

"Sorry. I thought I could handle this."

"Maybe you could. But you don't have to."

Deacon got her to the car and, while she leaned on the side of his Audi, opened the front passenger door. He grabbed his briefcase and gloves and tossed them into the back.

He pushed the button for the seat warmer and stood back to help Jess in.

"I had a towel—you don't want me to mess up your seat."

"Jess, the seat can be cleaned or replaced. I don't care. Please, get inside."

She suddenly bent over, panting, and he knew it was another contraction. He was helpless, unable to do anything of any use to her. He rubbed her back, making soothing sounds, and checked his watch. He might as well start timing these.

When she was able to stand upright again, he held her arm while she slid into the seat. She wriggled into the heat. He wasn't sure what to do about the seat belt, so he pulled it partway out and gave the buckle to her. Then he shut the door and almost fell returning to her van to get her bag and phone.

He wasn't sure he'd be able to grab the phone. It slipped twice between his fingers before he finally took a long breath and moved slowly enough to pry it out without it falling back beside the seat. He put it in her purse and picked up that along with the duffel bag sitting on the passenger seat. That had to be her bag of clothes and personal items for the hospital.

He shoved the duffel into the back seat of his car and handed Jess her purse.

"Anything else?"

She shook her head.

"Your phone is in your purse if you want to call anyone. I'll shut up the van and we'll be on our way."

He took one more quick glance around the van interior, looking for any items that had gone astray, then slammed the door shut. He didn't worry about locking it, because it wouldn't start anyway, but he'd grabbed the keys since they included her apartment door key.

Then back to his car and into the driver's seat. He turned to Jess. "You okay?"

She gave him a smile, not a hundred percent, but with enough Jess in there that he felt reassured.

"I will be. Thank you."

He reached over and squeezed a hand. "Let's go, because I am so not ready to deliver your babies in the car."

He got a chuckle, which he thought was a win in this situation, and put the car in gear.

It was a stressful drive. About every five minutes, Jess would lean over, panting, knuckles white where her hands gripped the dashboard. Deacon couldn't do anything, not even rub her back, because he needed to pay attention to the road. But his own knuckles were white on the steering wheel, as if he could somehow channel some of that pain into his own clenching hands.

Between contractions, Jess messaged her doctor and Rachel and Ryker. Her doctor sent instructions on what to do once they reached the hospital. Rachel and Ryker promised to get there as soon as they could.

Deacon wasn't sure they'd be able to get there in time. Jess's contractions were speeding up, and he could tell her pain was increasing. Jess did her best to hold in the moans, but she wasn't able to keep them all inside.

Rachel was Jess's labor coach, Deacon knew. But he had a sinking feeling that she wouldn't be there for Jess. He took a hand off the wheel and held Jess's in his. She gripped tightly.

"You okay?"

"Just peachy," she gritted out before another contraction consumed her and she squeezed his hand.

It hurt. It hurt a lot. But Deacon set his jaw and bore it silently. It had to be a lot less pain than what Jess was going through.

The trip to the hospital was endless. The needle on the speedometer kept climbing over the speed limit, and he had to force his foot off the gas pedal, not wanting the delay of a speeding pullover or to risk an accident. The roads were dark, shining in his headlights, trees tunneling the roadway. But he finally saw the outskirts of Oak Hill and knew they were getting close.

Jess was quiet.

"We're almost there."

She nodded. "Good. 'Cause I think the pushing part is starting."

Deacon had to take his hand back so he could wipe each in turn to remove the sweat. He wasn't ready to deliver babies. Then he let Jess grip his right hand again.

He followed the signs to the hospital and pulled up in front of the ER. Jess was clinging to his hand like a lifeline. He needed to get her into the hospital, fast, but he also couldn't leave his car here.

He spotted someone in scrubs standing outside the entrance smoking a cigarette. He ignored the contradiction of someone working here and smoking and instead hit the button to lower the passenger side window.

"Hey!"

The man turned to him.

"If I give you a hundred bucks, will you park this car for me?"

The guy looked around. "You talking to me?"

"Yes. She's in labor, and I need to get her in there."

"You're gonna give me your keys? You're not afraid I'll just take it?"

"Right now, I don't care."

Jess started moaning and panting through another contraction.

"Let me get you a wheelchair for her, and I'll come take your car. No money necessary."

Deacon waited till Jess relaxed and then removed his hand, now streaked with bands of red and white.

"Jess, we're here. I'll get you in a wheelchair and then a doctor will take care of you. Is your paperwork in your bag?"

"Yes," she gritted through clenched teeth.

Deacon got out, his new friend with the wheelchair almost to the car. Deacon grabbed Jess's bag while the man helped her into the chair. Deacon passed him the car keys and then promptly forgot him as he rushed into the building with Jess.

The waiting room for the ER wasn't too busy, fortunately. He didn't know the exact protocol for this, but he raised his voice. "Woman in labor!"

It got him attention. Undoubtedly a look at Jess assured them that this was serious enough. Another person in scrubs rushed toward them.

"How long has she been in labor? How far apart are the contractions?"

"I don't know—she thought it was Braxton-Hicks. The contractions are about three minutes apart now—" Jess's knuckles whitened as she grabbed the arms of the wheelchair, and her panting breaths told him she'd just started another.

"She says she feels like pushing now. She's expecting twins, and she's not due for another four weeks. I've got her paperwork in the bag here."

Another person came over and held a hand out for the paperwork. Deacon dug into a side pocket and found all the forms, filled out and ready, and passed them over, along with her identification.

"We're going to take your wife up to Labor and Delivery. You can come up as soon as you get the paperwork done."

They were gone with Jess before he could correct them as to their relationship. And then he decided he wasn't going to—not until Rachel and Ryker were here, at least. He had a better chance of learning how things were going if they believed he was married to Jess.

# CHAPTER EIGHTEEN

IT HURT. Jess's horizon was limited by the pain she felt and the hands moving her out of the wheelchair and onto a bed. Her clothes were taken off and a hospital gown put on. Then someone's hands were in her most personal space, but the contraction that wracked her body meant she didn't care. She didn't care if she was naked or not or who was around if they could just do something about this pain.

There was talk of pushing, and Jess could finally let her body take over. At some point, a familiar hand wrapped around hers. Deacon, she thought, and knew she'd be okay.

She heard them say there was a head. Part of her brain recognized that was a sign that one of the babies was almost here, but mostly, it was just pain and the comfort of Deacon's hand.

More pain, to the point she didn't think she could endure it, and then, relief, and the sound of a baby's cry.

"You did it, Jess!" That was Deacon's voice

in her ear. "You have a beautiful baby! Just one more."

No. She couldn't do this again. But her body contracted without her input, and everyone was saying push, and finally, another sweet pause of relief.

"It's over, Jess. You have two beautiful babies. A boy and a girl. They're good—you did it. You were wonderful."

"It's over? My babies?" she slurred.

A hand passed over her hair, and she leaned into it. "It's over. Here they are." Something was laid on her chest, and she knew what it was—her baby. A surge of love moved through her and she lifted her hand to touch. A second bundle, and she fought the exhaustion and drugs to touch...then, unconsciousness.

JESS CAME TO, senses barraged. She was in a bed, and her body felt different. Sore, achy, but no active pain. She'd never been so grateful.

Then she remembered that the lack of pain meant it was over. She'd done it. She'd given birth. She glanced down, and while her body wasn't as flat as she was used to, it was no longer round and stretched. She'd *done* it. She'd delivered the babies.

The babies. Where were they? She hadn't

imagined them, feeling them against her skin, had she?

A panicky look to the side, and she saw a bassinet beside her, and Deacon. He was sitting in a chair, holding something in his arms. He'd unbuttoned his shirt, and the baby, naked but for a diaper, was snuggled against him, a blue cap on the tiny head. Deacon was holding one hand around his head, the other holding the tiny bottom. Jess almost swooned again.

"Deacon?"

He looked up, an expression of wonder on his face.

"Hey, Jess." His voice was low. "Do you want to meet your babies?"

She nodded and watched while he stood, still carefully embracing the bundle in his arms. He stepped beside her and passed the baby to her.

There was a tiny red face showing beneath the cap. Eyes closed, mouth moving restlessly, bits of dark hair peeking out from under the hat. Jess didn't think she'd seen anything so beautiful in her life.

Deacon had picked up another small body from the bassinet. "Do you want to see Twin Two?"

Yes. Of course she did. She shuffled the first miracle he'd given her into the crook of one elbow, and Deacon gently placed the second baby on her other arm.

Same tiny red face, same dark hair. Pink hat.

Tears flooded Jess's eyes. "We did it."

"You did it," Deacon corrected her.

She looked up at him. "I remember the van wouldn't start, and you brought us here. Wait, did you really pay a guy to take your car?"

Deacon's cheeks flushed. "I didn't *pay* him. I had to get you inside, and the car was in the way."

So very like him. "Your car is probably gone now."

He shook his head and pulled car keys out of his pocket. "He brought me back my keys. The guy had no problem figuring out where we'd gone."

That really shocked her. "It's a day of miracles."

Deacon looked down. "Rachel and Ryker will be here soon. They were in Albany, so it took them a while."

Right. She'd done a bunch of the birthing classes with Rachel, but they had expected another week or two. This was the last trip Rachel had wanted to take out of Cupid's Crossing before Jess gave birth. Instead of Rachel, she'd had Deacon to help out. She tightened her arms around the tiny bodies she was holding. Deacon had done just fine.

"But you were here, so we were okay."

Deacon brushed a hand over her hair, and she wanted to lean into it. She didn't feel like being strong right now. "I'll stay with you till they get here."

Exhaustion dragged at her again. "I wish you could always stay," she breathed, and then she fell back asleep.

WHEN JESS WOKE up again, she found Rachel and Ryker in her room, each holding a baby.

"Hey." Jess said, pushing herself upright. "How long have I been out?"

"We got here about twenty minutes ago."

She shoved a hand through her hair, the strands sweaty and snarled. "Do I want to know what I look like?"

"You look beautiful, Jess." Rachel smiled warmly.

"Yeah, right." Jess didn't trust Rachel to be honest. Nice, yeah—honest, no. And there was no way she looked good after what she'd gone through.

"Your babies are beautiful."

Jess smiled, totally believing Rachel on that.

"Can I see? I only held them once." That

she could remember. With Deacon, who wasn't here anymore. And why would he be? He'd already done more than he had to.

Ryker stood, bringing over the blanket-clad bundle, this one with the pink hat. Impossibly tiny. Jess stared into the face of her child, love bigger than anything she'd known expanding in her chest. She had no doubts that she'd made the right decision about her pregnancy. Didn't matter what hardships were in store in future, this was the right call.

A nurse bustled into the room. "Ah, Mother is awake now. Excellent. We're fortunate that even though these two came early, they're big enough not to need the NICU."

Jess was grateful. At her last appointment, the doctor had thought the twins would hang on for a few weeks yet. When she'd realized she was in labor early, she'd panicked, thinking something might be wrong. That was before the contractions took all the attention she had, leaving no room for worry.

"So, I can take them home soon?"

"Soon. We just need to make sure everyone is recovering and healthy. Ready for nursing?"

Ryker stepped back quickly. "I'll go get… something."

Rachel grinned. "Want me to text you when you can come back with your something?"

Ryker nodded and was gone like a shot.

"Do you mind if I stay, Jess?" Rachel asked.

Jess shook her head. "Not at all." Jess would have been willing to bet money that Rachel was imagining a future when she and Ryker had kids.

There were a surprising number of things that could go wrong when nursing a baby. Since Jess didn't want anything sore or infected, she paid close attention to the nurse's instructions. And she'd already stocked up on formula as a backup.

When the babies were fed, Rachel offered to change their diapers, which Jess was happy to allow. With two babies, she was going to have lots of opportunity to change diapers in the future.

After, Jess got to cuddle the babies again, and despite the soreness in her body, she felt good. This was what she'd wanted. Her babies, with her brother and Rachel to help. Ryker had returned once he knew Jess was safely covered. He had his arm wrapped around Rachel, and they had a goofy look on their faces as they stared at her twins.

It was obvious they were as in love with the babies as she was. That wasn't a shock. They had to be the two most adorable creatures on the planet. She suspected it wouldn't be too long before her twins would have a cousin or cousins to play with.

Jess felt a sudden pang, because in an ideal world, she'd like to have someone she could share this with as well. Someone who would be going home with her, helping her, loving her the way Ryker did Rachel.

She swallowed and raised her chin. She knew from the beginning that she was doing this solo. And even if a certain lawyer had given her ideas about what it would be like to have someone, he wasn't here. He'd gone, just like everyone did.

She looked at Rachel and Ryker. Well, maybe not everyone. She was lucky to have these two, and she'd remind herself of that and not mope over something that wasn't going to happen.

DEACON STAYED TILL Ryker and Rachel arrived. He'd been holding one fragile body, bundled in soft cotton, and he'd felt tendrils of emotion wrapping around his heart. He wanted to stay here, holding this little snuffling baby and keeping Jess and the babies safe. He wanted to be here when Jess woke up and watch her face again as she held her babies. He wanted to help her get them home, see them using the cribs and highchairs he'd helped her assemble.

He wanted a lot, but that wasn't his destiny. And once Rachel and Ryker arrived, he had no excuse to stay any longer. Since Jess was sleeping, he asked Rachel to tell her that he'd be in touch later. Jess had said she didn't want to depend on him if he wasn't staying.

He wasn't. He had something to do elsewhere.

He'd passed the chair he'd been sitting in and the baby he'd been holding to Rachel. He'd waved off their thanks, knowing that it was late and he had a lot of miles to cover before he was back in New York. He wasn't going to get much sleep before getting on the plane.

His car was in the parking lot, the person he'd thrust his keys at willy-nilly having told him exactly where he'd left it. Maybe he was too cynical, but he'd almost expected the vehicle to be gone.

Maybe he wished it had been.

He opened the driver's door and sat down in the seat. The seats were cool now, the heat he'd put on for Jess long gone. He looked over to the passenger seat, where Jess had been curled up in agony just a short time previously. The car should be detailed. He turned the key in the ignition. The car started. All he had to do was put it in Drive and start back to the city.

He sat still. He was exhausted. Not as much as Jess, obviously, but going through that experience with her had wrung him out. That was probably why he was still sitting here, car not moving, when he was long overdue to be on the road. Maybe he was too tired to drive—at least, to drive safely. Maybe he should stay one more night. He could stop by the hospital in the morning, on his way, and see how Jess was doing.

He huffed a breath. No, he couldn't do that. There was a plane waiting for him in New York. Even if that wasn't the case, Jess had told him she couldn't depend on him if he wasn't going to stay. And she was right. Even if she wanted him to—but no, that wasn't an *if*. She'd said she wanted him to stay. And if he was honest, he wanted that, too. But how could he claim his happiness at the expense of so many others?

His phone interrupted his thoughts. Meredith. It was an effort, but he forced himself to answer the call. He didn't want to talk about the tournament, the firm or anything else connected to his New York life right now.

"Hello, Meredith."

"Deacon! Where are you?"

He sighed. "I'm in the car."

"Are you almost here?"

"No. I haven't really left Cupid's Crossing.
I'm in the parking lot at—"

Meredith cut him off. "You were supposed
to be here. What is wrong with you?"

Deacon didn't like her talking down to
him. He wasn't obligated to her. Just because
they'd made plans together didn't mean she
was entitled to know everything he did.

"As I was saying, I'm in the parking lot at
the local hospital."

Her voice changed. "Oh, no, Deacon. What
happened to you? Are you okay? Should I ask
them to delay the plane?"

Deacon interrupted. "Nothing happened to
me. Jess went into labor and her van wouldn't
start."

Deacon had never experienced a pause that
felt so accusing. He didn't like it.

"You could have called 911."

Irritation crawled under his skin. "I know
that, Meredith. I am a fully capable adult. I
called 911 and they couldn't get here in time,
so I took Jess to the hospital."

He could almost see her rolling her eyes.

"Then she's in good hands now and you should be here."

"She didn't have anyone who could make it in time to be with her, so I stayed till her brother arrived."

That was the least a decent person would do.

"Deacon, what's up with you and that woman?"

Deacon held on to his temper. "Nothing is up. She's a friend and she needed help."

"Well, her brother is there, right? So you're free to go."

"I know. I'm just a little tired."

"Deacon, the family is looking for you. Expecting you. This is where you belong."

He ran his hands through his hair, tugging to wake himself up. "Is it?" He really didn't want to belong there.

"Deacon, I know you have feelings for that woman. And yes, she appeals to your white knight tendencies, but you can't let that get away on you. If you're that worried about her, maybe we can find a place for her to work in the firm. She can file or something, right? Would that make it possible for you to get your head in the game? We have things to do. Big things."

Deacon didn't like how Meredith dismissed

Jess as something small, unimportant. How did a person decide the importance of another human being? Monetary value? Influence? Abilities? Shouldn't they be important just because they existed?

"She couldn't work for us, Meredith, because she now has two infants to care for. She can't afford daycare and an apartment on what we pay our support staff, remember? That's one of the big things we're supposed to be working on."

Meredith's sigh echoed in the car. "I know, Deacon, but to do that, we've got to get into a position where we can influence things. And once we've done that, daycare is on that list, along with a whole slew of even bigger things."

Deacon began to wonder if he even knew all the things that Meredith had on her list. And how she prioritized them. Once he got back, he needed to discuss this with her. He'd thought they agreed on how they wanted to bring necessary change to the firm. Daycare was pretty important if they wanted to make the firm more appealing to people with families, especially women, who often carried more of that burden.

Maybe he was the one who'd changed. After all, he might have considered daycare less essential before he realized that trying to promote and hire people who were responsible for children wasn't feasible if there wasn't a daycare option.

"Just don't marry her, okay? Keep her somewhere discreet if you must, but I've been putting out feelers. I think we've got a good chance of being in charge within the next year or two, but seriously, Deacon, we need to get married. It can be a marriage in name only, but before we change things, we have to work with the mind-set that's already making these decisions."

Deacon stared at the phone display on his car's dash. He'd told Meredith he wasn't interested in marrying her. Not for conventional reasons, and not for business reasons, either.

Meredith had her own agenda, obviously, and she wasn't listening to him. Was she more like the rest of his family than he'd appreciated?

He let his head fall back against the headrest.

"Meredith, we aren't getting married."

She sighed over the phone, and it sounded irritated, patronizing. "Deacon, do you want to change this firm or not?"

"I'm willing to sacrifice my working life for it, yes. But I'm not giving up my personal life as well. I'm allowed to have something for myself."

"I thought you were serious about this, Deacon. You didn't want to just ride on the family coattails and keep everything the same. I thought you were different. But you're trying to cut me out, aren't you? I do all the groundwork, and then you swoop in. Well, guess what, Deacon? They aren't sure they want you to take over. Not now, when there's an actual opening. They don't think you're experienced enough, and you don't have the necessary killer instinct."

Meredith's voice was cold, and it made Deacon's blood freeze.

He'd always known his family thought that about him. He was too nice. Too soft-hearted. He'd thought he could overcome it. He'd thought Meredith found value in him as he was.

He wanted to change the firm. He wanted to change the world, make it a better place, and he'd thought this was his predestined way to do that. But apparently either he had to to-tally change who he was to do that, or he had to commit himself in a legally binding con-tract to someone who perfectly fit the mold the firm valued.

If he became that person, would he ever

change back? How much was he willing to pay to follow through on this goal he'd assigned himself?

Not that much. Never that much.

"You know, Meredith, you're absolutely correct. I don't have the killer instinct, and I don't want it. I don't want to marry someone with it, either."

"What are you saying, Deacon? And be very careful, because some things you can't come back from."

Some things he didn't want to come back from.

"I'm saying that I've been fooling myself, thinking I could change that place. I can only do that if I change myself first, and I'm not willing to do so. I think…no, I know, that that's not the place for me."

"Deacon, don't do this! Don't throw everything away for that woman."

"I'm only going to throw away the things that don't matter to me, Meredith. And only to get something better."

# *CHAPTER NINETEEN*

JESS WOKE UP again when a nurse needed to check her vitals. She opened her eyes enough to see that there was daylight, so it must be morning. She'd been up in intervals all night, for feedings and body checks and probably just practice at depriving people of sleep.

She still felt like she'd been run over by a tow truck, but a smaller one than yesterday. So, improvement.

She pushed herself up, and the nurse asked if she was ready for the first twin to be fed. She was tired, but she'd made this commitment. She was going to take care of these two precious babies, and that meant pushing through even when she was tired.

For a few minutes, when it was just her and her babies, quietly nursing, the rest of the world and all her problems vanished. They were in a small bubble, the three of them, and she needed that to recharge and get ready for what came next.

What came next when visiting hours started

was a surprise. Deacon showed up with flowers (nice), a couple of blankets for the twins (nicer) and a meal from a local restaurant (nicest). Hospital food wasn't the worst, but again…far from the best.

"Thank you, Deacon. But you're supposed to be gone now."

Deacon smiled at her, a warm, soft smile that would have had her thinking ridiculous thoughts if she didn't know he was leaving and that those hopeful thoughts were just asking for heartbreak.

"I was, true. But you said you'd like me to stay."

Her cheeks warmed. "I had just given birth. I'm not responsible for what I said."

His expression smoothed into a blank mask. "So, you don't want me to stay?"

Jess fiddled with a loose thread on the hospital blanket. "You've got something important to do back in New York."

"I thought I did. But I'm reorganizing my priorities."

Jess did not think he'd ever reshuffle that list to put her near the top, so she didn't answer.

"Jess, if I didn't have to go back to New York—"

A very inelegant snort came out of her nose.

"We'll say hypothetically. If I didn't have

to go back, and I could stay, would you want me to?"

She pulled the thread hard enough to snap it. "You're a good guy. Of course, we'd like to have you here."

"I was asking *you*."

She glared up at him. "What do you want, Deacon? I know this hypothetical crap. You've been planning to go back since you got here, so don't mess with me."

Deacon frowned at her, brain obviously processing.

"You're right. I can't ask you for a commitment if I'm not making one. When are they releasing you?"

Jess didn't know what he was up to, but she was too tired to waste energy on that now. She was looking forward to leaving the hospital, but she knew things were going to get real once she was home.

"Later today. Ryker and Rachel are coming to get me and the twins."

"Okay. I have to go, but don't give up on me yet, okay?"

He set down the blankets and flowers on her table, beside the bag of food. Then he turned and left.

As Jess blinked back tears, she wondered when these hormones would finally get back to normal.

Rachel and Ryker hadn't come by in the morning, since they were busy getting car seats installed and organizing the last few things that Jess had thought she still had time to take care of. But when the afternoon waned and she was finally wearing her own clothes (maternity stuff that was now loose on her, but she wasn't back to prebaby clothes yet) and waiting in the required wheelchair, it wasn't her brother who showed up in her doorway.

Something inside swooped to a place it didn't belong, and her heartbeat sped up. She was glad she wasn't still connected to any of the hospital machines.

"Deacon? What are you doing here?"

"I'm here to take you and the twins home."

Jess shook her head. "I told you, Ryker and Rachel are doing that."

"Not anymore." He stepped back so the incoming nurse could place one of the twins in Jess's lap.

"Have you named them yet?"

She shook her head, accepting Twin Two from another nurse. Before she had time to muster up an argument, Deacon grabbed her bag and the one the hospital was sending home with her containing baby supplies and stepped behind her to push the chair.

"What are you doing?"

"I'm taking you home."

"I told you, my brother is—"

"I told him I was picking you up."

Jess didn't like what was happening to her emotions. She called up another argument. "But—the twins need car seats. And Rachel was going to pick up some stuff for me."

"It's taken care of."

"What do you mean, taken care of?"

But then they were at the front door, and Deacon had somehow managed to park his Audi right in front and not have it towed. It probably had something to do with more money and she should be offended by it, but she was too tired to argue.

They went through the automatic doors, and Deacon stopped the chair beside the car. He opened the rear door, and inside, there were two infant car seats set up in the back seat.

Jess just blinked as Deacon carefully lifted one twin from her arms. He pressed a kiss to the small forehead and then knelt on the edge of the seat. He pulled the belts out of the way and gently settled the bundle inside.

"I practiced enough times," he muttered. "This better work."

Under Jess's shocked gaze, he managed to buckle the baby inside.

"Yes!" He fist pumped, and Jess was sure she'd never seen him do anything so...so common.

He came back around for the second twin, and Jess watched in amazement as he managed to buckle her in as well.

With the twins secured, he opened the passenger door and held out a hand to Jess. She put hers in his, and he gently pulled her to her feet, then helped her sit. She noted that the car had been cleaned, and the seat showed no signs of her ride there while in labor. She wondered if it had been a mess—she couldn't clearly remember the previous day.

Deacon closed her door. In the rearview mirror, she watched him put her stuff in the trunk. He slammed it shut and slid into the driver's seat. He looked at the babies behind him, then at her.

"Are you ready?"

She nodded. Deacon smiled at her, and she was returning his smile before she consciously decided to do so. He pulled out of the parking space and through the lot, and they were soon on the road back to Cupid's Crossing.

Jess had every intention of making Deacon talk about what he was doing. She didn't want to make assumptions and get her hopes up just to be back where she started from. But the car ride was smooth and soothing, the twins were sleeping, and she was tired…

The next thing she knew, Deacon was parking his car at Benny's place, at the foot of the stairs to her apartment.

Jess rubbed sleep-stuck eyes, trying to focus on what was happening and what Deacon was doing, but by the time her brain was functioning again, he had already freed one twin from her car seat. The baby started to fuss, and Jess clicked open the seat belt and pushed open her door. She held out her arms, and Deacon placed the baby carefully in her grasp.

Jess gently jiggled the baby, uttering soothing sounds as she made her way toward the steps. When she looked over her shoulder, Deacon had the second baby out of the car and was gently rocking him as he closed the door.

He followed her up the steps to her apartment. Jess dug into her purse with one hand to grab her keys and unlocked the door. She stepped through the doorway, intending to drop on the couch and nurse the fussy baby, when she noticed the stuff.

An end table was positioned beside the couch, with a pile of receiving blankets and wipes on it. There were a couple of odd-shaped pillows on the couch—nursing pillows, she guessed from the shape. Some baby blankets lay over the back of the couch.

There were more things, but the baby was starting to cry now, so Jess sat down and prepared to follow the steps she'd been practicing.

She was vaguely aware of Deacon coming and going, but she was feeding one baby, and the other was now in a baby seat in front of her. Jess could already recognize the signs that Twin Two was getting hungry as well. When her baby girl finished, Deacon was there to pick her up, receiving blanket over his shoulder.

"Burping now, right? I watched a video."

Her heart turned over at the image of Deacon, in his suit, watching a video to learn how to burp a baby to help her. She watched as he carefully settled the tiny body against his shoulder and started to cautiously pat the little back.

Her boy twin was now near crying, so she leaned over to rescue him from the baby seat. Once he was happily nursing, Jess noticed a glass of water on the table beside her. She looked for Deacon and found him still patting

Twin Number One's back and heading to the room she had set up as a nursery.

There was the sound of a tiny belch. Deacon turned back to her, eyes wide.

"Thank goodness. I thought I was doing it wrong. I'm just going to change her diaper, okay?"

Jess glanced around the apartment, the one she'd thought she had another several weeks to get ready for babies. She hadn't bought diapers yet, since she'd planned to go to a big box store to get some as cheaply as possible. But seeing how many things had appeared, she suspected there were diapers in the nursery now.

"Do I have diapers now?" She pitched her voice loudly enough to carry down the hall without startling the boy at her breast.

Deacon wouldn't meet her gaze. "Well…"

Jess rolled her eyes. "And you watched videos about diaper changing?"

Deacon shrugged.

"Knock yourself out."

Jess turned her attention back to the nursing baby.

Deacon returned to the living room a few minutes later, clothing ruffled, but the baby in his arms appeared to be fully covered.

Jess tried to hold back her smile. "How did it go?"

Deacon looked down at the infant in his arms. "Babies are surprisingly wiggly. I'm afraid I spoiled a couple of diapers, but this one is good, I think."

Jess knew she couldn't count on this. But right now, exhausted and sore and overwhelmed, she was happy to accept any and all help.

Deacon passed her the newly diapered twin and walked away with Twin Two to burp and change. Jess took some precious minutes just to enjoy the drowsy, fed and changed, and now-quiet baby.

When Deacon returned, she asked him to sit. "I think we need to talk."

Deacon nodded and sat, her son cradled in his arms. Jess forced herself not to get weak simply because he was here and helping and looked so good holding her baby.

"What are you doing here, Deacon? You were supposed to be back in New York."

"I know. But things changed."

Jess raised a brow. "They did, huh?"

Deacon leaned back, Twin Two cuddled against his chest.

"Meredith called just as I got in the car in the hospital parking lot."

Jess wasn't surprised. Meredith struck her as an ambitious person, and not necessarily a patient one.

Deacon's hand rubbed up and down the baby's back. "She was upset that I hadn't gotten back to New York yet. I was supposed to attend a charity golf event."

"Rachel told me."

Deacon met her gaze, then turned his attention back to the baby in his arms as he continued.

"I told Meredith why I'd been delayed, but…"

Jess could imagine how excited Meredith would be. She thought Jess was trying to keep Deacon in Cupid's Crossing. Maybe she believed Jess had gone into labor on purpose?

Deacon sighed. "As she spoke…she was less the cousin I'd enjoyed as a kid, or the friend I thought she'd been, and more like the old guard at the firm. Definitely lacking in compassion. And she insisted we'd have to get married to be able to lead the firm, because everyone thought I was missing the killer instinct required."

Jess swallowed a sound in her throat. There were already enough people out there with killer instincts. Meredith was definitely one of them. Jess wanted Deacon to make those changes he wanted to back in the city, but not to change himself. She just wanted him to be happy.

Deacon shrugged, moving the baby and evoking a little rumble from the small body. He looked down, maintaining the soothing back rub, and the baby settled again.

"For what it's worth, I don't think you need a killer instinct."

Deacon's mouth turned down. He was staring at the wall, and she could tell his thoughts weren't happy.

"I told Meredith that I'd sacrifice a lot of things to try to make our family firm better. Corporate law isn't my first choice, but I worked at that, because I thought I could change the culture there. I wasn't going to sacrifice my personal life for a business marriage, and I wasn't going to change who I was. I don't have a killer instinct, and I don't want one."

Jess wanted to applaud him, but she had a baby in her arms. "How did she respond to that?"

Deacon turned back to Jess. "She wasn't happy, but it doesn't matter. I finally acknowledged that I'm not going to be able to make those changes I want, not without changing myself. And being here in Cupid's Crossing,

I've realized that I don't have to. I might not be able to follow in my father's footsteps, but there are more important things."

Jess's eyes widened. That was a big change for Deacon. "So what are you going to do?"

He smiled. "First, I'm going to warm up the casserole Rachel left for you. Next, I'm going to make sure you eat some of it. Then, if the babies are settled, you're going to get some rest."

Jess wanted to know what he was doing after that, but he stood up and set her twin in a baby seat. The baby was asleep, and Jess didn't dare disturb the infant. She let Deacon do exactly what he'd said he'd do. She didn't have enough energy for anything else.

# CHAPTER TWENTY

THE NEXT MORNING Rachel and Ryker came by. They brought more food and sent Jess for a shower while they cooed over the twins. They offered to take the babies for a walk in the stroller after they were fed so Jess could have a nap.

When she woke up, Jess found Rachel and her brother soothing the twins, but they needed to be fed, and that was on Jess. Ryker was a little uncomfortable with his sister nursing when he was there, so they left, promising to return soon.

Jess still could use some sleep but felt mostly human again. She opened her fridge, looking to see what food was in there. Based on how things had appeared in her apartment while she was gone, it was likely she'd find some surprises in there as well.

She was debating between reheating yesterday's casserole or opening something new when a knock sounded on her door. She was surprised to find Deacon again, with take-out in hand.

"I thought you might like some dinner?" he said.

For some inexplicable reason, Jess was self-conscious and just nodded and let him in.

He set the food on the counter and walked over to greet the sleeping twins. He squatted down, careful not to wake them, and Jess busied herself with opening the food while her insides jumped around in inappropriate happiness.

"Do you mind if I join you?"

Jess looked up. Deacon was watching her intently.

"Ah, sure. You brought the food, so of course."

He straightened up. "Only if you really don't mind."

Jess didn't think it was appropriate to tell him how much she didn't mind, so she reached up in a cupboard to bring out a couple of plates.

"Moonstone's?" she asked, noting that this didn't come from the diner.

"I'm celebrating," Deacon said.

Jess's hand froze on the takeout container. "Celebrating?" She suspected Deacon might have been tapped to lead his family firm despite what Meredith had told him.

Deacon smiled. "I'm the new lawyer for Cupid's Crossing."

"But you already—I mean, but you were leaving—what?"

Deacon took the plates away from her and moved to the table. "I told you yesterday that talking to Meredith made me revisit my plans. I decided that since I couldn't be the person needed to change things at the firm, I was free to do what I wanted. And what I wanted was to stay in Cupid's Crossing."

"Really?"

Deacon took the three steps necessary to join her in her kitchen space again.

"Really."

Jess couldn't meet his eyes. "Then I guess we're celebrating." She opened a drawer to get some cutlery. Deacon stood in her way.

"Are you happy about this, Jess?"

Two forks, two knives…would they need spoons? "Of course. You've been good for this town."

Deacon took the spoons out of her hand. "I didn't mean about the town. I meant you, Jess."

Jess made an inarticulate noise in her throat.

"Jess, at the hospital, you said you wished I could stay. And maybe you were just confused with everything going on, but I was hoping that your guard was down when you said that and that you really meant it."

When Deacon didn't continue, Jess scrambled for something to say. Something that wouldn't reveal how much she wanted him to stay, and that she wanted to be part of the reason. She drew in a shaky breath.

But he'd already exposed himself. He'd said he hoped she wanted him to stay. And he'd already permanently taken the position here.

She risked looking at him. He was watching her closely, worry lining his eyes.

It mattered to him. And when she thought back to all the things he'd done for her, with her. The way he'd supported her at the hospital. The way he looked at her babies.

Maybe she could finally take that risk again and trust someone. Let them in. Take a chance that he'd stay.

She swallowed against the lump in her throat. "I'm glad you're staying. I want you to."

His lips curved up. "You're a good friend, Jess, and I'll be your friend no matter what. But I was hoping we could be more."

Her hopes, which had screeched to a halt when he talked about being friends, sped up, bringing her heart rate up with them.

"I'd like that." Was she actually blushing?

When would she be done with these hormones messing her up?

"And I don't want to scare you, Jess, but I have plans. When Meredith said she and I needed to get married, I just couldn't. Because I didn't want to marry Meredith, not even as a platonic, business thing. When she talked about getting married, I pictured you."

Jess's mouth opened, but she had no idea how to respond to that. Twin One started to cry, and she was saved the chance of saying anything.

She picked up the hungry baby and settled on the couch to nurse her. Deacon picked up Number Two when he started to fuss and bounced him, speaking softly until Twin One was done, and they swapped babies. Like they'd done the first evening. Like it was a routine they'd practiced and worked out many times already.

When the twins were settled, Deacon didn't say anything further about the future, but there was a little bubble of happiness inside Jess.

DEACON STARED AT his phone, drew in a breath and hit the contact button to dial his father.

This wasn't going to be a pleasant call, but it needed to be done.

"Deacon."

"Hello, Dad."

"We missed you at the tournament. It did not look good."

Deacon stilled the hand that had been brushing his tie. "Something important came up."

"Meredith said you were delayed taking a friend to the hospital."

"I was."

His father moved on to the point of the call. "I think it's time you come back, Deacon. I'm planning on cutting back hours, and we need you here."

"About that. Um…"

His father continued, ignoring the interruption. "Meredith has a good head on her shoulders. I think the idea of the two of you marrying is an excellent way to ensure the future of the firm."

"Meredith wasn't supposed to mention that, because I didn't agree to it."

"She's a good lawyer and would be a good asset for you. Offset where you aren't as strong. Since she's busy at work, your mother could make the arrangements—"

"No!"

There was a pause, since Deacon had never raised his voice like that to his father, and they both needed to adjust to it. His father's voice was cold when he finally broke the silence.

"Is there a reason you felt it necessary to yell at me?"

Deacon closed his eyes and imagined Jess and how she'd respond in this situation.

"If I didn't interrupt you, I thought I might find myself married before we even ended this phone call."

The levity did not go over well.

"Was that supposed to be a joke?"

"Yes, but apparently not a good one. In any case, I'm not marrying Meredith."

"Why not?"

"Because I don't want to. I don't care for her like that, and I want a marriage where I actually love the person I marry."

He could picture the exasperated expression on his father's face. "Emotions can be messy and lead to unfortunate decisions."

Deacon shoved his shoulders back, determined to get everything out. "Also, I don't think Meredith will want to marry me when I won't be working at the firm anymore."

This silence was deafening.

"What did you just say?"

"I called to tell you I'm sending in my resignation."

"Don't be ridiculous."

Deacon clenched a fist. Of course his father would react like this.

"I'm not being ridiculous. I don't enjoy doing corporate law, and I'm not especially good at it. I've found that working as a small-town lawyer is something I both do well and enjoy, so I've taken on the position here in Cupid's Crossing permanently."

"You can't."

Deacon refused to give. "And yet, I have. I've purchased the practice here."

"You're a Standish. You work for Standish Legal."

"Not any longer."

Another pause while his father considered what he'd told him. "What's this really about, Deacon? Are you upset because we asked you to spend some time outside the city? Is this a temper tantrum?"

"No, it's not a tantrum. I actually am grateful that I came here. I've enjoyed these last months more than I could have imagined, and I've decided to stay. I know you would like your son to take over for you, but I'm not the right person for that. I've decided to stop trying to be who you want me to be and accept who I am.

"The firm needs to make some changes, and I thought I could be the one to implement that. It was something Meredith and I discussed. You should consider letting her lead. She's much better suited to the task than I am."

The line was quiet, but Deacon could almost hear his father's thoughts.

"Meredith said there was a woman there."

He was burning bridges, so he might as well burn the last one.

"Yes. Her name is Jess Slade. I'm going to marry her."

"You can't." His father sounded panicked, as if he finally realized how serious Deacon was.

"I can if she agrees. I'm hoping to convince her."

"Convince her? She's probably been working for this since you arrived."

Deacon was ready to hang up.

"You might hear that she just gave birth. Twins, and I'm not the father. You're going to suggest she wants me to provide security and money, but that's not it. I know who the father is, and Jess could get much more money from him if that's what she wanted, but she doesn't. I would like you to keep that in confidence. I'm only telling you because I hope you can meet her sometime, and I won't let you insult her if that happens."

A rustling sound. "Why don't you come home, and we'll discuss this. Be reasonable."

"No, Dad, I'm sorry. I'm emailing my letter of resignation as we speak, and things are going to be quite busy here. I'll send you an invitation to the wedding. It will be small, and if you can't make that, we'll see what works in the future."

"Deacon—"

"Goodbye, Dad."

He broke the connection. He'd just clicked Send on the email to Human Resources.

He hoped his father would consider what he'd said and talk to Meredith, but it was out of his hands now. It always had been, really. He also hoped he could convince Jess to take a chance on him. He hoped she loved him like he loved her. But even if she didn't, there was a weight lifted from his shoulders.

His life was his own now, and it was more exciting than he'd imagined. It could only get better.

THE NEXT COUPLE of weeks went by in a blur of feedings, diapers, baths and sleep. Never enough sleep. And visits.

Jess hadn't realized that she'd become part of Cupid's Crossing. Dinah, from the daycare, brought her some baby clothes for the twins and promised they'd be ready for her whenever she was able to come back. Mariah stopped by, making Jess self-conscious about the mess the place had become, also bringing some baby clothes and stuffed pink and blue horses for the twins. Rachel kept her fridge stocked with meals to reheat, and every day at noon Deacon stopped in to give her a chance to shower and then came by again in the evening. He'd send her off for a nap while he read to the twins. They were too young to understand what he was saying, but it made her eyes well up with tears every time.

If Rachel and Ryker stopped by when Deacon was there, they didn't ask any questions. It was like everyone expected him to be with her. Which she liked, but she was also a little scared. She'd started to hope that Deacon meant to stay, but most of the time he was here he was helping her with the twins. They didn't have time to be together, and wouldn't that eventually chase him away?

One night she went into the nursery from her bedroom to feed the twins, having heard them whimpering on the baby monitor. She nursed them back in her room, changed them and managed to get them settled again. There was a light on in her living space. Deacon must have forgotten to turn it off when he left. He'd shooed her off to sleep after the previous feeding, promising to clean up the kitchen for her.

Deacon had left the light on. He was stretched out on the couch, sound asleep, in his suit pants and dress shirt. Jess felt her heart turn over and knew she'd fallen in love with him. She was just so afraid he wouldn't stay with her. With this family she now had.

But she was grateful she'd had this time with him, and she didn't know how she'd have gotten through these first weeks without his help. She grabbed a blanket and pulled it up over his shoulders. She couldn't resist dropping a kiss on his cheek.

Then she went back to try to get a few hours' sleep before the twins called again.

The next morning, she dragged herself out of bed to answer the twins' call. Deacon met her in the nursery, picking up one twin and rocking him while Jess picked up the other and settled in a chair to feed her. Deacon walked out to the kitchen with his twin, and Jess heard him filling up the kettle.

Deacon's twin was starting to fuss by the time Jess had finished with her little girl. Deacon came back, and they swapped babies. Deacon walked the hall with the twin until she'd fallen asleep, and he set her in her crib as Jess changed the little boy.

Jess was getting pretty adept at working one-handed. She was able to get herself a cup of tea while bouncing her baby and left it on the counter when she returned the baby who was dropping back to sleep to his crib.

She took a quick stop in the bathroom before heading back out to the kitchen. She ran a brush through her hair and splashed some water on her face. She couldn't do much else, but she didn't want to look like a nightmare to Deacon. She wasn't used to him being around first thing.

She liked it. She just wished she looked better.

When she came back out, Deacon was sitting on the couch where he'd spent the night. The blanket was folded up, and he was leaning forward, hands playing with something as he stared at the ground.

"You okay? I know that couch isn't the greatest to sleep on."

He looked up at her. "I'm fine. I hope you weren't upset that I fell asleep here."

Jess shook her head. She'd thought he looked adorable on the couch, but that probably wasn't what he wanted to hear.

Deacon looked at the floor again, and his

fingers kept toying with whatever he had in his hands.

"I've been waiting. I talked to Ryker and Rachel, and we were trying to find a time when I could take you out."

"Out?" Did he mean a date? A walk?

"But I don't want to wait." He stood up and crossed over to where she was blowing on her tea. It wasn't hot anymore, but she was keeping her hands busy, and it was an excuse not to look at him.

"Jess, I liked being here at night to help you. I loved waking up with you and the twins. So, I'm not going to wait to take you out for a nice dinner. I'm going to—"

With shock, she realized he was going down on one knee. One knee? What was he— Wait, was that a ring box?

Oh, sweet saints. He was proposing?

Deacon caught her hand, and she set the tea down so the other was free as well. "I love you Jess, and I love your twins, and I love this town, and I want to be part of all of it. Cupid's Crossing, and your family. Would you marry me?"

Jess's mouth opened and shut again. This was nothing like Thomas and the impulsive trip to Vegas. She knew Deacon. He wouldn't be doing this if he wasn't all in.

"Are you sure?" she finally asked.

Deacon smiled at her, open and loving. "Absolutely."

Jess looked away, blinking back tears.

"Jess?" Deacon now looked worried. Jess dropped onto her knees in front of him. "Of course it's yes. But you're taking on a lot, Deacon Standish. People are going to wonder about you."

Deacon framed her face in gentle hands, as if she was something precious. No one had ever treated her like that.

"I don't care about people. Just you. You're the one I love."

Jess put her hands on his, feeling the strength in them. Not muscles or calluses. But hands that would be there for her. They'd already been through some of her worst times. If that hadn't scared him off, she trusted that he would stay.

"Well, I love you too, and I'll try to be my best for you."

"You're what I want, Jess. Just the way you are."

Suddenly a baby's cry split the air. Jess pressed her lips to his and then stood, Deacon following her up.

"You'd better get yourself ready for work."

"See you at lunch?"

"I'll count on it."

# *EPILOGUE*

"WHY DID WE decide to move homes with two babies?"

Deacon looked up from where he was changing Emma's diaper. "Because we needed a bigger space for the twins and there wasn't going to be a good time to move?"

Jess frowned at Deacon while she jiggled George on her hip. "*You* said you wanted a home office."

"I did. I want to work from home when I can. I don't want to miss anything. And when you want to, you'll have a space to take classes online."

Jess gave up her grumbling. She couldn't believe they were moving into one of the nice houses near the park. Sure, Deacon was the town lawyer, so he was expected to live in this kind of place, but she'd never imagined she'd ever be living in one of these homes.

But she loved the thought of her kids growing up here.

She continued to search one-handed in

the moving box labeled Baby Clothes. She wanted to find the outfits Rachel and Ryker had gotten for the twins, since they were expecting her brother and his wife shortly.

Deacon had insisted on hiring movers so that Jess only had to pack things. She'd argued that they could easily move their stuff with the help of friends, but Deacon vetoed that idea.

Jess was only working part-time at the daycare now, because the twins needed time with their mom.

The past months had been challenging. Adapting to the twins was one thing. Getting married was another.

They hadn't done a fancy wedding. Jess didn't have the energy, and Deacon's family was so upset that he'd quit the firm and proposed to Jess that they hadn't wanted to attend. There'd been a small service, though Mariah had made sure it was still pretty nice.

Jess still expected to wake up one of these mornings and find it was all a dream and she was back over Benny's place, just her and the twins. But she had a ring on her finger, and every morning she woke up with Deacon.

"Here they are." She tugged and found the coordinated outfits. Deacon took Emma's outfit and put it on with commendable dexterity. He was a very hands-on father.

Jess wrangled George into his outfit and even managed to change her own clothes before Rachel and Ryker showed up with food for the potluck dinner they'd begun to share on Sunday evenings.

Jess passed George to Ryker while she took the casserole dish from Rachel. Her brother was great with the twins, despite his earlier squeamishness with the whole nursing thing, but today, something was different. Rachel watched him with the baby and blinked back tears.

Jess set down the dish and turned to examine her brother and his wife.

"What's up with you two?"

Rachel and Ryker exchanged glances. Ryker smiled that soft smile he reserved for Rachel, who broke into a big grin.

She turned to Jess and Deacon. "I'm pregnant."

Emma started to cry when shrieks and congratulations echoed loudly around the room. Rachel and Ryker had brought sparkling water to toast, and the twins were passed from person to person as they set the table and sat to enjoy the food and each other's company.

Rachel was due about the same time as the twins would turn one. Jess foresaw some busy Aprils with birthday parties and anniversaries. She was onboard.

Rachel and Ryker didn't stay late. Rachel was tired, something Jess remembered well from her own pregnancy. Rachel and Deacon had the office downtown to open in the morning. Jess was off on Mondays, but there was laundry, unpacking more boxes and enjoying her time with the twins.

Once Emma and George were in their cribs and asleep, Jess let her body lean against Deacon. "I'm so glad they're sleeping through the night finally."

Deacon wrapped his arms around her. "I had no idea how much I'd come to treasure sleep."

Jess twisted in his arms and leaned up to kiss him. "I'm so glad you've been here to help."

Deacon tightened his arms around her. "Do you know it was a year ago today that I got a flat tire on my way to Cupid's Crossing?"

Jess tilted back her head to look at him. "Really?"

He nodded. "That flat tire was the best thing that ever happened to me."

Jess rested her head on his chest, hearing

the thump of his heartbeat. She wrapped her arms around him. She remembered being tired and almost driving past the guy in the fancy suit standing at the side of the road.

She was so glad she'd stopped. She'd had no idea that when she'd told him to pay it forward, it would end up like this.

"Best thing that happened to both of us."

\* \* \* \* \*

# Get 3 FREE REWARDS!

**We'll send you 2 FREE Books plus a FREE Mystery Gift.**

**FREE** Value Over **$20**

Both the **Harlequin® Special Edition** and **Harlequin® Heartwarming™** series feature compelling novels filled with stories of love and strength where the bonds of friendship, family and community unite.

**YES!** Please send me 2 FREE novels from the Harlequin Special Edition or Harlequin Heartwarming series and my FREE Gift (gift is worth about $10 retail). After receiving them, if I don't wish to receive any more books, I can return the shipping statement marked "cancel." If I don't cancel, I will receive 6 brand-new Harlequin Special Edition books every month and be billed just $5.49 each in the U.S. or $6.24 each in Canada, a savings of at least 12% off the cover price, or 4 brand-new Harlequin Heartwarming Larger-Print books every month and be billed just $6.24 each in the U.S. or $6.74 each in Canada, a savings of at least 19% off the cover price. It's quite a bargain! Shipping and handling is just 50¢ per book in the U.S. and $1.25 per book in Canada.* I understand that accepting the 2 free books and gift places me under no obligation to buy anything. I can always return a shipment and cancel at any time by calling the number below. The free books and gift are mine to keep no matter what I decide.

Choose one:
- ☐ **Harlequin Special Edition** (235/335 BPA GRMK)
- ☐ **Harlequin Heartwarming Larger-Print** (161/361 BPA GRMK)
- ☐ **Or Try Both!** (235/335 & 161/361 BPA GRPZ)

Name (please print)

Address                                                                 Apt. #

City                              State/Province                        Zip/Postal Code

**Email:** Please check this box ☐ if you would like to receive newsletters and promotional emails from Harlequin Enterprises ULC and its affiliates. You can unsubscribe anytime.

> Mail to the **Harlequin Reader Service:**
> **IN U.S.A.:** P.O. Box 1341, Buffalo, NY 14240-8531
> **IN CANADA:** P.O. Box 603, Fort Erie, Ontario L2A 5X3

**Want to try 2 free books from another series!** Call **1-800-873-8635** or visit **www.ReaderService.com**.

*Terms and prices subject to change without notice. Prices do not include sales taxes, which will be charged (if applicable) based on your state or country of residence. Canadian residents will be charged applicable taxes. Offer not valid in Quebec. This offer is limited to one order per household. Books received may not be as shown. Not valid for current subscribers to the Harlequin Special Edition or Harlequin Heartwarming series. All orders subject to approval. Credit or debit balances in a customer's account(s) may be offset by any other outstanding balance owed by or to the customer. Please allow 4 to 6 weeks for delivery. Offer available while quantities last.

**Your Privacy**—Your information is being collected by Harlequin Enterprises ULC, operating as Harlequin Reader Service. For a complete summary of the information we collect, how we use this information and to whom it is disclosed, please visit our privacy notice located at corporate.harlequin.com/privacy-notice. From time to time we may also exchange your personal information with reputable third parties. If you wish to opt out of this sharing of your personal information, please visit readerservice.com/consumerschoice or call 1-800-873-8635. **Notice to California Residents**—Under California law, you have specific rights to control and access your data. For more information on these rights and how to exercise them, visit corporate.harlequin.com/california-privacy.

HSEHW23

# THE NORA ROBERTS COLLECTION

**40% OFF!**

Get to the heart of happily-ever-after in these Nora Roberts classics! Immerse yourself in the beauty of love by picking up this incredible collection written by, legendary author, Nora Roberts!

---

**YES!** Please send me the **Nora Roberts Collection**. Each book in this collection is 40% off the retail price! There are a total of 4 shipments in this collection. The shipments are yours for the low, members-only discount price of $23.96 U.S./$31.16 CDN. each, plus $1.99 U.S./$4.99 CDN. for shipping and handling. If I do not cancel, I will continue to receive four books a month for three more months. I'll pay just $23.96 U.S./$31.16 CDN., plus $1.99 U.S./$4.99 CDN. for shipping and handling per shipment.* I can always return a shipment and cancel at any time.

☐ 274 2595          ☐ 474 2595

Name (please print)

Address                                                                 Apt. #

City                          State/Province                  Zip/Postal Code

**Mail to the Harlequin Reader Service:**
**IN U.S.A.:** P.O. Box 1341, Buffalo, NY 14240-8531
**IN CANADA:** P.O. Box 603, Fort Erie, Ontario L2A 5X3

---

*Terms and prices subject to change without notice. Prices do not include sales taxes which will be charged (if applicable) based on your state or country of residence. Canadian residents will be charged applicable taxes. Offer not valid in Quebec. All orders subject to approval. Credit or debit balances in a customer's account(s) may be offset by any other outstanding balance owed by or to the customer. Please allow 3 to 4 weeks for delivery. Offer available while quantities last. © 2022 Harlequin Enterprises ULC. ® and ™ are trademarks owned by Harlequin Enterprises ULC.

**Your Privacy**—Your information is being collected by Harlequin Enterprises ULC, operating as Harlequin Reader Service. To see how we collect and use this information visit https://corporate.harlequin.com/privacy-notice. From time to time we may also exchange your personal information with reputable third parties. If you wish to opt out of this sharing of your personal information, please visit www.readerservice.com/consumerschoice or call 1-800-873-8635. Notice to California Residents—Under California law, you have specific rights to control and access your data. For more information visit https://corporate.harlequin.com/california-privacy.

NORA2022

# #483 TO TRUST A HERO
*Heroes of Dunbar Mountain* • by Alexis Morgan

Freelance writer Max Volkov recently helped solve a mystery in Dunbar, Washington, and now he's staying in town to write about it! But B and B owner Rikki Bruce is perplexed by another mystery—why is she so drawn to Max?

# #484 WHEN LOVE COMES CALLING
by Syndi Powell

It's love at first sight for Brian Redmond when he meets Vivi Carmack. Vivi feels the same but knows romance is no match for her recent streak of bad luck. Now Brian must prove they can overcome anything—together.

# #485 HER HOMETOWN COWBOY
*Coronado, Arizona* • by LeAnne Bristow

Noah Sterling is determined to save his ranch without anyone's assistance. But then he meets Abbie Houghton, who's in town searching for her sister. Accepting help has never been his strong suit...but this city girl might just be his weakness!

# #486 WINNING OVER THE RANCHER
*Heroes of the Rockies* • by Viv Royce

Big-city marketing specialist Lily Richards comes to Boulder County, Colorado, to help the community after a devastating storm. But convincing grumpy rancher Cade Williams to accept her advice is harder than she expected...

# HARLEQUIN
## PLUS

Try the best multimedia subscription service for romance readers like you!

---

## Read, Watch and Play.

Experience the easiest way to get the romance content you crave.

Start your **FREE TRIAL** at
www.harlequinplus.com/freetrial.